THE BARON RETURNS

The Wentworth Family Saga

Book One

Graham Ley

THE BARON RETURNS

Published by Sapere Books.

20 Windermere Drive, Leeds, England, LS17 7UZ,
United Kingdom

saperebooks.com

ISBN: 978-1-80055-569-3

*In memory of my mother, the novelist
Alice Chetwynd Ley*

CHAPTER I: SKETCHES OF THE FAMILY

Devon, 1795

The long French windows looked out on to the small formal garden, its intricate walks bounded by low box hedges, and beyond to a rose path culminating in an arbour with a climber, on which the new stems were just visible. Behind the garden was the wide Devon orchard, with little in the way of leaves but brilliant blossom on the early pear trees. The drawing room was warm, thanks to a well-tended fire, but the weather gave signs of being cool, the sunshine that lit up the blossom alternating with ragged light cloud.

The young woman standing by the French windows was looking out through them, but seemed preoccupied with something other than the view. Her lips were pursed slightly, and there was a furrow on her brow. She was standing very still, her left arm hanging by her side. She held an open book lightly in that hand, and her fingers drummed in an absent-minded manner on its cover, which her thumb was tucked behind. She was in the first years of her twenties, and was dressed in a beautifully embroidered caraco shaped to her figure over a white linen petticoat, finished with a broad ivy-green sash around her waist. Her blond hair was pulled loosely back over her neck, with fashionable ringlets to the side of her head.

'A penny for them, Bella.'

The voice came from a younger woman who was sitting with her sketchbook at a small table in the drawing room. It was clearly a loved voice, because Miss Arabella Wollaston broke from her reverie at the window with a smile, although she hardly moved or even turned her head.

'I doubt they are worth that, Amelia. Indeed, I hardly know what they are myself.'

Miss Amelia Wentworth glanced meaningfully across at her mother, who had looked up momentarily from her reading in a comfortable chair by the hearth, and who raised her eyebrows without great commitment to any opinion before returning to her book.

'It may not be a matter of what they are, but of whom they concern, dear Bella. Or at least,' Amelia said as her friend looked in a rather challenging way across to her, 'that is how I find it in myself. But come, you must not squint, it will bring lines around your eyes, and you will have to go to great expense to remove them. There, you see, I have darkened this cottage doorway far too much, and the haystack has no body to it — it looks as if it would fly away at the first sign of a breeze.'

Amelia put her sketchbook and pencil down in a show of dissatisfaction, and rose to cross to her friend, whose warmth readily drew her to her side. She herself was simply dressed in a high-waisted yellow muslin with the addition of a neatly pleated bodice, and her dark hair was swept up and tied with apple-green ribbons.

Her approach did now capture Arabella's attention, and Amelia took her by her free hand as if to bring her away from whatever, or whoever, it was that was causing her distraction. She decided to treat her rather like a little girl, and conducted her solemnly to the more comfortable chairs by the fire, next to her mother. They both laughed as Amelia sat her down on one of the striped covers.

'And now, Bella,' Amelia remarked, 'you must tell us both what you make of Mary Wollstonecraft. Come, you have had the book with you all morning, although I fear it may not have had your full attention. Is she not stirring? Do you not feel your spirits rise?'

Arabella felt the heat of the fire pleasantly although she had not missed it before, and she found herself stifling a yawn. At this, both Amelia and her mother Sempronie offered a mock gasp, Sempronie with her hands laid lightly in her lap, both resting on her open book. She was a woman of intriguing beauty, her coiffure far more *bouffante* than those of the others, her gown less to the fashion of the moment, but ample in its folds of green satin. Her complexion was the same as her daughter's, but her hair shimmered between deep chestnut and a hint of raven, while Amelia's was of the chestnut hue only.

Arabella felt that she should erase the memory of her lapse of manners, and at least make an attempt at the tone of a salon. 'I fear I am under scrutiny, and this tribunal will not let me off lightly. I shall tell you honestly that I find it difficult to trace her argument. It seems there is too much on Rousseau and the Spartans, an odious people. She is wordy, a little like a sermon. You see, I have failed you.'

'But there is a case to preach, do you not agree, *Maman*?'

'*Pour moi*, before I went to Québec and met your father, I used to dream of a life in nature. It was not difficult to think of these things in Brittany. So, a woman who is free, who lives by reason, yes, that appeals to me still.'

'I would be free and have my reason, assuredly. But we cannot all be at writing for a living, as she is. So what would she have us all do?'

Sempronie raised her book in one hand. 'Yet here is one who succeeds at it famously. Amélie will always be reading the latest cry at the bookseller, and I have from her here Mrs Radcliffe and her *Mysteries of Udolpho.*'

'There we are, I have it!' Amelia exclaimed, apropos of nothing and to the surprise of the others, who had been expecting more on this topic of conversation. Her spontaneous vivacity was in character, and amused both her mother and her friend. Sempronie was visited by the memory of her own younger self, whom she saw remade in so many ways in front of her eyes; while Arabella was charmed by a quick volatility that was so unlike her own more purposeful energies.

Amelia had jumped up and gone to tidy up her table, removing her sketchbook, charcoal and graphite pencils quickly onto the chair.

'That is it, you see, we must look at *your* sketches, *Maman*! I vow that Bella has never seen them, have you, Bella? Oh, she so far exceeds me that you will wonder at them. A whole life is in them. There, I have cleared a space, and I shall go to fetch them.'

Sempronie was now standing, and she reached for the bell. 'We must let Thomas carry them in for us. I shall ring for him. The portfolio is heavy and … how do you say?' It was unusual for her to reach for a word in her adopted language, but this one was perhaps unusual and obscure.

Arabella sensed her difficulty. 'Might I suggest "bulky", *madame*, or you might want "cumbersome", undoubtedly a more elegant word? But perhaps Amélie and I could manage it together?' Arabella reached out to restrain her friend as she moved towards the mahogany doors that opened from the drawing room into the library.

'Miss Wollaston, I am obliged to you, in your debt, *sans doute.*' The older woman curtseyed to her frivolously, amused by the passing play on the two languages. In that slight gesture, there was a world of grace.

Arabella swept after Amelia, who had pushed back the doors emphatically and almost run on into the library. The long shutters had been closed to protect the volumes on which the sun might shine, and as she folded them back the light sprang into the room, picking out the muted colours on the spines of the books opposite. As Amelia went to the far end of the room, Arabella paused by a padded chair that stood next to an oak desk, darkened by age. There were open books on it as well as closed, including Paine's *The Age of Reason* and works by Burke and Rousseau. She saw a notebook and was suddenly filled with curiosity as to its contents. But a voice came from the other end of the room as her hand rested on it, her other lying on the old frock coat that was draped over the back of the chair, her fingers idly running over the collar.

'Come away from Justin's desk, and your fascination with that old coat of his, and help me with these portfolios. I know it is here somewhere, but there are others as well. Ah, no, here it is! Oh, you are no help at all, Bella, and I knew I should do it best by myself.'

This last was a little unfair, because Arabella was now pushing aside the larger volumes and portfolios on the deeper, lower shelf where Amelia had been occupied. But her friend's discovery was in fact on the shelf above, a worn and fragile sleeve of board tied with faded ribbon, on a smaller scale than many that were more modern. This she grasped as one might hold a prize, turned triumphantly to Arabella, grabbed her hand unceremoniously, and almost ran to the doors, pulling her light-heartedly along with her, to Arabella's sudden delight.

'Now you shall see. It is all here, and you shall learn pictorially of us all, and of Kergohan, the *manoir*, and Brittany. My mother has pictured it all, all of it and everyone! You cannot let your concentration drift away. I shall examine you on it all afterwards, and you must get the faces right, although I know there is already one on which I cannot hope to trip you.'

Arabella had just then let go of her hand. 'You may trip yourself if you run on like that, miss.'

Amelia had reached the table, where she was joined by her mother. 'Come, don't be sombre, Bella. I shall not tease you.'

'And birds will not fly,' said Sempronie. She untied the ribbon and opened the portfolio. 'Oh, these old things. Are you sure you want to join us in this, Arabella? You may well prefer to sit by the fire with your book, and I for one should not blame you.'

'She shall not,' said Amelia. 'It is as well that she knows more of our wider family. Come, gather round, the light is good here. See, I know this, this is the view of the *manoir* from the woods. It is little changed. And this is the orchard, in full blossom. Oh, how you have caught it, *Maman*! *Grand-père* had replanted it, so you say, and do you remember when Justin became drunk on the cider? That was so much later, and while you scolded I remember that *Grand-père* just laughed! And here they are together, *Grand-mère* and *Grand-père*, I can just recall *Grand-mère*…'

Arabella was intent, as Amelia had expected, but also studied in her politeness. 'So that is your *manoir*, *madame*? In the southern part of Brittany, I believe?'

'Yes, that is Kergohan. That view is from many years ago now, but it had changed little when we were there last.'

'And you grew up there, *madame*? Your childhood was spent in that idyllic setting?'

'It was. Until my mother died, and my father took me with him from Lorient to Québec. We returned, thankfully, after I was married to Wentworth, Justin's and Amélie's father, and from that time forward until recently, this house and Kergohan shared us as we chose. But I ceased to sketch some time ago.'

'Ah, look at this! You have given us a family portrait in front of the *manoir*, *Maman*, and how one can pick out the characters. *Grand-père*, looking older, dear Papa looking so young and handsome, and you are not here because you are drawing, but who are these two with them, and the child?'

'That is my father's sister, Catherine, my aunt. And the small boy in the little coat is my cousin Laurent. That dull man next to him is his father. He was from the town, as you can see from his clothes, which I did not really know how to draw. His name was Guèvremont. We did not like him. She was much younger than my father. We did not like each other, and my father was sad. *C'est dommage, mais…*'

As she turned the drawings, a bust of a young man appeared, and Arabella started and placed her finger on the sheet. It was alarming, as his face was familiar. Amelia drew in her breath, brushed Arabella's hand away, and closed the portfolio promptly, with an almost desperate look at her mother. But Sempronie, who had missed no part of this, would not be disturbed.

'I can see from your face, Arabella, that you perceive the family resemblance. He is indeed like Justin, and so much like his father, whom you will not remember. I am glad that I drew this of him when I could, although Amélie believes wrongly that the image will haunt me. I hope it does not trouble you, my child. Let us look at it again, briefly.'

Amelia was pale, but she opened the portfolio again at the sketch.

'Yes, that is my son George, Justin's and Amélie's younger brother. He is in his midshipman's uniform, although not much of it is visible in this bust. It was drawn in the summer before … before we lost him. That reminds me,' she continued, 'that we must invite Captain Yeo again to visit us. Yes, and your father, Arabella. They are known to each other. Let us make a dinner of it, or rather let Justin make it an engagement. There are others, too…'

At this moment Sempronie was sufficiently observant to see that a blush was spreading over Arabella's neck, and she feared that in some way the mention of her father, or perhaps it was the captain, had been indiscreet. She had been distracting herself and her daughter from painful memories with that impromptu plan for a dinner, and feared that she had inadvertently caused upset to another. But her eyes then followed the direction of Arabella's gaze, which was resting on the drawing that Amelia had pulled forward to cover that of her lost brother George, and she thought she understood. It was time to leave the young to whatever feelings were moving them. She thought of refreshment, the warmth of the fire, and of writing dinner invitations that might be delivered promptly.

'It is assuredly a good likeness of Justin, as your attention to it testifies,' said Amelia archly. She bent to thumb through her own portfolio lying on the chair, and pulled out one of her own sketches, which she laid alongside. 'My mother's eye is wonderfully sharp. Do you not marvel at the way she has caught the indentation of the cheek, and the curl of the eyebrow? My own of him here is inferior, although I would of course bow to you as an expert observer.'

'Justin is so like his brother,' said Arabella softly, ignoring her friend's gentle jibes, or perhaps unaware of them. 'I had not known. It must have been so hard for you both, so soon after the death of your father.' She continued more brightly, 'No, I think you have the thrust of Justin's mouth better, the lower lip is fuller just as you have drawn it … and the way his eyes drift off past one, into some unknown, distant perspective. But perhaps your mother has caught that too, now I look twice.'

'Perhaps she sees the child in the man more than I do. But for your part, I do not doubt that you see the man. *Tiens*, let us finish with this. One may become positively maudlin with the pictures of those one loves. Shall we play cards? You always win, Bella. I think it is your father's influence. The military are sheer devils with cards.'

'Your language, please, child!' Sempronie remonstrated from her place by the hearth. 'And what would you know of the military? Little enough, *j'espère*. We should think of refreshment.'

'Not yet, *Maman*. Perhaps you would sew, Arabella?'

'No, I shall not knit a stocking. I cannot abide it.'

'But you can play, Miss Wollaston, unless I am much mistaken. I heard you play in your father's house, in front of quite a gathering, and you sang to us too. As you know, Justin has provided us with a piano, so that Amélie may pursue her practice. Indeed, I believe that he bought it soon after we were with you on that occasion.'

'And so much for *my* lessons and practice,' added Amelia under her breath. 'He will not be hoping to listen to me. I am like a cat running over the keys. But you have played for us before, Bella, and now is a good time again. Please, Bella, do! I shall stand with my hand on your shoulder as you play, smiling down on you, as if I were your beau.'

The mood had taken Arabella, and she approached the piano in a relaxed frame of mind. She briefly grasped her friend's hand as it was laid on her shoulder, played first a newly published sonata by Haydn, and then sang an aria by Handel, both off by heart. Her accomplishment was evident. As she sang, the sky darkened, and her voice rose slightly as the wind lashed the rain against the window.

CHAPTER II: AT THE SERVICE OF HIS COUNTRY

The church stood in a small group of trees, on a small hill above a valley that dropped away into a wooded combe, running down towards the sea in the distance. It was dark and gloomy in the churchyard, and the rain fell heavily, whipped at times by gusts into slingshots that stung both face and hands. In the distance, there was a small farm across the valley, but the landscape was otherwise bare and desolate, thin pasture and scrub giving way to rock. The Celtic crosses bore witness to the fact that men had come here over many centuries to worship. The church itself showed signs of neglect, with patchy stonework and missing slates testifying to a lack of ready money in the parish. Saint Petroc was no doubt devoutly loved, but he was used to poverty in this region, and the bare living that his clergymen shared with their parishioners.

The scene was peaceful, in its wild way, and not much could be heard apart from the sound of the rain and the wind in the trees, just the occasional bird chirping a sharp song of annoyance at a rival, and what could have been the distant bleating of sheep, floating uncertainly across the valley. To the side of a buttress there was a slight movement, and a man who had been standing in its shadow lifted his head, giving away a tension that had been suppressed in stillness. Nothing of his face could be seen clearly, but his hat and his ample cape shadowed his movements as he looked around the churchyard and then stepped forward into what was left of the daylight. He moved away from the wall, and walked firmly but lightly round the corner towards the other side of the church and the porch, apparently satisfied that he was alone. His hand rested on the latch for a moment, and when he opened it he seemed more concerned that he was not being watched than he was for what service might be progressing inside. He slipped in, and the door quietly shut behind him.

He was wet through, and muttered slightly at the rain dripping off his clothes and hat onto the floor. But satisfied that the matting would soak it up easily enough, he shook his cape briefly, and pulled his hat off his head. The light in the church was dim and rain dripped heavily in some darkened corner. But there were signs and faint smells of recent rites, only a few days old if that, although it was hard to guess of what precisely the smell was composed.

Places that have had life passing through them strike us differently from those that have stood empty, and instinct tells us enough to know whether to be alert or at ease. The man seemed sure that there would be no one else in the building at that moment, and he strolled up the south aisle, stopping to look at memorials on the walls and the roughly lettered tombstones under his feet. He paused in front of an elaborate monument on the north side of the chancel, and looked up at the plaster or alabaster sculpture of the kneeling woman in her Elizabethan or Jacobean ruff, and the row of kneeling children in the panel beneath her, ascending in size, both boys and girls. He set himself to count them, smiling.

He had got to nine, in a rather distracted way, wondering pointlessly how many years had been between the third and the fourth, who appeared to be very different in size, when he swung away with a hissed intake of breath. The wooden rood screen was in a bad state, broken in parts and eaten with worm in others, but it was still standing and marked a barrier between the nave and the chancel. He chose to stand in the corner where it joined the chancel wall, in what was a patch of deep shadow that extended down from above his head to the floor around his feet. For a second time, he stood stock-still, but he threw his hat on the floor before pulling up the hood of his cape to make sure his face did not catch any of the chance light. In this position he could just glance towards the door, but since he was on the same side of the church he could not be seen by anyone on entry. Ultimately, his place of concealment would be exposed, but it was better than nothing. And so he waited, with a patience that seemed almost habitual.

What he had heard was the soft whinnying of his bay mare. She was tethered securely away from the lane and at the back of the small grove of trees that surrounded the churchyard, and he had been able to rely on her for an early warning of other animals. How many there were was another matter, but any rider in this remote spot was enough to put him on his guard. Still, it was less worrying than the silence and stealth of unseen legs and feet, which had nagged at his sense of unease outside. The mare would not mind a pedestrian, or even a small crowd, since she was a sociable beast, but ever since she had foaled she was nervous of others of her species, alarmed and prepared to guard her ground. The thought of the foal made him smile, but that faded as he heard the grind and clatter of harness and wheels, and more whinnying from other horses outside in the lane.

A flash of light through a window, with the clouds hurling off to the south briefly, showed little other than the intentness on his face. Then the shadows pulled back around him. He could now distinctly hear the complicated running of a carriage, not a cart, and sounds that similarly had nothing rural about them, including one that he thought he recognised well.

He waited, but without the tension that had possessed him earlier in the churchyard.

As he expected, the door was pushed back, and the heavy tread of boots came to him in his hiding place as they progressed up the aisle. A figure swung into view some feet from the font, and he heard what he thought was a muffled oath. Then a voice cried his name, unmistakably his name, with impatience. He stepped from his hiding place and threw back his cape, pulling at the fastenings as he swept it from his shoulders and over his arm. The man by the font made a grunt of momentary surprise but also of satisfaction, and he too pushed his cloak aside. As he stepped forward he came into a good patch of light, and it was obvious that his uniform and powdered wig were of a piece with leather shoes of the finest quality, and stockings and breeches that were dusted with flecks of dried mud. Well back from him, just by the door, stood another figure who kept on his black cape, but under it there was a glint of metal. Another man left, and pulled the door to behind him.

'Damned weather, Wentworth, although I shouldn't say that here, I suppose, or I'll be damned myself.' The man paused, waiting for an answer, and then: 'You are Wentworth, I suppose, or I'll be damned even more. Say something, man! Don't stand there like a statue! Let me have your name or there'll be consequences.'

Justin glanced at the dragoon by the door, who was motionless but quite alert, and reckoned quietly that there must be more dragoons outside, apart from the other one he had seen. Uniforms and wigs like this did not come unattended down country lanes in Cornwall. He bowed quickly and smartly to the man who had spoken to him. 'Yes, my lord. At your service.'

'At the service of your country, I hope you mean? Well, Wentworth, do you take a seat, or shall I stand? They may be hard, but there are plenty of them.'

Justin nodded slightly and moved round into the nave, opposite the admiral, and both sat down on pews. Justin let his eyes drift towards the altar, waiting for the other to begin.

'I trust you know my name, Wentworth, or we shall be at sixes and sevens before we start. Tell me, man.'

'Lord Haworth, I believe.' Justin smiled briefly, and looked to the side at the admiral's profile. His face was sharp, his nose prominent, with white skin stretched over it like parchment. He had dark eyebrows, searching eyes, and a thin, hard mouth which was capable of a severe smile. Justin had seen the type before, many times: a commander, of men and machines, a sailor who had become used to land, but who saw his own estates infrequently, living in clubs and hotels in the city. The last part was a guess, but the first was a certainty, or so he thought. He knew the name, but not the man, because —

'So, Yeo rode over and made us acquainted, in a kind of a distant way?'

'He did. He seemed amused to be a messenger.'

'Be damned he was, yes, I'll be damned! We sent post to him, but we didn't want any post seen at your doors. Precaution, you know. These are hard times. He'll have me for making him an errand boy, I'll be bound.'

There was a silence, which Justin vowed he would not be the first to break. After all, he had ridden God knows how many miles through rain and mud from Chittesleigh to meet this man, and it was straining his sense of loyalty when there was so much to do on his estate, on the verge of spring.

'Well, you'll want to know why you're here, Wentworth, and I'll get on to that. How is your mother?'

Justin looked across at Haworth, who was staring ahead, apparently unconcerned by his own question, and scanning the altar screen as if he had an interest in those ancient carvings. Everything told him he should now be on alert, if he had not been before.

'Fine woman, Wentworth. Met her when she was in town with your father many years ago now. She has survived him without too much ennui, I trust. Winters are bleak and long.'

'She has our local acquaintance, m'lord, which is adequate to her social needs, and the parson is attentive. And my sister is still with us at the manor.'

'Yet I dare say your mother misses her home country from time to time, sir, or I'll be damned. And her estate there. Yes, who wouldn't miss his own country, Wentworth, no matter how long away, don't y'think?'

Justin felt his face tighten, but kept a light smile in place. So that was it. The slip into colloquial language could hardly mask the probing comment, and in a flash he was back at school, taunted with 'Frenchie' and fighting back until his knuckles bled, and he was beaten by the schoolmaster for his aptitude in self-defence. He braced himself for what was coming next, but the admiral surprised him.

'But no matter about all that.' Lord Haworth got up and moved to the pulpit, as if to give himself more authority for what he was about to say, but he did not turn round. He shifted his shoulders slightly inside his uniform coat, and when he spoke it was quietly. 'You've heard about our setbacks in Brittany, I'll be bound.' Justin remained still and silent, but watched him closely. 'And about Granville and Savenay, where Westermann boasted of taking the battle to women and children? Dammit man, Westermann is a ghastly Republican regicide with a murderous bunch of uniformed rogues, butchering peasants and their innocent families on your doorstep in the Vendée, and you have nothing to say?'

Haworth had now turned to face him, and Justin looked him in the eyes before he spoke in a firm and even voice. 'I know about the Vendée, and the regiments the Republic sent out to put down the uprising. With half the French court in exile in London, an *émigré* on every street corner, how could a man not know, my lord? But Granville I know nothing about, except that it is a port.'

'Yes,' said Haworth, 'Granville is a port. I shall tell you, but I'll be brief. Back in the month of February 1793, some six months after the murder of the king, the bastard Republic tried to raise some three hundred thousand men for its renegade armies. Instead of that, they got themselves an uprising. Some call it the Vendée, some speak of Chouans, but it's an uprising whatever you care to name it. Your Breton peasants for one part, and those of the lower Loire for another, standing by their priests of the old church, and embracing loyalty to the new king in exile. A bloody struggle, fought out in woods and farmsteads, across the whole of the west of France. God spare us from anything similar here.'

'Granville, my lord? What is the Channel port of Granville to the uprising?'

'Was, Wentworth, was, or was meant to be. We were to support the uprising, to send transport ships with arms and exiles to the port of Granville. But it came to nothing. The Chouans were holed up in a town just inland. The plans were there, but it was poorly done.' Haworth sighed and shifted his weight.

'You want to do it again, and better this time?'

Haworth smiled, but his face showed little pleasure, just relief that he was beginning to be understood by this taciturn younger man. 'You have it, Wentworth. A mind that follows through the line, I see, a good naval tactic for a landsman.' He came and sat down on the bench again. 'I have little time left. The day is wearing on, and my inspections down on the coast finished an hour ago. If by chance I am being watched, I do not want to be missed for long.' He pulled on his sleeves, and then looked across the aisle at the other man. When he spoke, his voice carried as much stern authority as he could muster. 'You speak the lingo, Wentworth, and by repute you also know the Breton dialect too. You grew up there, you have land there, and you know the country. We want you to go in and speak to people that have influence. That is the sum of it.'

Justin grasped the top of the pew in front of him with both hands and stood up slowly. He seemed relaxed, but there was a trace of anger in his voice. 'The land I know is far from the Channel and from Granville, my lord. Our estate, my mother's estate, is in the south of Brittany, a patch of land near Lorient and Vannes. How can I be of use to you and the Admiralty? I am a soldier, sir, not a naval man, and my commission has lapsed.'

'We are not talking of Granville now, sir, but of other plans. I cannot tell you more. You must speak to Windham. As Secretary at War, he holds the reins.'

'To Windham?' Justin swung round to face Haworth, a flush of anger showing. 'Or do you mean to Wickham? You would have me a common spy, out of uniform, one of his sly mercenaries? I might have to ask you, my lord, what you take me for?'

'Don't raise your voice to me, Wentworth! You can get off your high horse. I said Windham, and I mean Windham. But I know how you served out in Quebec, when the French came into the war against Washington and we feared for Canada too.

You learned to speak the languages of the local tribes, they tell me, and fought skirmishes in the woods, so they say. Be damned if that was all in uniform, but it was your duty, sir, to the king, and you were glad to do it.'

Justin lifted his hands from the bench-top and took the anger out of his voice. 'That was a long time ago. I'll thank you, my lord, for your company here. It is a long way to Chittesleigh and my manor, and as you say the day is late.' He turned to pick up his cape and hat, and stepped into the aisle. He swung the cape on, faced Haworth, and bowed. 'Your servant, my lord.'

Haworth acknowledged his bow without standing, and spoke mildly. 'They said you would be difficult, and I was not inclined to disbelieve them.' Justin did not respond, but walked away to the door. 'Think about it, Wentworth.' It was a command, rather than an invitation. Justin halted and made as if he would turn his head, but changed his mind and looked at the dragoon guarding the door. The dragoon moved quickly aside, and Justin went out.

Lord Haworth picked up his cape, threw it over his arm, and strolled towards the entrance. He took a last look at the church, and as the sun abruptly cut in through a window, he passed through the door. The dragoon clipped his heels and followed him, and the door shut on its latch. The sun flashed in again briefly and then was gone, leaving the church caught in the dusk and quiet. Outside there were the sounds of wheels, a shout or two, and horses' hooves gradually fading away, and then all was silent apart from the wind in the trees.

Justin took care to stay for the night in Launceston, at the King's Arms Inn in Southgate Street, just by the old gate. He had no fear of losing his way in the dark as the miserable afternoon gave way to a dreary dusk, and in any case the bay mare would have found her way home once they were within smell of Chittesleigh. But he had learned to be cautious many years ago, and something in this unwelcome summons and meeting had raised all those old instincts, as far from the sharp-scented forests of North America as Cornwall and West Devon might be. It was hard to imagine danger in the occasional squat cottage, looming out of the dark like a mute beast, its thatch dripping like the cattle on the moor, although all might gaze at a horseman as the evening drew in, and mutter a little if there was no recognition. It was more that he wanted to be seen, in a town that he visited often enough to be known, and to sit in a public place taking his refreshment. This he did by avoiding the snug and taking a weather-beaten table and a creaking chair in the main bar, a man simply relaxing with a pint of claret and his landlord's best beef and pudding. As he told the landlord, William Palmer, for all to hear, he was in the town to speak to the wine merchant in the morning.

An old campaigner, Justin had tracked around the town before he rode in, making his approach from the direction of Holsworthy rather than the west. It was all probably quite unnecessary, and to no obvious purpose. But somehow it satisfied him that he was taking precautions, on his guard against a threat that he now obscurely sensed lay over him, and perhaps his family. After all, he was their only guardian. His father was dead, his brother had died when young, his sister was unmarried, and were he to go then his mother would be hard pressed to cope with the loss, practical woman though she was, and shrewd when called upon. She had been through much with his father after they met in Canada, and her possessions in Brittany had brought her grief and anxiety in recent years. But she was not to be daunted by conflicts or by hostility; it was bereavement that delivered the greatest wounds.

That press of thoughts had been far more to the front of Justin's mind than any sense of immediate danger to himself, or real apprehension that he was being followed, or that his rendezvous with Lord Haworth had somehow been observed in that remote location over the border in Cornwall, although it had been fixed through intermediaries. That is what danger meant as you grew older, he reflected as he drank his wine, while scanning the faces and bearings of those who came into the bar. Every blow or cut may hurt your nearest and dearest as much as you, may threaten them more than your own life might be valued in the scales either of justice or eternity. He laughed briefly as he realised how morbidly philosophical he was getting, probably as a means of distracting himself from wondering what on earth this whole enterprise might signify for him.

The next morning's activity was perfunctory. He settled his bill and duly walked through the main square above the castle to the wine merchant, who was only a little surprised to see him, since he would have expected him in another month or so. But Justin found an easy reason in the entertaining he had done recently, and he made some changes to his standing order for wines from Bordeaux and Gascony, which pleased the merchant, because those Justin chose were more expensive and flattered the merchant's recommendation of them. He left the merchant beaming and making hurried entries in his ledger, and walked back across the square and along Southgate to the King's Arms, whistling 'Greensleeves'. The ostler at the inn was a lean and oily man, with hands like the leather of the reins he gripped with ease, and yet he was civil enough, holding the stirrup without looking for the tip that he was given as a matter of form. Justin looked up unobtrusively as he turned his horse in the yard, scanned the windows, smiled at the ostler, and rode out of the yard with a quick sideways glance at the door to the inn. He rode down the hill, past the castle walls and the gate, and out towards Okehampton, and then on to Chittesleigh.

Soon after he left, a bulky figure in what looked like an old soldier's coat came out of the inn, spoke briefly to the ostler and laughed aloud with him, and asked after the public stage to Tavistock. What he heard seemed to satisfy him, and he went back in to wait, scribbling the words *Nothing much* in a grimy pocket-book.

CHAPTER III: DEATH IN THE FOREST

The Breton forest was momentarily quiet. The sun had broken through the clouds, and was now slanting down between the trees, and the canopy was glistening. Even the birds were quiet. The new leaves barely rustled, but there was an uneven patter of raindrops on withered leaves on the ground. Old sweet-chestnut shells lay mixed with the dried acorns, and the few remaining berries of the holly trees shone a polished red in the light. A red squirrel paused in its ascent up a trunk, its head tilted slightly to one side, as if listening for a sound that was so noticeably absent, apart from its own, swift movement.

Then the silence was broken. Softly at first, as if there was nothing; but the squirrel knew, and was suddenly nowhere to be seen. Then again, the same indistinct sound. The birds were just now beginning to be heard, not alarmed, but stirring after the rain. The sound was undoubtedly movement, still blurred and intermittent, but it was gathering pace, as if stumbling towards this clearing. It was a wild and careless noise, hardly that of an animal of the forest, but rough and incompetent, with the ground trampled, sticks snapping, the rushing sound of undergrowth and smaller branches being pushed aside. Along with it, and gradually, could be heard a gasping, ugly intake of breath, and parts of what became a recognisably human voice, muttering, sobbing, and cursing.

By now the birds were sounding their alarm calls, one or two flitting from branch to branch on the edge of the clearing, the blackbird running straight across it, as always in charge of its territory, even in fear. But as the man burst out of the undergrowth and into the open space, it clucked and rattled for the last time as it scuttled through the leaves and flew quickly into the trees. It need not have worried; the man did not see it, even if he stared wildly about him.

It was hard to tell his age, although he was slightly balding in the middle of his tousled hair. This was because his face, where it was not covered in grime and smeared in sweat, was scarred with bloody scratches from the undergrowth, which here was thick with brambles and scattered with gorse, apart from the low-lying branches that must have swiped at him as he forced his way through. He was wearing the bright blue uniform of the Republican army, muddied and torn in places, and had the good fortune of some half-decent shoes, a rarity in those parts. Of his musket, there was nothing to be seen, and instead he clutched in his left hand a very small knife, such as a man might use on campaign to cut up his bread or meat, if he was very lucky. He kept hold of it as he fell to his knees, listening as if he was certain that he would hear something that would terrify him.

That strange quiet settled on the clearing again and spread to the whole forest. Nothing moved. His head turned from side to side, and perhaps he was just listening, but he also seemed to be looking for something, searching the glade for some helpful sign. He stood up again, wiped his hand across his forehead, muttered dimly and then half staggered and half ran across the clearing, first to one side and then to another, always away from the direction in which he had come. Then he stood stock-still and lifted his head again, his hand inadvertently gripping the knife so tightly that the knuckles stood out white against the blotched skin. He mouthed a curse and stared back where he had come, then turned and rushed headlong into the undergrowth, on what was the bare outline of a track.

But he had not gone more than a cart's length in when he was brought up short, the veins standing out on his neck. Great breaths dragged out of his lungs. What he had heard was just the sound of a little owl, so low it was almost mute, at a distance. But although he was from the city — his beloved, scruffy Paris with its wondrous, crowded streets — he knew that owls do not hunt in daylight, and he also knew with brutal certainty what he would hear next. The first owl cry was answered almost immediately by another and another, on the left, to the right, one behind, one or two or more in front, mostly distant, but some close. The effect on him was blind panic. He broke through his paralysis, and started forward with nerves and sinews tight. But as he lifted his right foot off the ground, he felt his left foot caught, and looked down in horror to see a forearm and a dark hand grasping his ankle with a grip like iron. He screamed like a beast, and the scream penetrated into the depths of the forest.

The robin, the *rouge-gorge*, perched on the yellow gorse. The rain began to fall again, gently. It was a mild spring. Grosjean stood up, grinned, and wiped his long hunting knife on his breeches. His beard had raindrops in it.

The road home seemed like all roads home, familiar and friendly, increasingly so as the mare got keener, and its pace firmer. There was always a rhythm in the beat of the hooves, and tunes came and went in Justin's mouth, perhaps to match them, perhaps to set up a counterpoint. As he drew near to Chittesleigh, he turned off down a lane to the hamlet which sheltered one of his tenants, to speak to him about the matter of a plough and a lame plough-horse, and the problems of a loan from a neighbour. There was a good welcome at the farm, as always, with the tenant's wife insisting on him eating butter, and the children staring at his boots and the long cape with its several collars. It was a short detour, but reassuring after dragoons and admirals in the rain, and he rode on nodding and speaking to those he passed in the fields, down on through and over the hill into sight of the manor.

The sun was welcome after yesterday's torrential rain, even if it was fitful, and the glass in the larger windows of the west wing shone, in contrast to the darker outlines of the older east wing. They had built much of it in old Henry's time, or perhaps it was that of Elizabeth, he had forgotten precisely. But the heart of the manor was even older than that, coming to the Wentworths through marriage with the daughter of a line that claimed to be Norman. His father had felt it was too old and dusty for a young wife, and so when he had married Justin's mother he had renovated the west wing in contemporary fashion, enlarging the windows on both floors, and creating a modern drawing room in which his wife could welcome other women of standing in the locality without undue embarrassment. The plasterwork was delicate, ranging round the edge of the ceiling in a display of simulated fruit and animals, and the furnishings were of a piece in quality, with mahogany and walnut and the fine lines that those with income liked, because they marked out a change from the grim sturdiness of the previous age, which somehow reflected its cruelty, or so his mother felt.

Chittesleigh faced south, and Justin rode round behind it to the stables, where Jem was waiting with a warm welcome as he took the bridle. Justin's other mare also gave its greeting to the returning mount from behind its door, and bustled briefly to the opened hatch just to show its pleasure. Justin spoke to it, and looked over the bay he had ridden to check it was uninjured by what had at times been a hard journey on unfamiliar roads and tracks in inclement weather. The women used to complain that he always greeted his horses before he greeted them, and he had seen his sister at the window as he came down, so he only jumped a little when she placed her hands over his eyes after sneaking up behind him. Jem grinned and led the bay off to be stabled with its enthusiastic companion, and Justin held Amelia by the hands, and tried to smile a little to please her.

She looked at him with an amused but penetrating stare, holding his attention in the way that she did when she chose. She had done it since she was a child, and he could not easily resist. 'And why so stern and grave?' she asked.

He smiled some more, and with an effort relaxed his face. 'Serious matters in Launceston,' he said. 'The vicar's cat was trodden on by the jailor's pony, and the whole place was in an uproar. It's as wild as the ragged coasts in the far west of England, you know.'

Amelia looked at him again, shrewdly this time, but decided to drop her scrutiny. 'I doubt if those in Cornwall would thank you for calling them English, but we shall let that pass.' She took his hand to lead him towards the house, and he did not resist. 'Mother has kept to the arrangements and invitations for dining, Justin. It is as well that you were no later. She will want your voice if the hall is to be set as it should be. Thomas can be slow, and the other is not the most willing in kitchen work.'

'No wonder that he is not always, with a leg that can pain him. But he came recommended by Miss Wollaston's father, who was anxious for us to give him room.'

'Well, in that case I shall leave him without reserve in my brother's capable management, while I keep all my natural spirits for restraining the unwanted *esprit* of the *formidable* Miss Arabella Wollaston, whom he fears so much.' Amelia on occasion amused herself by echoing some of her mother's French expressions, something to which Justin himself was not averse.

'Miss Wollaston is your schoolfriend, Melia, and I would charge you not to forget it. That accounts for her presence here. Unless, of course, we were also to add to that your irrepressible desire to tease me mercilessly on a topic of your invention. Her father is our neighbour, and one must be hospitable. Besides, in these difficult times it is as well for us to know how each other thinks.'

They were strolling along the back of the manor through the garden, which despite changing fashion was still cast in its original design, with low hedges of box and stone paths, a little like a maze but one in which one could see one's way. There was a sundial centrally placed, and there were stone benches in various locations beneath the more substantial plants and small trees. Behind it and the rose arbour lay the orchard, which was breaking into blossom, the apple trees following the pear trees. The scene was one of tranquillity and beauty, and they walked on slowly, arm in arm, lost in their own thoughts.

CHAPTER IV: PATRIOTS ALL

The dinner at Chittesleigh came off as was to be expected, namely in good humour when all parties knew each other tolerably and respected each other's station in life. That is to say, all had sufficient manners to avoid any unpleasantness that may be incidental to conversation, even between those of the same standing. The food at the Wentworth table was always of good quality, dependent on the season, taken in some part from the estate at the home barton or from its tenants, but supplemented with purchases made in the local towns, or in the spring and autumn from the fishing ports on the northern coast of Devon. The family did not go to the expense of hiring a French cook, although they were more numerous since the troubled state of France had sent the dependants of great houses abroad. They kept to the local arts of Jem's wife, and a young lad who seemed to have a penchant for baking and roasting meats and fowl.

These were all points noted in casual conversation by Sir Francis Wollaston and the other guests, who on this early spring evening numbered also his daughter, Arabella, the naval Captain Frederick Yeo, known to both the Wollaston and the Wentworth families, Thomas Darke of Fishley in the local town of Hatherleigh, and Cradock Glasscott, its vicar. The wines were good if not exceptional, as Sir Francis used often to remark to his daughter on the journey back to Alverscombe in the carriage, rather to her irritation, although she was in most respects suitably fond of her father. It was an observation hard to take as authoritative from a man who had good reason to observe mild temperance in his habits.

After dinner, the women went first into the drawing room in the west wing, in the form established at Chittesleigh, leaving the men to linger over their wine in the dining room in the old hall, and to share a few thoughts on the state of the nation. These were mostly of a conventional kind, and drifted easily into speculations on the likely quality of this year's harvest. But Justin became alert when Sir Francis suddenly mentioned the Breton insurrection at Granville, some eighteen months back in the early winter of '93, and the failure of the British to support it properly.

'Your concern, sir, takes what special form?' the vicar had asked, quietly smothering a yawn brought on more by the wine than a lack of proper interest. The French revolutionaries were godless, even if many of the priesthood they had displaced were of the mistaken faith, God rest their souls.

'Mr Pitt was surely to be commended for his refusal to become embroiled in the struggle, Sir Francis? We have no army that can fight with the revolutionary French, with their enforced conscription.' Thomas Darke was a broad-faced man of strong local roots, who despite being a landowner looked for all the world as if he had stepped off one of the ships of Francis Drake or Hawkins.

'A war has been declared, and a war cannot be fought by sea alone. These are regicides, Thomas. We should be mistaken if we did not do what we can to encourage revolt or resistance. After all, sir, resistance from within is cheap, in taxes and in blood, and the Bretons are willing. Is it not so, Wentworth? You have land there, I believe.'

Justin was standing by the hearth facing into the room, while the others had remained sitting, and they all looked to him as he spoke. 'It is by right my mother's land, as you say, but now it is apparently for her cousin to protect both manor and the estate, and many headaches it must be bringing him. The Bretons in revolt may be both violent and unsparing, yet will hardly be a match in open warfare for the troops of the French government.'

'You call it a government, then, Justin? You would give it legitimacy?' Sir Francis was not indignant, just lightly inquisitive, and Justin momentarily distrusted that tone more.

'They are making laws, creating armies, drawing taxes, taking lives and property as they choose. We have seen this before, gentlemen, and we proved unable to stop it then in our own possessions in the American colonies. I doubt we can stop it now, whatever our revulsion. Our concern must be to make sure it does not cross the water.'

'Meaning, sir?' The vicar was again curious, despite the wine.

'Meaning that ideas may cross the water and even the ocean, Mr Glasscott, and no blockade even by His Majesty's navy may prevent them.'

There was a general mutter at this as each protested, looking to each other, but Justin continued speaking.

'These are much the same ideas that brought revolution to America, and American success has endorsed them and sent them back to where they came from. Paine is now at home in Paris and Rennes, as much as Voltaire and Rousseau were in Boston and Philadelphia. I trust we shall not see the frame of a guillotine on Hampstead Heath, but no one should imagine that the challenge of ideas may not rattle casements in London, and some of our larger and growing towns. Yet there are those who predict that it will be the industry in these new boroughs that will change all our ways, even more than ideas.' With these last sentences, he looked at them directly, and he saw they were shocked, not at the speaker, but at what they knew to be true in part, although they had great difficulty in making sense of it all. He had hoped that a short, opinionated speech delivered quickly would put an end to this discussion, but he was to be disappointed.

'This is far from the question of whether we go in to Brittany,' said Sir Francis slowly and deliberately, as if he was not going to be distracted by the larger issues introduced by Justin, 'or indeed how. That is the current, urgent question.' He had looked away from Justin towards the others, but the younger man was convinced that the words were directed at him. 'It will be troubling Mr Pitt, you can be sure of that, as well as Windham, who would like to make a success of any further intervention. But gentlemen, I can see from our host's demeanour that we have been far too long over our wine. It is time we ventured across to the drawing room, and rejoined the ladies.'

Amelia drew Arabella to her, took her arm in hers, and sauntered across the room to the fire-screen by the hearth, where her brother was talking to Glasscott, the vicar. They were in the drawing room with the gentlemen, who had brought into the scented room a strong odour of wine. Amelia always disliked that intrusive smell, but it made her mother laugh at the frailty of men before Bacchus.

Arabella looked on Sempronie Wentworth a little as a mother, since her own had died many years ago and suddenly, collapsing while out riding. It was, as Cradock Glasscott had said at the time, in his first year at the Hatherleigh church, a warning to them all that in the midst of life there is death, and that God calls us to him when it suits his inscrutable design. As a girl looking on at the sombre scene of burial, Amelia had wondered how any kind of design could be called inscrutable. Ever since then she and Arabella had found it hard to believe that Mr Glasscott really knew the full and accurate measure of what he was saying, although this was an observation they tended to keep to themselves.

'It was, indeed, difficult, but at least… Ah, the young ladies. Miss Wollaston, Miss Wentworth.' Glasscott bowed slightly, as befitted his station in life, which should not show too much deference to attractive young women, even if they did come from the gentry. 'You will no doubt do me the honour of helping Mrs Glasscott and the ladies of the town to prepare the church for the solemn festival of the passion of our Lord? She is always most appreciative of the presence of members of our most distinguished families. There is such a difference between careful discrimination and — how might I put it? — misguided enthusiasm.'

'I trust, Mr Glasscott, that you are not doubting our enthusiasm in praising our discrimination. We should be most sorry to lose at the same moment as we gain.'

'Not at all, Miss Wentworth, not at all. You have always been most enthusiastic in your participation. Ah, I see Sir Francis is beckoning to me. With your indulgence, Wentworth, and yours…' The vicar bowed quickly, crossed the room, and joined Sir Francis suddenly and to the latter's surprise, who nonetheless welcomed him to the close conversation he was having with Captain Yeo.

'Glasscott is deserving of rather less of your wit, Arabella, and more of…'

'Our discrimination, I suppose.' Arabella smiled back disarmingly at Justin, who had made the mistake of faltering as he tried to think of a mild term for respect. Faced with these two, he was constantly provoked to remonstrating, and also painfully aware of how rarely he could keep up with such ready tongues. 'And I do like to entertain the notion that by now I am deserving of rather less than "Arabella", Mr Wentworth.'

Justin made the mistake of being momentarily confused. What did this perplexing young woman mean by being less than herself? He smiled and pursed his lips in complete puzzlement, but fortunately help was at hand.

'Brother, how many times must we insist that you call our good friend "Bella" as she prefers, and not as custom dictates? It is a mark of friendship that we may dispense to a degree with those formalities that we find both tedious and cold. It is some years since this was requested of you…'

'And yet we see no reformation.' Arabella looked directly at Justin, who glanced only briefly back into that challengingly beautiful face, and then found that he had to scan the other parties in the room. He caught the eye of his mother, whose attention had been on his small group for a little while now, while she spoke easily with Thomas Darke of the horseracing of which he was inordinately fond. She laid her hand gently on Darke's forearm, in the manner that had most men finding room to praise her to their womenfolk and gain sharp looks in return. She left him in mid-sentence to join her family group.

'Now, Amélie, you have been leading our dear friend Bella astray in making light work of our good churchman, I see? *Le pauvre homme* means well, and he has been very kind to us, even if his manner has at times more of the hoof than the feather. Now, Justin, you must leave me to discipline these *méchantes*, who are so much worse when they are together, and we must encourage Sir Francis to pay his respects to his present companions, and reunite himself with his daughter. Come, I shall call to him.'

As many had done before, Sir Francis came when he was called, perhaps the more promptly in that he was a widower.

He had always entertained hopes of one day appealing to Mrs Wentworth's need for companionship; but he saw, as others did, that her son unwittingly stood in the way, all the more so since he chose to remain unmarried. But he was not a man to pine after what he could not have, and he had other preoccupations.

'Mrs Wentworth,' he said, 'madam, I am honoured as always, and I'll be blessed if I don't run up like a spaniel whenever you call, don't I, Justin, eh? Like a puppy, and that's a thing! 'Tis your French blood, madam, that has us all at your mercy, the charm of your race, which is at its highest in you because it is least assumed and most natural.' Rather pleased with this effusive flattery, he beamed at them all, ignoring his daughter's motions to him to be silent, and Amelia's lightly quivering lip as she looked across at her brother. But Sir Francis was no fool. He was intrigued as well as charmed, and like the solid Englishman he was, he knew he did not understand the degree of affiliation that this remarkable woman had to her own country of birth. 'Madam, tell me the story of your name and ancestry again. I am like a sieve for knowledge; it spills out as fast as I gather it. Forgive me, madam, your full name, if you will honour me…'

'…is Jeanne Sempronie de Guèrinec, *monsieur*. And you will ask me again how it came to be Sempronie, and I shall tell you willingly that it is taken, as you did suspect, from the Romans.'

'Ah yes, some imperial family, rich and haughty, I'll be bound, with its portraits in marble in some lofty hall in Rome staring down at us lesser mortals.' He laughed good-naturedly, and there indeed was nothing hostile or slighting in his tone. But he was, nonetheless, corrected from an unlikely source.

'Sempronia, Sir Francis. Aristocratic, certainly, but of the radical faction, as I recall: the family name of the Gracchi, who fostered a revolution of the poorer classes.' It was Captain Yeo, who had come up behind the women and spoke between them. 'At least, as I recall from my schoolroom history of ancient Rome. But you would know better than me, Justin.'

'And I, *peut-être*, would know best of all. You are right, Captain, and as I have before informed you, Sir Francis, unimportant though it may be amongst the concerns of life, it was my father who named me thus, since he admired the family of the Gracchi greatly. He was, as they say in France, of the *éclaircissement* himself, even though a Breton, which is far from the salons of Paris.'

'And you, madam, as we all know, suffer so much from those radical factions that now oppress your country. A sad irony.' Sir Francis shook his head solemnly.

'There are those amongst them who will still maintain the principles of humanity and moderation without the lapse into savagery, my good Sir Francis. I am sure my cousin, who now takes care of our estate at Kergohan for the family, is one of those.'

'But your son, as we all know, is a patriot. Thank God, what proved to be the desperate fate of the Gracchi is not for him.'

'But you may die as a patriot, *monsieur*, as well as a revolutionary.' It was a statement rather than a question from the lady of the house, and by her side Captain Yeo went pale.

'Madam, it is all too true. Your son George was a patriot, and under my charge, by God. My sorrow is not as great as yours, Mrs Wentworth, or that of his sister and his brother; but it is grave, and time has not lessened it.'

'A naval man may be forgiven for his milder oaths, I suppose.' It was the voice of the vicar, who with Thomas Darke had come across to join the larger group. 'But we are not used to this language of the wind and the rain in our sheltered rooms, Captain Yeo.'

'Ah, patriotism, to which we all must offer our services if called. God will bless the memories of those who are dear to us all, madam.' The group had begun to break up, but Sir Francis continued speaking to Captain Yeo, and to Justin's back as he withdrew with his sister. 'But I wonder if it is always given to us to recognise when it calls, in its different guises, and its variant duties. For that, sir —' he turned to Captain Yeo as Justin momentarily slowed in his step — 'we shall need the help of your ancient Romans and their virtues. To answer the call: a very Roman, and a very British virtue, I believe, sir.' Captain Yeo nodded at his words, looking distractedly across the room at Jeanne Sempronie de Guèrinec as she talked to one of the maids, while Justin kept walking towards the portrait of his father, which hung benignly above the hearth.

CHAPTER V: CONFRONTATION AND COURAGE

Babette pulled the shirt out of the bowl and wrung it out with strong hands and wrists. She glanced across the yard and out into the dusty court, around which the other cottages stood, and down the lane, and yawned.

'Gilles!' she shouted. 'Come here, you little weasel, you shrew, you mouse! Come and get a beating.'

'Why should I get a beating?' The voice came from nearby, probably somewhere in a loft amongst the straw, she thought.

'For what you did last time, which I've forgotten, or for what you are doing now, or for what you are going to do very soon if I don't catch up with you, Jesus and Mary be praised.'

A young lad of about fifteen years came running round the corner, with a grin on his face. 'What is there to do? There is nothing here, anyone can see that. Nothing to clean out.'

'The cow and the pigs are in the woods, you fool, where the servants of the devil can't get them.'

'Which servants of the devil?' Gilles kicked a stone across the yard with a clog that all too plainly showed signs of that habit on its toe.

'The soldiers, you fool.'

'You know what, Babette?'

'What now, weasel? Hang that shirt on the wheel.'

Gilles took the shirt from her and swung it round. He ran over to an old cart wheel, leaning in the sun against the side of a thatched barn. But he faced the handsome young woman as he was hanging it up, grinning, at a safe distance. 'I saw

Grosjean was here, and he had his hand on your arse, Babette, and he was laughing and whispering in your ear, Babette.'

Babette looked at the bowl she was carrying, as if to see if she could swing the water in it at him. 'And then you saw me swipe him, you little rat, didn't you, and saw him rub his cheek for all that big man's beard of his. Hah! Our father left me the cow and the fields, and poor, dumb Tangi to work them. What need do I have of Grosjean and his black beard?'

'What need then do we have of Guareg and his leg?'

Babette, stopped for a moment, and then threw the water away in a wide arc. 'His bad leg, you mean. He can't help that, little weasel.'

Gilles came across and grabbed a buckwheat biscuit before she could stop him. He dodged her hand as she tried to clip him, and stood by the door as she put the bowl down. 'But he eats so much. They must be glad to be rid of him at home.'

Babette laughed. 'So the spoon tells the pot it is dirty, is that it? When did you stop eating?'

'But I'm yours, or our mother's, may the two Marys bless her and save her soul. He's not. He's from Plugarec'h, not here. Why have we got him?'

'Because we have pity, as the Lord told us to, you fool. Now get out of my kitchen before you do more damage than a rat… And because we are fools, with the biggest fool Grosjean amongst us, for our sins,' she added under her breath as Gilles slipped outside, kicking his clog against the doorpost. She stood at the door in the sun. It was sharp, beginning to have some real heat in it now, making the crops grow at last, although a long way from ripening. A hard time for food, apart from biscuits and milk, and some of the plants that grew wild. But that would change. She smiled, and in a relaxed mood looked left down the lane towards the woods. Her smile vanished. She stood absolutely still and looked again, bringing her hand above her eyes in concentration. *'Mère de dieu, et tous les saints glorifiés… Les bleus… Gilles, Gilles, ven-ci!'*

She whistled loudly for the other women in the cottages, or behind them in the fields, but sent Gilles out to them anyway, and to stay away. There had to be some women here, in the cottages, but the others could run and hide. Curse Grosjean and his pig-willed plans. They would surely find Guareg.

But then she saw that it was too late to worry. The bluecoat she had just glimpsed in the trees had turned into five or six, and they were dragging a man between them, his legs trailing along the ground, until they hit him, and he tried to walk a few steps again. Most had muskets, but there was one in front with a sword, and gold tassels on his coat. Babette spat on the ground.

'Voir les connards en file,' she said to herself, without caring much about who heard her. But she turned round quickly as another woman came out of the cottage opposite and ran across to her. Babette gripped her firmly by the upper arms. 'They have him, Yaelle, it's too late now. Shut your mouth or you will be dead too.' And backing this up, Babette clamped her large palm over the young woman's mouth, avoiding her teeth but gripping her jaw, her other arm tight around her shoulders. 'Shut up or we're all dead, including Gilles.'

The woman looked up at her with fearful eyes, and then forced her head around to look towards the lane, at the far side of the court where the Republican soldiers were now appearing. Two other women who had been in their cottages came out slowly and stared, too late to flee into the fields. The soldiers threw their prisoner down. Two of them pointed their muskets at him, while the others pointed their muskets at the women, who had gathered together, silent and expressionless.

The captain put his tricorne back on his head, covering the fair hair above his short, military pigtail. He was young, but no younger than some of his generals, and like them he was already hardened. He looked at the women as if he was looking at something from the Middle Ages, and despised them because their respect was only for priests and aristocratic landowners, their *seigneurs* over centuries of ignorance. It was their fault that they clung to the past; and it was not his fault that he was an unforgiving present. He had not wanted this war in the west, of patriot against traitor. He spoke harshly. 'Do you know this man?'

Silence. One of his soldiers, the sergeant, laughed. The captain looked at him, and then strode forward, right up to the women. The sergeant followed behind him, leaving his musket.

'You heard me. You understand French well enough when it suits you. Or I'll bet that some of you do. Do you know this man? What was he doing in your woods?'

One of the women pushed forward urgently, before her arm was grabbed, this time by Yaelle. 'What have you done with our pigs?'

The captain looked at the sergeant, who laughed again. 'Nothing, you Breton bitch; the only pig we found was this one. He grunts well enough.'

At this prompt, one of the soldiers kicked Guareg on the ground for good measure, and grinned back.

The captain went over to Guareg and grabbed him by the collar, pulling him onto his side and showing the wound on his leg, which had opened again bloodily and was covered in dirt. 'Do you see this? Have any of you been tending to this man? You know what this means? It means he has been fighting the soldiers of the Republic, that he is a rebel, one of your village army of Chouans or whatever you call these traitors —

enemies of the constitution and of liberty, murderers of honest men!' There was fire in the captain's voice now, and his face was red. He stared in fury at the blunt hostility of the women, and raised his voice. 'Do you know what happens to traitors? To rebels? By decree of the Convention? You know what my orders are? What is the law?' He quickly raised his arm and clicked his fingers. The soldiers pulled Guareg to his feet. 'For your sake, we will do it out of sight.'

He clicked his fingers again, and swept his arm across his body to indicate a path between two cottages across the court. The soldiers dragged Guareg quickly past the women and down between the cottages. The captain paused to look at the group of women, and then swung out behind his soldiers. There was not long to wait. The order rang out, and straight after it two shots, cracks like a beam going in a house.

The women did not move, aware of the watching soldiers and the sergeant, who was still smiling. He came up to Yaelle, and gestured to Babette to stand well away from her. He was a burly man with a scar on his forehead, a heavy-boned face, brown with grime and the sun, and strikingly white teeth, with only two missing in the lower jaw. Yaelle stared at him, transfixed, and he put his broad hand up to her cheek and pinched it between his fingers, still smiling.

'So, you don't know him, do you? But I bet you do know a man, don't you? And if he won't do, perhaps we will, eh?' And as quick as lightning for a stocky man, he grabbed her by the hair with one hand, pulling her head back, and shoved his other hand into her blouse, turning to smile at his men as she wriggled, and then staring with the same smile into the face of Babette, who smiled back at him. Just as suddenly, he released his hold as the captain and the two soldiers came back down the path between the houses. The sergeant turned to his captain. 'Captain, this one knows more than she is saying. We should perhaps ask her some questions, away from the others, inside one of these pigsties? There may be more of them in hiding.'

The captain said nothing, but signalled to two of the soldiers to take hold of Yaelle.

Babette stepped in front of him, slowly and deliberately, half-smiling and fixing him with her gaze. 'Let her go.'

'Why should I let her go, woman?'

'Because she is innocent, town-boy, unlike you.'

The captain looked at her, and past her at Yaelle, who was still mute but terrified, and struggling slightly, as if she feared that worse would come if she struggled more. He looked round at the cottages, and at the wheel with the shirt drying on it. 'Let her go. Some biscuits. You'll find him at the back. I'll let you dispose of him.' He took off his tricorne, smoothed back his hair and wiped his forehead, then replaced the tricorne. 'Biscuits. Quickly, before I change my mind.'

As the air in the drawing room became more oppressive, Arabella went first to the closet, where her maid was in attendance with warm water and crisp linen. She was in the habit of retiring quite often when in company, not so much out of need, although she liked to wash her hands when in hot rooms, but because she could in that way not be caught inextricably in conversation. Despite her charm and social graces, she had an independence of mind that at times could not bear to be submitted without relief to talk of hounds and hunting, or indeed of fashion and family. All of these things she accepted well enough, but in small doses as topics of polite conversation, or she became impatient. It was fair to say that she liked her own company, and that of her friend, and would rather hear about her pursuits of sketching or reading than those she was often expected to admire.

And it was for those reasons that she liked the house at Chittesleigh and its members, the wonderful mother with her sharp but kindly eyes, and her beloved Amelia, who was prepared to consider the disturbing ideas recently proposed by Mary Wollstonecraft with some favour. Their conversation together was always stimulating and a delight. But, somehow, when the men were present it degenerated, and here she blushed, partly in irritation, because she was aware she herself was at fault. She knew that she did flirt relentlessly with Amelia's brother Justin, or rather that she tried to attract his attention, despite her constantly renewed intentions to behave in a more mature and sober way. What is more, she was convinced that he despised her for being no more than a person of her kind, a young woman of standing, of estate and income far beyond his, for all that his tenure of the land was older than that of her family. So, infuriatingly, the less interest he showed in her, the more she tried to draw him out.

In her embarrassment and humiliation she knocked the ewer slightly, but with a small cry and with quick and practical hands she caught it before it toppled, and before her maid could intervene. She found their French porcelain delightful, part of the beguiling atmosphere of this remarkable house that haunted her, no matter what other grand mansion she visited, either here in Devon, where there were several known to her father, or in Bath, or in town.

Perhaps the house was on her mind, or perhaps she did not want to return to the gathering in quite this mood. But, however that was, she turned up the staircase that led to the domestic rooms above, where she had so often stayed as Amelia's guest. She walked up the treads lightly and quietly, lifting her skirts, and reached the top of the flight, with the corridor leading off to the women's rooms to the right, and to the left towards Justin's large chamber. Just at that moment, something caught her eye and she paused, concealed by the large, polished wooden post that marked the top of the staircase.

She had indeed been observant, and what she saw made her puzzled and wary. Along the corridor she could just perceive a man's back, hesitating briefly by the door to Justin's chamber. She had no idea who it was, and instinctively she held her breath and drew back further, with a sense of mystery and suspicion. She heard the floorboards creak, and for one dreadful moment thought that the man must be coming towards the stairs and her place of concealment, so she turned as if to run down the stairs, or at least pretend that she was coming up them. But the sound ceased.

The man might have been there for a legitimate purpose, but she stepped forward, perversely convinced that he was not. She trod lightly but firmly down the corridor, and could see that the door to Justin's room was still open. She had been down the same corridor many times, but never to this point. She pushed the door slightly. Across the room was a writing desk. There were papers on it, and several of the small drawers at the back of the desk were open. Could the man have been rifling through Justin's papers? Her heart started to pound. She could not resist the story she was telling herself, and so she crossed the room.

She had expected to see a stolen key suspiciously in one of the locks, or even a sign of split wood or breakage, but instead her attention was drawn to the papers. A quick glance told her that what was on the desk was a collection of bills and estate correspondence, requisitions for fodder and hay for horses, and something to do with wine. She suddenly felt ashamed and glanced round, and saw for the first time and with embarrassment the bed with its coverlet to one side, and what must be the door to Justin's closet, also ajar, an inner sanctum which made her even more nervous.

But her lively imagination pulled her back to what lay in front of her, and she reached with a slightly trembling hand for one of the papers, a letter that was squashed into an open drawer. With an indrawn breath, she realised that it was in French, in a hand that was not Justin's. She spread it out, feeling her mouth going dry. She knew that her own knowledge of French was poor; but that surely was the word *armée*, and further down she could trace the terrifying words *la mort du roi*. Was this what the man had been looking at? What could it all mean?

From below she heard the sound of voices. She folded and pushed the letter hurriedly back in the drawer, and swept across the room to the door as she heard steps briskly coming up the stairs. She was not quick enough. She was outside and had her fingers on the brass handle, her back to the stairs, but she had to turn to put a brave face on her awful indiscretion.

Justin smiled at her. 'I'm afraid it closes with difficulty. But, forgive me, I am forgetting myself: perhaps I should ask you how I may help you? I must suppose you are looking for something. A mislaid reticule, perhaps, or a shawl for the draughts, or possibly something for my sister? These old houses are hardly warm even in the late spring. You must, of course, in any case have mistaken your way.' He came forward, still smiling.

She trembled, lifting her hand from the doorknob, and blushed from her neck to the roots of her curled hair, feeling the uncomfortable sensation but, as always, unable to control it. She could, however, just keep her voice steady, and she resolutely cleared her mind. 'No, sir, you must forgive me for creating a poor impression of myself with you. I had wished to go to Amelia's room, but saw that your door was open, and thought that I myself would have wanted it closed. Now, with your permission…'

She gathered up her skirts decisively, and made to move past him in the corridor. But instead of his usual politeness, he did not stand completely aside as she attempted to pass, so that she almost brushed into him and had to put up her hand towards his shoulder to prevent a collision. With a sudden movement, he took her wrist in his, firmly although not roughly, and turned her hand to look at the palm. She flinched and gasped as he spoke again, this time with a harshness with which she was totally unfamiliar.

'A fair hand, my lady, far too fair to do your father's dirty work, I have no doubt.' He released her.

She looked at him in astonishment and mounting anger. 'Sir! I must ask you to stand aside, if you please!' She swept past him towards the head of the stairs.

He smiled again grimly, but did not much lower his voice. 'No, what could I have been thinking of? Impossible, quite impossible.' And as she looked round for a final time, with her eyes blazing, he added, 'Far too fair.'

Although it had seemed like an age, it had been scarcely ten minutes since Arabella had left the drawing room and the company. But on her return, Amelia looked over with some concern from where she was sitting, in conversation with Captain Yeo. Amelia frowned slightly, noticing that Arabella looked flustered and a little flushed, and she also wondered where her brother was at this moment. She continued talking to Yeo about life in the West Indies, which he knew well, because she was drawn as ever by the need to get a better picture of the world that her brother George had known as a midshipman on that fateful service on HMS *Lucretia*. But her attention was now drifting from the conversation, and she kept glancing worriedly over to Arabella, who had joined her mother, while her mind would not let up on where her brother could be.

But it all proved to be about nothing, as there he was again at the door, taking in the scene at his ease, enjoying the spectacle of women and men conversing together without exaggerated formality. That was his mother's wish, and his, although he had pleaded that the men should be allowed to go apart to smoke in the library if they chose, and indeed to partake of stronger spirits for a while. Amelia could sense that this was now the time for that separation, and rather than wait for a hint she politely detached herself from conversation with Captain Yeo and drifted over to her mother and Arabella, whom she surreptitiously scrutinised. Something was clearly amiss, and she wondered if it was anything to do with her brother, and the odd coincidence that he and Arabella had been absent at the same time. But even to imagine this seemed faintly indecent, so she dismissed it as an absurd fancy of her own.

Once in the library, the conversation amongst the gentlemen ranged casually amongst their usual preoccupations. To their credit, as provincials who would rather think of tenants and their parishioners, and of hunting rather than of debating, they made a show of keeping up with events of national importance. There was the trial of Paine in his absence, and the arrest of others accused of sedition. But, as Thomas Darke reminded them while the bottles went round, not all the support for reform had come from those of the artisan class, trouble-makers in their nature.

Sir Francis listened with interest. In an inexplicable manner, he always asked for port, although he seldom drank any of it. It was one of his stranger habits which he never explained, and Justin had learned to humour him. Here again he raised his glass and looked at it, conscious of his audience, who tended to defer to him, gratifying his sense of his own importance in the county. Captain Yeo was inspired to reach for the decanter himself, which he was lifting as Sir Francis spoke.

'Of course, many of these ideas come from America, where they can rage unchecked. But one can spend time overseas and not be subject to such unreason. I mean, you have listened to the colonists, but you yourself would give such madness little encouragement, eh, Justin?'

The company was silent. Justin looked up at the painting of his father, and then allowed his eyes to rest on Sir Francis. When he spoke, it was softly. 'I doubt, sir, that any in London would trouble themselves to listen to me. I venture there so seldom.'

Captain Yeo raised his glass. 'Gentlemen, a toast to His Majesty. I give you King George, long may he reign.'

They stood, in the wisps of tobacco smoke, and against the crackle of the fire and the flicker of candlelight, and pledged their loyalty, each with a thought of what he held dear in his heart.

'You should know, gentlemen,' said Sir Francis after they had all sat down again, 'that we have had warning to keep a check on the local publicans, in case they are allowing seditious meetings to take place on their premises. The Home Secretary tells me that in some cases there are men posted — I take it you know what I mean? Not, of course, in our villages, but in our towns. Such as Okehampton, and indeed Launceston.'

'I myself have misgivings about the numerous Frenchmen who have come to these shores, the *émigrés* or whatever it is one is supposed to call them. You cannot tell me, gentlemen, that they do not conceal amongst them some who are intriguing for those whom they claim to be escaping.' And with that Glasscott shook his head, lost in a reverie of foreign perfidy.

'Do you mean espionage, Cradock?' It was Thomas Darke, looking all the more like Sir Francis Drake in a thunderous mood, Justin thought, now that the spirits were bringing blood to his face under that beard. 'Spies, man. Damned spies? Is that it?' And in an emphatic gesture, he banged down his glass on the table, spilling its contents slightly, at which he stared in rather a glazed manner.

Spies who may be all the more likely to succeed in their aims if their enemies are drinking port, Justin mildly observed to himself.

'Spies there must be,' said Sir Francis, 'although I doubt that many are to be found amongst the ranks of the *émigrés*, or in London, where they cannot do much harm.' He raised his glass to look at it, as if to confirm that it was still untouched. 'No, it is not there that we should look for them.' With that enigmatic statement, he looked over his glass at each man in turn, finding puzzlement in all.

'Where then, Sir Francis?' Darke asked.

'Where they can mix with their own kind, Thomas, with the enemy within our walls. That is where we should fear them, gentlemen, and take every action to guard against them. That is Pitt's view, and that of many of his ministers, I'll be bound.'

During this last, solemn speech, the door to the library had opened behind Sir Francis, and following Justin's gaze he turned his head to see his lovely daughter staring at him, with what looked almost like fear in her eyes, her face drawn and pale. It was most unlike the Arabella he knew.

'Whatever is the matter, Bella?' he said, forgetting the company he was in, and reverting to the language that he used at home. 'Is the chimney on fire, or have you seen a ghost on the stairs? Come on, speak up, we were … just concluding,' he added, becoming more conscious of his indiscretion in speaking to her in male company with such a degree of familiarity.

'I had come to ask you, Father, to think of concluding, at the request of Mrs Wentworth. She thought the message might come all the more lightly and easily from your own daughter.' She smiled wanly, and disappeared from the doorway.

'Indeed,' said Thomas Darke, 'we should be rejoining them, if only to give our farewells.' He pushed back his chair and headed for the door. 'A charming young woman, Francis, most worthy of you, sir, most worthy. Your servant, Wentworth.'

The vicar and Captain Yeo followed, each with a bow to Justin, as if to thank him for his hospitality. Justin held the door for Sir Francis and gave a slight bow. But Sir Francis held out his arm.

'No, sir, after you. I shall come after you.' He watched Justin through the doorway, scratched his nose in thought, and strolled out behind him.

CHAPTER VI: UNDERCOVER IN BRITTANY

The sea hurled itself against the rocks, flinging up towers of spray, and the waves rolled heavily, ready to crush those who judged badly. But the landing was clean enough, the scrape of the keel on sand and grit, the hands that held his arms, one from inside the boat, one from outside on the beach, and almost lifted him clear of its edge into the slack of the backwash. The rough greeting, the lamp in his face, the rasp of the boat as they rammed it back into the surf. It could have gone much worse.

This northern edge of the Breton land that claimed him was dark, brooding and unfamiliar, and the ways they took had been long and hard. They passed him from hand to hand, and each clapped him briefly on his shoulder, with half-heard laughter or grim muttering, much of which he did not catch. For some of the time they made their way through thick woods, caught with bramble and gorse, often at night when they feared detection, but also during the day, when the light spread through the trees and showed him how little he knew where he was. They called him 'baron', and insisted on it even when he told them it was hardly wise, although none knew at this distance from his estate in the south whether it was true or not. On other days they half walked, half ran down lanes and tracks, partly covered by high banks and hedges, cutting through fields when this seemed right.

They passed few people, and those few they did they greeted casually, and walked on. Once, one man stood in their way; he wore a dark hat and clogs and held a pitchfork, poised by the hay he was feeding to his cattle. There were three with him at that time. They had picked him up in the ruins of a hamlet near Plumaugat, and had proudly shown him their spire, gleaming in the distance after a shower of rain. Something about this man with the pitchfork worried his guides, and two gave a curt greeting and hustled him past through the gate, one on either side, shielding him from view, while the other went right up to the farmer. He had heard low voices, and looking back as the three of them paused for a moment he saw their companion thrust his face in close. He heard a grim and guttural sound, saw a finger raised, and then a smile, a farewell tossed behind him as he came back to join them. They said little, but their pace was sharper for a mile or two.

Days and nights it proved to be, as he had expected. What he had not guessed was that while they might feed him at night, they would only take him to shelter and rest during the day, in isolated clearings and hamlets. Here he could sleep for some hours in a woodshed or *cabine*, tucked away but comfortable enough with straw or hay. It was easier to keep watch during the day, to pick up reports from others about what he came to realise were troop movements. *Les bleus*, they called them, amongst other fouler names, and he began to accept that the soldiers of the new republic were everywhere, or at least might be appearing anywhere across the centre of the region, in small but dangerous detachments. Whether they were looking for him specifically he doubted. Realistically, how could they know about him and his mission? But at the least he would be taken for an *émigré*, an aristocrat who had returned to foster the rebellion, and the penalty for that was harsh and instant.

And then it had rained. What would Brittany be without the rain? Paradise, he had heard them say jokingly, and the mud and the dung clung to his boots and his legs across the fields, the woods providing cover of a sort, and the chance to scrape clean and rub off what he could with grass and leaves. Something in the air had told him he was getting closer to what he knew, and that was relief of a sort. Morbihan was warmer, as if the south of the region lay sloping into the sun, while the north had always to fight off the Channel air, the mists and the unseasonable cold. His clothes began to dry, but somewhere just on the edge of La Trinité, in a stone house on the outskirts of the village, he had been bustled into the kitchen at the back and then into a small room, where a man they called Yann — lean, shaven, confident in his leather jerkin — had shown him to some fresh clothing. Crisp, dry shirt, strong breeches, a jacket that proclaimed some well-being, and a hat that signified the traveller. They gave his boots to the boy to clean, and the whole looked well enough. When he came back into the kitchen, the others had gone, and so had the boy, the boots standing by the hearth.

Yann went into the yard, and he heard the noise of a cart, the grinding of the wheels on the cobbles, the clip and shuffle of the pony, Yann's voice and another. Then the door opened, and Yann shut it softly behind him. He looked up, seemed to approve of what he saw, and smiled. '*Seigneur*, we are close. This is La Trinité, the house of a friend and patriot. Outside is LeGoff and his wagon, who will take us through the Lanouée forest, and down into Josselin through the Saint Martin gate. We shall go together.'

'Wagon?' Justin looked up as he knelt down to pull on his boots. 'Why travel in a wagon?'

Yann frowned and ran his hand through his hair. 'Because it is safer, *seigneur*. We can slip into the town.' He breathed deeply. 'They all know LeGoff; he is there all the time. They will not question him and his cart. He comes to collect produce. We can get close to the *rue des Vierges*, where we shall meet.'

'So what is this?' Justin pointed to his new clothes. 'And you? Do they know you in the town?'

'One or two, perhaps, but not well. I call to see my cousin from time to time.'

Justin took a moment, and then spoke patiently. 'These clothes mark us out, Yann. People notice, they look, they remember.'

Yann bent down, and when he stood up Justin saw the knife at his belt. He walked to the table, and turned round with a beaker in his hand. 'We shall pass as merchants, visitors, men from Pontivy, calling, if anyone asks, what … on a trader who supplies tanned leather for cutting. There are many such here. Business goes on. It will pass.' He paused and raised the cup to his mouth. 'And so will we.'

Justin ran his tongue across his lips and looked at him. 'If you say so.' He walked over to the table and put his hand on the jug. 'And who do we meet? I have to meet people who know, Yann.'

'People who know will be there. It is very dangerous for them, but they will be there. And then they will disappear again, send back word. You will encourage them with what the English will bring.'

The pony shuffled outside, and the cart rattled.

'We should go, *seigneur*,' said Yann. He put the beaker down and moved to the door. 'Are you content?'

Justin nodded. The door creaked open, and he walked out into the sun.

CHAPTER VII: THE REPUBLIC TAKES CHARGE

The silk of her dress brushed against the bars of the balcony, but the sound of voices came through the open windows, concealing her sigh. It was, she decided, a sigh of boredom, but none the less potent for that. These men! Constant talking, and none of it about her, as it should have been. The rest of the women were matrons, after all, and their sense of *la mode* was even more provincial than her limited purse could afford. Her father was kind, but he disapproved of *la luxe*, and he told her firmly that *la politique* dictated some restraint. Not that they were likely to be thought to be aiming above their rank. Their rank was not low, and the family she hardly knew had a name, and an estate. Land. Always land! Always on her father's mind, and what did she care about this land?

Still, he was dear to her, and she turned towards the window to see him in the large candlelit room so full of talking people. There was no sign of him for the moment, so she tutted and let her gaze drop on to the wide street below, wide for Pontivy, although it hardly compared to Rennes. As she did she was spotted by two lounging soldiers, their hats hanging loosely by the straps in their hands, and the white bands on their blue uniforms not quite aligned as they should be, she thought. They passed a word between them, and one called up to her, but his face fell as she heard movement next to her, and saw a suntanned hand that laid hold firmly of the balcony rail. The two men below scuffled away, keeping to the nearside of the road. Her eyes met those of the officer, as he surely was, and he spoke quietly and with deference, she was pleased to note.

'A thousand apologies, *m'demoiselle.*'

'*De rien, m'sieur, ou capitaine, peut-être? Je ne comprends pas les rangs militaires…*'

'*Oui, c'est capitaine, Capitaine Leroux, à votre service, citoyenne.*' He smiled a little as he used the word, as if he expected a young woman who had chosen to wear silk to be slightly above the common jargon.

'*Citoyenne*, why not? I quite like the idea. Perhaps men will listen to me now I am a *citoyenne*, officer? What do you think?'

'I am sure that they do already listen to you, *m'demoiselle.* Why would a man not do that?'

She pursed her lips as she thought about that, and then slowly but surely shook her head. 'I do not think they do, Capitaine Leroux. But I think you are living up to your rank and profession, because you are choosing to be *galant* in a town that is new to you.'

Before he could answer, another voice spoke from just by the open windows to the room.

'*Galant?* I had expected you to be exact in the pursuit of your duties, Leroux, but I was not sure that the Republic had time to be *galant.*' And to his daughter: 'I was missing you, Joséphine.'

It was her father, and to pacify him as much as to discipline the soldier, she moved to his side and slid her arm into his.

'Papa, the estimable captain is treating me like a lady and a citizen at the same time. Do you not think that is clever? Do not be severe on him.'

The captain bowed, but as if he was not sure if he should do so, and nodded to the older man. 'I should leave you,' he said, and was gone through the open windows into the crowded room and the candlelight.

'Now, Papa, see what you have done! The only good-looking man in the assembly, and you have sent him about his business when he was close to flattering me. Why, he must be thirty years younger than the rest.'

Her father looked indulgently at her. 'That is because they are men of affairs, and my friends, burghers of this town, thank God, and the military are here to protect us and our interests. That is the meaning of the Republic, at least in Pontivy, *ma fille*. At least, we continue to hope so…'

His daughter removed her arm impatiently, and drew him towards the windows. 'Oh, don't lecture me, Papa. What do I care what the Republic is in Pontivy, or elsewhere, come to that? I know there are many who oppose it…'

Her father interrupted her quickly. 'We don't speak of that, Joséphine, at least not here and not this evening. We are building bridges tonight, because that is what we have to do. Now, come with me. The air is chill.'

The two of them moved through into the room, and Joséphine looked for the captain, but although there were other uniforms in the room he was nowhere to be seen. With another sigh she moved over to the refreshments placed on a small table, and smiled as daintily as she could at the men who were thirty years older, to please her father, and considered the possibilities of the other military men available.

The room was indeed crowded. Matrons there were, good, reliable wives who knew what was expected of them on this occasion, for the most part and perhaps unusually standing by their husbands, whose faces were grave, some not a little strained. And in small groups there were other men, wearing the tricolour flash conspicuously, but dressed for the most part plainly. The army was sweeping west again, and south from Pontivy, against the uprising, and it had to be supplied with necessities closer to its sphere of operations than Rennes. So the Republic had sent these commissioners as well as its soldiers; few of their accents were local, and some were distinctly Parisian, for those who knew the capital. There were deals to be done, faces to be put to names, traders and commodities to be identified at one and the same time.

A portly figure, with prominent, round eyes and bushy hair either side of a shining, bald head came into the centre of the room, looked around him, and coughed in a significant way. He was holding a tiny bell, which looked incongruous in his thick and hair-backed hands. Joséphine stifled a laugh. His mayor's chain of office sat on his chest next to a tricolour flash, and he raised the bell. Joséphine cast another glance around the room for the captain, who had become a temporary obsession in the dullness of the occasion. He was still nowhere to be seen. The mayor rang his bell, which tinkled in the dying conversations, and it had its due effect in almost total silence. To an extent, they all had been schooled, although this was all new to them, stepping stones across an unknown marsh. Still, there was perhaps strength in numbers. The mayor cleared his throat, and by now some of the Republican commissioners had gathered around him.

'*Mesdames, messieurs,*' the mayor began. 'It is both our pleasure and our duty to welcome the representatives of the Republic into this assembly of the loyal citizens of Pontivy.' At this he stopped, as if unsure of what to say next, and gestured to the figures to his side, who regarded him with a degree of condescension, and who were for the moment not going to help him out. The mayor stuttered, but seemed to gain impetus from a thought. 'The extent of our welcome must be apparent to all from the hospitality that has been extended to our visitors, and from the desire of all those who have been engaged in what we trust will be fruitful conversations to provide the appropriate means to restore order to our distressed and, in some respects, misguided province.'

He removed his handkerchief and wiped his forehead, smiling graciously at the lean commissaires and at all in the room. The ladies sensed their opportunity and smiled back graciously in turn, looking also to each other and setting up something of a hum. Joséphine now spied the captain, trapped between two matrons in maroon and lace. The corners of his mouth just managed a smile, but after all her efforts she chose to pretend not to see him. How dare he absent himself for so long?

'If I may, Mayor...' The Parisian accent was harsh and ugly to those used to the softer sounds of the west. Their faces tightened, and the silence in the room deepened. It was clear that the others deferred to this man, and the mayor plainly knew his authority, because he swallowed palpably, and managed what could only be called a weak grin.

'Let me remind you,' the Republican commissioner continued, 'of the reasons why we are here.' His glance took in the room, but he was fixed on a point in the centre of the largest candelabra, as if it offered a greater source of light than the minds of his audience. There was a tone here that reminded Joséphine of something she could not quite recall.

'You must be aware that the administrator for the office of the *Domaines Nationaux* recently wrote to mayors and municipalities, to provide lists of empty properties, and of the *émigrés* who have vacated them. That is, vacated them by deserting across the Channel to the enemies of the Republic in England.' His eyes now deflected from the candelabra and took in the room, aiming at individuals to secure his point. 'The armies of the Republic must be provided with what they need. And so, citizens, the Republic must legitimately finance its forces with funds drawn from the traitors who have deserted their country. Confiscation of property is necessary, and lists are required.'

It was a short speech of no mean force. He could have managed much more, and he was plainly very well-practised. At that instant Joséphine had a flash of recognition: her former governess, a thin woman with a rasping voice, like a bitter east wind tearing at the chimney. In common with the commissioner, she had used a tone that had you resolutely in the wrong, whatever you had done or not done, as if you were in front of Saint Peter himself. If the commissioner's audience felt that they were in the wrong, they did their best to conceal it. The speaker had hardly concluded before the voices of the good citizens of Pontivy rose around him, whether in protest or enthusiasm it was hard to say, but he had stirred them. His fellow commissioners were ready to stand by him, and began to disperse into the room as the clamour increased, so the mayor took his chance. It was possibly his finest hour, and he surprised them all with his volume.

'Gentlemen, Citizens! Citizens, please! I am sure no one is accusing you, or our municipalities, of neglect. The authorities, represented in our presence by Citizen Thibodeau and his companions, have every right to expect that we should pursue those who are enemies of the Republic. But as you well know, our dear province is sadly in disorder, chaotic, lawless, highly dangerous to any representative of the Republic who goes unarmed. You must let this be known to those who are here with us now, and encourage them to instruct the army and its officers to record all that they find as they venture into our villages and suppress the savagery that has possessed them.'

He had finished, and before a further impossible task could be found in addition to that which was already facing them, he grabbed hold of the right hand of Thibodeau, and then went the rounds of the other representatives. He was followed immediately by the burghers, shaking hands, offering reassurances, bewildering those commissioners who were from Rouen or Le Mans or the suburbs of Notre Dame with details of likely properties, notorious *émigrés*, obscure regions and manors and chateaux of this strange, backward land of Catholics and royalists. The mayor eventually introduced Joséphine's father to a tall man standing next to Thibodeau, who wore a larger than usual tricolour, and hid a lisp when he spoke, which was always softly. He gave his name, which was Morin, and asked for a repeated introduction, as if his mind had been elsewhere. Joséphine's father was not slow to respond to this prompt, and his manner was purposeful.

'Allow me to introduce myself. My name is Guèvremont, Citizen, Laurent Guèvremont. I have an interest in timber in Pontivy and along the Blavet, which I have been discussing with one of your companions. We are strong on timber here in central Brittany, and may with help transport it well.'

Morin seemed distracted, less interested than Joséphine's father had hoped, but Laurent had learned to be patient, and this out-of-town clerk would not disturb him from a long-held purpose. Timber was for the moment not really on his mind.

'Allow me to say, Morin, that I know of a *manoir* which now stands empty. The family has long since gone to England, with small likelihood that they will return. I have an interest in this manor, and would like to negotiate…'

Here Laurent began to lose his way, and Morin who in his lethargic way was no stranger to greed was quick to respond. 'Negotiate, *Monsieur* Guèvremont? I am not at all sure that the

Republic negotiates. You must speak at some point to the procurator, who would handle the auction. But nothing of that kind has been arranged yet. Where is this property?'

'To the south, citizen. It is sadly in a contested area, like so many.'

Morin grimaced in distaste. 'Then you must wait for the army, Guèvremont. The details might be given to my colleague Thibodeau, or his secretariat, and I believe Captain Leroux has been in the south, and will be returning. You might speak to him. He may be able to secure it for all of us, but above all, of course, for the Republic.'

Laurent sensed that this was enough for now. He inclined his head slightly, in what in former times might have been a bow, a gesture accepted by Morin with good grace, and started to sift amongst the military uniforms for a face he could barely remember. He need not have worried, because when he caught sight of his daughter half hidden behind some shielding matrons, there was an officer at her side.

The drumming of the rain on the canvas over them had now slackened to a pattering, but the floor of the cart was already wet, with runnels dashing from one side to the other, back to front, at the pitch and lurch of the unsprung wheels. Justin shifted his position once again, grateful for the sacks of buckwheat that gave him some support, and found himself unintentionally giving Yann a prod in what was probably his shoulder. But nothing passed between the two men, no sound or word, which was probably beyond the strict call of caution, since the noise was almost deafening — the rattle of harness and hooks, the whole consort of creaks and groans of the axle and the shafts, all conducted by the whistles and calls of LeGoff at the reins. At one point, LeGoff pulled up and cracked jokes with another driver, and the sounds of human activity began gradually to increase, the track underneath the wheels sounding louder as they ran over a harder surface.

Yann pulled himself up alongside Justin, put his finger to his lips unnecessarily, and whispered, 'We're now coming in to Josselin, at the top. They call it Saint Martin.' He raised one crack of the canvas a fraction, and levelled his eye with it. 'Yes, the northern road, running in to Saint Martin. Soon, the smell of bread…' He pulled himself down again. 'We shall go down to the bottom of the *bourg*, quietly. LeGoff will lead the horse. *Compris?*'

'Yes. And then?'

'We must get out by the wharf on the river, opposite the *lavanderie*.' Yann paused, as if he was thinking of something for the first time. 'The women will be there, but it doesn't matter. They don't miss anything, and they talk like a spinning wheel, but by the time they see their friends we shall be gone.'

He put his fingers to his lips again as they felt the cart slow a little, and heard LeGoff return greetings. Yann as usual was right; Justin could now smell bread, and it was good.

'The *boulangerie* at the top of town. We are in. No more.' He slid down, and they both were silent. They heard snatches of conversation, and the roll of the wheels over paving as the cart ran past houses that gave back an echo, the world outside closing in over them. The jolting was bad, but they had nothing in particular to fear. The cart suddenly came to a stop, and LeGoff went to the head of the pony to take it down the slope. It was quieter here. Yann lifted the canvas again, and then put his mouth to Justin's ear. 'We are passing the church; round behind it, to the east.'

Justin said nothing. He did not know the town well. It was just a childhood memory, no more, and mostly then of the towering chateau above the river Oust. In the discomfort, his mind drifted back to an image of his father, standing at the foot of one of the towers with his brother, the town bridge behind them.

'We are going down, by the side of the chateau walls.' There was a pause, in which there was little sound apart from the harness and the pony's hooves on the stone. And then, just faintly, the sound of women's voices and water, and behind them men's voices, distant scraping, creaking, something that could or must be the roll of barrels, more carts. Surely this would be the *lavanderie* at the bottom of the stream by the river, and the wharf? LeGoff shouted greetings again, and they passed by the women at the washing stones, turning to the left into the sounds of the wharf. Justin felt his arm gripped tightly, and Yann's voice close to his ear yet again.

'We are there. We will roll out of the back of the cart, out of sight behind a booth, and then quickly back up the hill, as if we have come ashore here, off one of the wherries. Keep close to me.' He kept hold of Justin's arm until the cart came to a stop. 'Now,' he said, and slid out from under the canvas. Justin swung his feet out, pivoted on his right arm, and stood up. For a moment, the sunlight was blinding. Steam came in wisps from the canvas on the cart and on the booth, and the smells were strong — of tanning and timber and, in the background, rain, buckwheat and other grain. The booth was at the back of the wharf, by the side of the hill that had been cut into to provide the flat ground. Yann swung quickly away up a path that climbed into the parish of Saint Nicholas, to the side of the chateau. Justin had little time to take in the massive shapes of the capped turrets, and no time at all to glimpse the activity at the wharf. The two men climbed silently together.

Once in Saint Martin, they worked their way to the Ploermel road, and turned left towards the centre of town. The carvings on the house beams stared out at them, as did one or two of the townsfolk, notably at Justin. He passed by without observing them, Yann's arm casually in his, Yann distracting attention with a nod here and a word there. The chateau was strangely silent, the Duke an *émigré*, the apartments empty. But they were by now overshadowed by its walls in a street that grew narrower, with the sun shut out from it. Yann stepped up to a door to the side of a glover's shop, its shutters open, the odorous display of tanned and dyed leather laid out on the counter. He tapped lightly, swinging his body back out to watch the street. There was a man in dark clothes and a cap standing in the shadow opposite, and a brief nod between them both seemed to signal that all was fine. The man took off his cap, scratched his head, and strolled off just as the door eased open. Yann and Justin went in. It was a narrow, dark passage, the only light coming from the back. As they walked towards it, they passed a recess on the left, a doorway to the back of the shop, and at that moment Justin felt his arms seized in a grip of relaxed but immense strength. He was about to protest when Yann turned round to face him, and lifted his hand in restraint.

'They will search you for weapons. It is to be expected.'

And so they did, the one who patted him down being short and wiry, his narrow face half-lit, with quick hands that had done this kind of thing before. Nothing was said, but the small man went on between him and Yann, with the other following behind. The small party turned to the right and climbed a staircase, loudly enough to give notice of their approach, if any were needed. A door opened at the top, with sharp daylight whitening the room beyond. A gruff word or two was exchanged but no more. The two guardians, who Justin thought of as the glover and the bear, took their places either side of the door. And bear it surely was, Justin observed, now that he could see him: he was above normal height, the size of a mature tree, and had a bronze beard and sharp eyes beneath bushy eyebrows that matched his beard.

The room held a plain table and a bench, with one simple chair and a stool on the nearer side. There was nothing else there to be seen. The window faced south, across the wall to the upper storeys of the chateau, the shutters were thrown back, and there was another door in the panels of one of the walls. The men who faced him were both of middling height, one older, of middle years, and one younger, but by no means a youth. They had been travelling, there could be no doubt of that: mud splashes, damp on their collars, a mixture of sweat and dust just visible on their faces. If this was a welcoming committee, then no one had told them, because they were not smiling but staring very hard, first at Yann, and then at Justin. Justin waited, rehearsing now what he had come all this way to say, and wondering not for the first time if it would satisfy his listeners. He found that he was swallowing as if he was preparing to speak, but the older man got in first.

'Good morning. Please do not sit down right now, or you will have much to explain.' He spoke quietly in Breton, waved his arm invitingly to the chair, and with his companion sat complacently on the bench on his side of the table. They both continued staring at Justin, who remained stock-still, staring back at them. There was a pause.

'I shall have much to explain in any case,' he replied in Breton. Beside him, Yann grinned, and they all broke into laughter, handshakes all round, the glover and the bear joining in.

'Deniel, fetch us the cider.' This to the bear. 'Baron, we wish to hear what you have to tell us. You have come from Puisaye and the *émigrés* in England. What does he have for us?'

Justin sat at the table next to Yann. The bear came back in with a tray, a pitcher, and four glasses, which he placed on the table. This was town life, thought Justin. Glasses, indeed. 'No, not precisely from Puisaye, although he knows what I have to say.'

The other men ceased smiling and leaned slightly back, with their hands spread on the table. 'If not from Puisaye, and the *émigrés* in England, then from whom?' the younger asked slowly, spacing out his words deliberately. The older man poured cider into glasses.

'*Yec'hed mat!*' He raised his glass, and they echoed and followed his lead.

'From the English government.'

The younger man frowned, and pulled a name from his memory. 'Do you mean from Windham? The English minister Windham?'

If Justin was surprised at this knowledge, he tried not to show it, but his glass halted halfway down to the surface of the table. 'I would rather not mention names. But you may take it that I am not a spy.'

'Well, Baron, with all respect, what are you, and what use are you to us?'

Before Justin could answer, there were confused shouts from down the road. All four got to their feet at once. Quite distinctly, although muted by the buildings in between, there had been the crack of a musket. It was followed by another. The bear turned and went swiftly and silently out of the room. The glover peered down into the street, and called out to the watcher with the cap below. They all heard the first words of the reply, and looked at each other. The glover swung back round to face them.

'*Les bleus*,' he said. 'A detachment has come across the bridge, from the Vannes road, through Sainte Croix. They…'

But his words were cut off by shouts from the other direction outside.

'They are coming up from the river both ways. I shall conduct you to safety —' this to the two rebels — 'and you, Yann, take the Baron. We must go separately. It will be fine if we are quick. You should go that way, through that door and then down.' He pointed to the door in the panels, but as he did so there was banging at the front door. The glover shrugged his shoulders, and motioned to the two men he was to guide to sit down again, and drink. 'You are cousins of mine. Deniel will talk them away downstairs. Or so we must hope.' Then to Yann and Justin, urgently: 'Go, go! Up through the town and away. We can do no more for you. You must run. Through there. Quickly now!'

On the far side of the panelled door was a room in which there were two wooden box-cots and children's clothing scattered on the floor. A steep staircase led down from here to the back of the house, where they found a heavy, bolted door in front of them. Yann put his hand on the bolt and listened. As yet, it seemed quiet outside. He pulled back the bolt cautiously, and they stepped out into the street and the square, framed by the ancient timbered buildings surrounding the stone church. People had begun to gather in front of the church, at the bottom of the main street that led back up to Saint Martin, and Yann and Justin quickly headed into it. When they reached the corner of the church, five Republican soldiers came up into the square, pushing through the crowd, who gave way to them. Indeed, one or two of the voices cheered '*Vive la*

République, vive la Convention nationale! A shopkeeper came out with a flagon. But the soldiers pushed it away and went on past, scanning the faces of those who were less enthusiastic.

Yann grabbed Justin's arm and threaded his way up the street, but just as they were getting out of the crowd he ran right into a burly blue uniform, who had come out of one of the bars, smelling a little. There was an apology and an attempt at goodwill, and Yann eased the soldier round in what he hoped was a friendly way, pushing Justin away with his free hand. Justin slipped behind those closest to him, a woman with a pannier and two children, beyond them a black mule and its sun-browned owner, and then stepped into the dark entrance to the church. He heard another crack of a musket, and then more, and cries came echoing into the porch, only softened as he steered his way further into an aisle, hearing instead of the shots the prayers of those inside, the candles guttering around them, with a glimpse of a priest's garments moving nearer the altar.

Then they forced their way in, clattering with disrespect, flinging swearwords casually as if to prove their freedom from rite, branching out to go down the nave and the left aisle, six of them or more, staring into the faces of worshippers, one grabbing a candle as if to see better, some with muskets balanced, others with them slung, and a hand on the bayonet. Justin had no idea where to go, unless there was a rood loft, a staircase up to it near the tower. He had never been in here before, and found himself in his urgency dominated by the plan of English parish churches, which he knew instinctively would be wrong, would let him down. He did feel panic now, the beat of his heart hard against his ribs, sweat under these stiff, awkward clothes, cursing that he had no weapon at all, although much use that would be to him against five or six. He almost stumbled forward into the depths of the church, searching the walls for the entrance to a curving, stone staircase, glancing back and across at the flashes of blue and white moving closer.

Suddenly, there in front of him was the tomb, its recumbent statues white in the gloom, the space around it inviting, high enough to conceal him at least if he crouched, although where he would run to was impossible to say. As he knelt down, one hand on the cool marble to steady himself, two of the soldiers came swinging loudly into the chapel.

'*Sacrée merde!*' one said loudly, and the other laughed. He heard them step up to the tomb, and the priest come rustling after them.

'My children,' began the priest.

'*Quoi? T'as enfants, père? Dieu te perdonne, mon brave!*' They found this far funnier than it was, and when the priest began to mutter something placatory about '*citoyens*', the soldiers asked him bluntly whose tomb this was. One of them scraped his feet perilously close to the upper end of the memorial, and Justin cowered down without shame, his heart pounding.

'Olivier de Clisson,' said the priest, '*marèchal de France*, and adviser to the king.'

'*Alors*, that is for you, marshal and adviser, and for your king.' Justin saw the barrel of the musket raised high above the other side of the tomb, and heard the butt crash down on the heads of Olivier and his wife. A sharp crack was followed quickly by another, as a piece of marble sprang from one of the tomb figures and ricocheted against the stone wall of the chapel, coming to rest by Justin's boot. At that moment, a shaft of light shot in on the tomb as a door buried obscurely in the outer wall was pushed open with loud shouts, and in flowed a section of the citizenry of Josselin, burghers and women who looked likely to be their wives, overwhelming the hostility of the soldiers with indignation, some pushing and accusing, swelling round both sides of the tomb. It was Justin's chance, and he took it. Lifting his hands to show that a man dressed as respectably could never be involved in desecration, he edged his way towards this heaven-sent opening in the wall, down the steps into the street beyond, out to the open air, along the quiet path away from the church across the square, and thankfully away through the back streets to the east of the town, heading for Ploermel, and preferably for the village of Saint Servant across the river Oust.

The two *bleus*, who rapidly found they had bitten off far more than they could chew, backed slowly out of the chapel into the body of the church, where they were joined by their companions, and there was more shouting and shoving than fighting, protests and insults changing hands, until a new body of blues came in through the church door, followed by a sergeant, who saw to it that they propelled the good burghers out into the street, and about their lawful business. The sergeant scratched his chin, went through into the chapel, and looked at the heads of the nobles on the tomb.

'*Tant pis*,' he muttered, and strolled back to join his men.

At that point, the chapel doorway opening to the street was briefly darkened by another uniformed blue and white figure, who walked to the tomb and surveyed it. He bent down suddenly, and picked up something from the floor, which he weighed in his hand as he stood in the light. It was Captain Leroux, and he was holding Olivier de Clisson's nose.

Justin crossed the river at Saint Servant, and cut away south and west. But what came to him again and again, and made him fearful, was the strong impression that they had known that he was there.

CHAPTER VIII: THE STEWARD OF KERGOHAN

The carriage ran lightly along the road in the sunshine, with the two friends glad of each other's company, the springs capable of absorbing the light shocks that came from a good surface on a rural toll road, the leather seats padded enough for sufficient comfort. Jem had charge of the pony, who was stepping out with some verve, fresh from being condemned by rain for too many days to shuffle discontentedly in his stall in the stables at Chittesleigh. Jem's familiar presence did not inhibit the young women.

'Well, Okehampton will be a step-up from Hatherleigh, I have to say, which is a poor sort of a place.'

Amelia would not take this slight of her home town even from a good friend. 'I'll have you know, Bella, that I shall not hear my dear Hatherleigh dismissed, although I dare say it has not the appeal of the tar and fishbone odours of Plymouth, which are evidently so close to your heart.'

This was rancourless banter, and it passed the time cheerfully enough.

'Plymouth has its charms, Melia, my love, but before I tell you about the wonderful stuffs of Exeter and its grander trading houses, please share that wrap with me rather more than you are doing at present. I find the air on the edge of your beloved moor rather chill, despite these bursts of bright sunshine.'

Before her companion could respond to this with the goodwill she doubtless felt, Miss Arabella Wollaston reached a firm hand across and pulled it unceremoniously towards her. The two friends laughed and wrestled a little, before they rested back on their seats. Amelia placed her hand in that of her friend, where it received a warm squeeze.

'I wonder where he is.' Amelia spoke quietly. 'It has been weeks now, and still nothing.'

Arabella glanced at her companion. 'Well, there is nothing unusual about nothing, you must admit, not where your brother is concerned. As I might claim to know only too well.' She grimaced with some theatricality as she said this, and it made Amelia laugh, as she had hoped it would. 'But as I was saying,' she added, 'before I lived to hear Plymouth insulted, Okehampton has the merit of being on the London road, which Hatherleigh cannot contest, and apart from the diverse inns and their claims to comfort which do not concern me, that means there are at least one or two opportunities for orders or purchases that can divert us a little. I am inclined to seek a mate for this riding jacket, certainly if I stay, as you seem to wish, but I am fussy about the wool as well as the trim.'

It was indeed a good, warm short coat, green with hand stitching and a waistband, which lay on the seat between them, but Amelia ignored it. 'I do wish you to stay, and only go to come back again. What would I do without you?' Her hand was squeezed again, and the carriage began to run down the hill into the town, with Jem pulling on the pony's enthusiasm, who knew the routine well enough to have the scent of hay from the ostler already in his nostrils.

'Amelia, without me you might find yourself a pack of admirers, which would give you better company than a spinster in the making, such as I am.' Again the theatricality, designed to distract but also veiling the beginnings of an apprehension that now troubled one who believed that she knew what she wanted, yet was as far from it as she had ever been. They had not parted on good terms, to say the least, she and Justin Wentworth. She was mortified to recall that incident when Justin had found her on the upper floor at Chittesleigh, sneaking along the boards by his room. She flushed with shame even now as she thought of it.

They were pulling into the yard of the Red Lion, which was more Jem's and the pony's choice of hostelry than any preference on behalf of the young women, but was central enough. Jem jumped down and lowered the stair for them, and they descended with a spring in their step. He had picked a good spot, so their path to the main street was short and clear of fouling, and they headed without debate to the left towards the draper Altringham, the best of no fewer than three of that trade in the town.

'And now, my dear,' said Amelia, 'we can turn our attention to fitting you out as becomes your impending spinster status, I have no doubt. Shall we order you a mantua gown? Surely you will demand the stiffest of whalebone-hoop petticoats, or I shall be most disappointed in you.'

The two friends walked happily to the draper's door arm in arm, parting as they went through. They were greeted unctuously by Altringham himself, who despite the conversation to date began immediately to talk earnestly to Miss Wentworth about silks and muslins. Arabella gazed idly about her and laid her riding jacket on the counter, behind which a young assistant was clearly too overawed to address her purposefully by himself. Leaving him to wonder what precisely he was meant to do with it, she drifted across to the window, preoccupied far too much with matters that pained her, and with the image of a man who could not be induced to pay her anything but hostile attention.

It was with that mortifying scene in mind, yet again, that her eye was caught by a figure that seemed urgently familiar, crossing the street to pass in front of the shop. How could he be so familiar when he was so inconspicuous? Preposterous. She frowned, looked away as if to dismiss the intrusive idea, then looked back again sharply, watching his back as he ambled down to one of the river bridges, close to the grand White Hart Inn across from the Red Lion. It was then that she realised that she had instinctively turned away so that he might not see her at the window and recognise her. It dawned on her that this was the very man at the core of her humiliation at the manor. The man who had been in Justin's rooms, unless she had been so terribly mistaken. Or was she mistaken now? Was she still trying to justify her mistake, to ease the pain of that confrontation with Justin, who had so scathingly suspected her?

It all proved to be too much for her, and for that impulsive spirit with which she was plagued. With a glance to see that Amelia was still deeply engaged in stacks of fabric with the draper, she almost strode out of the door and up towards the White Hart, occasioning one or two disapproving looks from women for whom her youthful temperament would have had little time, despite her respectable upbringing. She even found herself skipping to keep up at one point. Stepping over the crossroad at the junction, her skirts caught briefly in the mud and mire. It was because she was keeping her eyes on the man's back while trying to maintain an air of casual progress, a combination that might have tested the more experienced tread of the man whose heart she wished to ensnare. But she was sure-footed too, and when the figure turned into the inn she did not hesitate to follow him, of necessity aside into the private rooms, where a small bell stood on a counter. She rang it instantly.

The delay was infuriating. He might be anywhere, but reflection reassured her that if he had come to this place then he would stay for a while, and a pounding sense of intrigue insisted that he must have business here. The wood in this room was dark, but there was some padding on the chairs, and a sufficient air of grandeur for a relatively important country town. There was movement at the door.

'Ah, there you are. Fetch your wife, my man, and quickly too. Don't stand there gawping, and do not presume to ask me questions. About your business, go!' The landlord, who was used to a slower pace of life, and to a kind of tolerant if condescending respect from local gentry, recognised a visitor from the London road and decided to defer to his wife. She had followed him into the room, hearing the raised female voice, a cap crushed in her hands. Arabella ignored the woman for the moment and glared at the man, waving him out of the door imperiously. He went without resistance, and in some relief. Arabella now turned her attention to the wife, who had chosen deference and silence for the moment, and remained standing there, motionless.

'Some refreshment, my woman, as promptly as you can. And…'

The landlady shifted her posture slightly, not enough to offend, and in her desire to be prompt interrupted Arabella. 'Begging your pardon, ma'am, but would that be the beef we have just off the spit, or there is a cold ham…?'

'Beef? Cold ham?' The scorn was driven by urgency. 'What do you think I am? One of your moorland squires, ravenous after the Sunday service? What I need is … broth, woman. Broth will do very well.'

The woman considered mentioning that she had no broth prepared, but wisely thought better of it. Kitchen could surely manage something appetising. 'Yes, milady. Will you be comfortable here?'

'I shall be comfortable,' said Arabella, 'when you show me to the closet.' She looked squarely at the woman.

'Yes, indeed, milady, if you will wait here for just a moment, Agnes will show you and attend,' the woman said, as lightly as she could without, she hoped, hinting at the absence of anyone waiting on this person of quality.

'Well, be quick then.' It was an abrupt rejoinder, but in keeping with that kind of urgency, and it served the purpose of getting the landlady out of the room. Arabella waited for less than a minute, and then rustled on after her through the door. Behind it was a corridor that had the sounds and smells of the kitchen through openings and passages to the left, an empty storeroom through a broken-down door to the right, some stairs that bent back on themselves further along to the rooms upstairs, and then a draught of colder air gradually displacing the warmth. Wherever the closet might be, it was no concern of hers, and she was instead playing with one of her father's favoured oaths as she began to despair of gaining any further sight of the man on this wild-goose chase, let alone of what he might be contriving. Just at that point, the corridor made a right-angle, and what was plainly an outside door framed by cracks of light brought it to an abrupt end. She listened before she pushed it slowly outwards, and mercifully it did not creak.

The door led into the yard of the inn, or one part of it, under and at the back of a lean-to with a sagging roof that was stacked with the detritus of stables: an old tangled leather harness, a cart with one wheel and a snapped shaft, some broken bales of straw. Of no interest at all. That oath of her father's edged a little closer, but stuck in Arabella's throat as she heard voices in the yard. She shrank back by the doorjamb, but the oath crept back to her when she saw it was a stable-lad crossing the yard, and tossing comments over his shoulder. He stepped smartly in between the two doors of the large barn opposite, but as her eyes followed him vanishing into the dark of the interior another movement caught her attention. She pulled herself further back into the shadow, partly shielded by the door and out of sight, and two men walked across the yard. She felt her heart beat loudly as she confirmed that she did indeed recognise the profile of the man from the manor. There could be no doubt about it. He was that sneak, and if he had had no business being in Justin's room before, he might well be up to no good here. Her instinct was sound, even if she was no closer to knowing what else was afoot, and despite being at the back door of an inn, under completely false pretences, she felt more at ease.

She put her hand on the door, ready to return to the broth she did not want and a public closet she most certainly had no wish to visit, when her eye fell on the other conversant in this pair, who had his back to her. He was what she inwardly described as a burly man, wearing a worn coat that looked military. But as he swung round to leave the yard, the oath that had been so long suppressed forced its way silently to her lips. For as he turned, his face revealed beyond any doubt that this was a man whom she had known for many years. He was in her father's service.

'And there she was, skipping along the high street, and up to heaven knows what mischief, while all the time I was deep in muslin and silk with Altringham, thinking Bella was in a corner of the shop entrancing that poor young man…'

Amelia was entertaining her mother with an account of the foray into the hazards of Okehampton town while Arabella sipped her chocolate, unconcerned by her friend's teasing, but also a little preoccupied on her own account.

'I am sure Miss Wollaston was quite at her ease, *ma chère*. Skipping is not altogether proper as an expression, my love.'

'But *Maman* —' Amelia was not to be suppressed — 'if it was not skipping, as you insist, then it was dashing, I declare. Why, her skirts were dipped in…'

'Yes, we are obliged to you, Amélie, for this colourful sketch taken from the life.' Her daughter had run across to her and taken her mother's arm, her face alight with the fun of it all. Arabella remained sitting, the small table in front of her, her cup poised above its saucer, her eyes on the windows that opened on to the formal garden. 'But, miss —' and here her mother lightly tapped her daughter's arm — 'we are to have a visitor within minutes, and proprieties must be observed.'

'Ah, I suspect from the tone of your voice that this will be monstrously dull.' Amelia left her mother and went to sit next to her friend on the chaise, compelling Arabella to smile and slip aside gracefully to accommodate her. But Amelia had still failed to gain her full attention.

Arabella frowned slightly. 'Should I then leave you, *baronne*?'

'You shall do no such thing.' Amelia placed her hand on her friend's arm.

'That is gracious of you, but there will be no need. The word monstrous is not for polite company, Amélie. At two o'clock, we are to meet the steward from Kergohan, who has written to us. By chance he was resting at Okehampton before he comes to see us. I have had a letter from him there. He says he is not living at Kergohan.'

'Kergohan, Mother? Then perhaps…'

'No, my love, he will not have seen Justin, and you will recall that we do not know where your brother is. This gentleman, *Monsieur* Le Guinec, was appointed by my cousin, Laurent. No doubt he is most efficient. Now Thomas must take those things away, if you are refreshed, Arabella. Please ring for him, Amélie.'

It was a matter of a moment to remove the chocolate. Arabella went to stand by the garden windows, while Amelia engaged in the further impropriety of trying to whisper something to her mother, standing close to the small screens by the hearth. All Sempronie did was shake her head, and look over to the clock that stood on the wall across from the door. At that moment, a deep-toned bell rang out towards the front of the house, and Sempronie and her daughter took a stand in front of the hearth screens. Footsteps came down the hall, and Thomas knocked and entered.

'Mr Le Guinec, my lady. From France,' he added rather superfluously, perhaps slightly proud of his pronunciation. He had had some practice with Breton names before in this household. 'He is here for his appointment, as he says. Shall I show him in, *baronne*?'

This last was to show to all that he knew the subordinate status of the man who was now standing behind him, just visible through the doorway, dressed in an odd combination of brown and black with a white neckerchief tucked neatly in his waistcoat, and impeccable boots, despite his travels. As Thomas stood aside to let him through, Le Guinec revealed a broad forehead, with impressive black hair waving behind his ears, although now receding on either side of the peak, and salted with grey. He had large, practical hands, but meticulously groomed, and in one he was holding a manilla folder tied by blue tape across and down. He bowed ceremoniously to Sempronie and Amelia, with just the hint of a flourish at the end. Arabella, who had remained silently at the window throughout, turned her head to look at him, and, more idly, at what he was carrying.

'*Madame la baronne*, may I present myself? And this will be the Miss Wentworth? While this young lady…?'

'Allow me to present to you Miss Wollaston, daughter of Sir Francis Wollaston, and our dear neighbour.'

Le Guinec repeated his bow, with less of a flourish. It seemed possible he regarded the daughter of an adjacent aristocrat as something of an irrelevance to his mission. '*Madame la baronne*, I offer to you my apologies for my failure to come to England before. But, alas, circumstances have not been propitious…'

'We are aware of the difficulties, sir, only too well. But let me send for some refreshment for you…' This with a motion of her hand to Thomas, who had stayed in the room for precisely this eventuality, but Le Guinec declined. He had, he said, been amply rested and refreshed at the White Hart in Okehampton. At the mention of the inn, Arabella looked up quickly, and began to come out of her reverie.

'As you wish, *Monsieur* Le Guinec,' said Sempronie, 'but do let us allow you to be seated.' And so saying, she and Amelia swept aside the skirts of their morning dresses to sit in two of the carved chairs near the hearth. Le Guinec took a pace towards the third, but then came to a halt and stood to its side, holding on to the gilded wood with his left hand, while he kept his package in his right.

'With your permission, *baronne*, I shall continue to stand.'

Sempronie inclined her head to him. By the window, Arabella took a step or two towards the chaise longue on which she had been sitting, but chose to remain upright.

'I have chosen to come to report to you at the instigation of *Monsieur* Laurent Guèvremont, who has employed me to replace the services of Mael Sarzou, the steward whom you left in charge of the *manoir*. Sadly, Sarzou became indisposed, not I hasten to add to a dangerous degree —' this because Sempronie had gripped the arms of her chair as if to rise, but slowly eased back — 'but sufficient to make him consider yielding his office.'

There was something in his tone or in those words that made Arabella look across to him, but his face was relaxed, waiting for the expression of sympathy which duly came.

'I trust, *m'sieur*, that you will convey our most sincere sympathies to Mael in his distress. He is, I hope, well looked-after, and…'

Le Guinec clipped the train of thought. 'Absolutely, *baronne*, *Monsieur* Guèvremont has him in his own keeping. He is cared for well, although away from the estate and from the duties of office that no doubt contributed to his indisposition.'

Once again, Arabella scrutinised the face and manner of the steward, as if she expected to detect some sign in them; but the steward was placid. She came closer to sit on the chaise. Less troubled than her mother by Sarzou's retirement, Amelia found the opportunity to slip in the question that had been at the front of her mind from the beginning, barring what might be considered an impertinent query concerning Le Guinec's strange cravat.

'*Monsieur*, I admire your spoken English hugely. It is a great skill, and must have taken you long to perfect.'

Le Guinec bowed slightly to the young woman. '*M'demoiselle*, I was a customs clerk in the port of Morlaix when I was a boy until I was —' and here he laughed — 'more than a young man, when *Monsieur* Guèvremont found me, and brought me into his affairs. I perhaps know more English than is strictly proper, if you will forgive the allusion to something beneath your notice. Men of trade and of the sea have their … how shall we say it? Lively expressions.'

'Indeed, so they do.' Arabella spoke for the first time, and for that reason if no other it sounded to Amelia and her mother a trifle mysterious. Le Guinec again bowed to her, but was not to be deflected.

'*Madame la baronne*, I feel I should come to my business with you. I am informed to my profound disappointment that the Baron is away from Chittesleigh at the present time. This had not been anticipated.' He paused, as if to suggest by his silence that in some way the Baron had no right to be absent when he had taken the trouble to come visiting, but he was interrupted in his complacency quite sharply.

'Informed, sir? You intrigue me. There has been no prior correspondence between us, to my knowledge. Who might inform you?' The atmosphere in the room had changed, since all three women were now ill at ease, even if it was the oldest of them who had posed the question.

'Correspondence there could not have been, *madame la baronne*. The state of the nation, as one might say, prohibiting that across a troubled land. As I say, I was surprised but will not be dejected.' He smiled deferentially. 'My journey will not have been made in vain, since I can report to you, *madame*.'

'But by whom were you informed, *monsieur*?' Sempronie remained politeness itself, a tone of mere curiosity masking her determined insistence.

'But by those here in the hall, *madame*. Your man told me the master was not at home, and another stopped in passing by to add that he had been away for some time. But no matter, let us not delay on this. It is a pity, but it is not decisive.' Le Guinec began to untie the package he had been carrying from the beginning, as if it were precious. He knew that he had their attention, and so he chose to pause and look questioningly at the two younger women. 'What I have to say, *mesdemoiselles*, will be dull, I am afraid… Perhaps I should only trouble *madame la baronne* with my report?'

Arabella was determined to betray no reluctance to leave the room, and the two friends passed through the door that clicked behind them, taking each other's arm gaily. Sempronie felt relieved, because she needed her full concentration in matters of business, and was not inclined until she knew what they were to share them with the Wollastons. Her gaze rested on a leather-topped mahogany table with elegant, curved legs that stood just back from the window, with two high-backed Chippendale chairs to its sides.

'Would you care to place your papers on a table, *Monsieur* Le Guinec? This will do well enough, I am sure. You will forgive me if I am seated.' She went across the room ahead of him and sat down, leaving most of the length of the table for his presentation to her.

He was, after such a protracted introduction, remarkably brisk in his delivery. He now spoke in French, without hesitation or permission. 'As you must be aware, *madame la baronne*, the *manoir de Kergohan*, your son's inheritance through you from your father, has been a victim of the tragic convulsions engulfing our country. So it is that the *manoir* has been neglected, perhaps even deserted, in the last two years.'

Sempronie was pale, but did not stir. 'This we know, *monsieur.*'

'Indeed. It has been my duty to attempt to preserve the patrimony of the estate from marauding hands. In this —' he held up one of his own hands, as if to show he was no marauder — 'I have been successful, but largely through the careful policies of my employer and your cousin, *Monsieur* Guèvremont. His interventions with those representatives the Republic has dispatched to our region have managed to distract them, to postpone what in other instances has been the sequestration of lands and the confiscation of goods. It is unlikely, *madame la baronne*, that this can continue.'

'So I would understand, *monsieur*, if we expect the Republic to remain in place.' Her voice was to a degree questioning, but also resigned.

'We do, *madame*, I am afraid. And that is all I have to report.' There was brief silence.

'All, *monsieur*? You have come all this way just to tell me this?'

'*Monsieur* Guèvremont was insistent that, despite the dangers, I should make this journey to speak to you in person, and inform you of what we feared, and what we had been doing. It seemed respectful, and the proper thing to do.' He coughed and bent forward over the table, opening the folder. 'But here, in addition, are some papers detailing the sale of small quantities of timber, and some of the *eau de vie* in the cellars, negotiations made carefully by *Monsieur* Guèvremont in Pontivy. The limited sums raised have for the larger part gone to support the tenants and their families on the estate, and to the provision of guards at the house itself, to prevent any unlawful removal of its contents.' He stood back again, leaving her to crane forward and inspect the bills of sale, which to his surprise she chose to ignore.

She stood up, placing her hand on the back of the chair, and looked down at the documents and then up at the steward. 'And how did you get here? I must have forgotten. There were dangers, you said?'

Le Guinec smiled. 'There were dangers.'

'But not here in England,' Sempronie persisted.

'No, *madame*, I am an *émigré* myself, if any question me too closely. And I have a letter written in English for my predecessor, Sarzou, with the Baron's signature, which he wrote for just such an eventuality of travel in these difficult times.' Here he patted his pocket. 'It is a kind of pass.' And then, allowing a momentary glimpse of his vanity, he added, 'Besides, I speak the language well, which disarms prejudice.'

'And how will you return?'

'To France, you mean, *madame*? I may return again here if it is necessary.' He smiled again, as if enjoying his confidence in his powers. 'As I informed the young ladies, with a tale like that of Othello, I have from my younger days many friends in Morlaix. There are always boats and cargoes to many, many places. It is a short journey inland from the coast to here, and well known to many.'

'*Monsieur*, if you will forgive me, I am fatigued. You will convey my greetings to my cousin, Guèvremont, and encourage him from the Baron and myself in his efforts to protect Kergohan.'

The steward bowed to her, swept his papers together into the folder, and marched towards the door.

'You will return directly to France?'

He swung round, with his hand stretched out for the handle. '*Bien sûr, madame la baronne*. What would delay me now?'

He left the room. Sempronie remained motionless for some minutes, with her head in her fingers. Then she brushed her temples with them lightly, and crossed to where the bell stood on the mantlepiece. She rang it briefly. The door opened, and Thomas came in. He bowed, closed the door, and waited without speaking.

'Thomas, you have seen that gentleman?'

'Yes, my lady. I believe that he has left by the stables.'

'Did you speak to him, Thomas?'

'I address all visitors, my lady.'

'Yes, Thomas, I understand that. I mean did you converse with him?'

'I, my lady? I do not converse with visitors, my lady. When he arrived, I informed him when asked in the entrance hall that the Baron was not at home, and that you were, as he had expected, receiving visitors. When he left, we said nothing at all.'

'And did you talk to anyone else in the entrance hall? Someone who passed by? Or did *Monsieur* Le Guinec talk to anyone?'

Thomas took in a deep breath, and his height increased by half an inch at least. 'I do not talk to passers-by in the hall, my lady. I do not talk to passers-by in any circumstances.'

Sempronie seemed reflective, as if something was not quite right.

'Will that be all, my lady?'

'Yes, that will be all.'

The air was crisp, the sunshine watery but the weather fine, and Arabella had the propriety — she amused herself at the memory of Sempronie's exaggerated concern — to be riding with her groom. This she always did when she was making a journey, although in this case she was combining necessity with pleasure. Alverscombe Hall was a good hour and a half from

Chittesleigh, even if she cut across country, much of which was her father's or Justin's land. It was true that it was remote in parts, although this was Devon, for heaven's sake, and barring talk of smugglers or wreckers, who belonged more naturally to the wild tracts of Cornwall and its notorious coast, the idea of a fierce encounter was ridiculous. Or so she said to herself. But she was troubled more than she had ever imagined she would be on her own land, in her safe, stolid towns, with friends around her, who were indeed more than friends, who loved her like a sister, perhaps even a daughter, although she was not so sure of that.

Her chestnut bucked his head momentarily, and she heard the groom draw rein behind her for an instant, but she had the horse on a measured tread again without anything more than a short break in the pace. He would have seen a rabbit poke its head out from the high hedge that ran along the banked lane, while she could let her eyes range above it and across the landscape at low, rounded hills and a patchwork of fields, some pasture, some arable. The lane opened on to a small triangle of grass with an ancient granite cross at its centre, and a step for a preacher. Across to the left was the large bulk of Dartmoor, alternately presenting massive, rounded hills and heaped mounds of jagged stone, with the smoothed towers split by time resting on their summits.

The chestnut snuffled and pricked its ears, and her own attention was caught by a figure riding across the more open land to the south. In the near distance there was one of the many farmhouses that were unsure of whether they belonged to moorland or more domesticated pasture. Suddenly her nervous state had an object, and in an instant she told Andrew to stay by the cross and set the head of the chestnut at a pace along a hedged byway, a soft green-lane that was silent and gave her cover, and would bring her up close to the side of the building. In keeping with her determination to see and not be seen, she leant forward slightly across his neck, and blessed herself for her dark riding-cap and coat. It was exhilarating, but she knew that at heart she was still angry and confused. Things were being done around her by people who were close to her family and she was told nothing, left to suspect but not even to know what she suspected. Yet again, it was humiliating, and she breathed in the warmth of her horse's neck and tightened her grip on the strands of its mane. It was ridiculous that horseflesh was so trustworthy, and men so deceitful.

But with that thought she pulled up abruptly, in the shadow of a lonely hawthorn that gave her cover, and a good view of what she had come to feel was her target. Her own progress had been good and urgent, that of her quarry slower, but he was now approaching the farmhouse, and her heart jumped and continued to beat strongly. This rider was none other than that steward from Kergohan, Le Guinec, his strange white cravat unmistakeable, his swept-back hair confirming his identity. She was transfixed, but her horse breathed contentedly after its exercise as she swept her hand absent-mindedly down its neck. What was the man doing here? What was he doing in Devon at all? And then she quickly swung her hand down on to the chestnut's muzzle, to stifle any response as the rider's arrival was greeted from behind the farmhouse by excited whinnying. She was close enough, the wind still enough for once, to hear the stamping of the horses, and above it from the same hidden source the sharper jingle of metal on a bridle, momentary but decisive. She could recognise instinctively the sound of a complicated harness, but as she hung on to that somehow incongruous perception the farmhouse door opened and the rider began to dismount, a lad appearing to hold his bridle and lead away the horse.

Le Guinec headed to the door, and out came the man she knew only too well by sight, who she was sure worked at Chittesleigh, but of whose name she was ignorant, as of his status there, except that he had had the brass at least to make free with the rooms of the master of the manor, even if she could not know if that was by permission. But her suspicions were flying now, harking back to the conversation she had seen taking place at the White Hart, with the involvement of her father's retainer, whom she half expected to see here too, as if in some kind of nightmare assemblage of all her unsolved mysteries.

But to her complete astonishment, it was not his burly figure that came to join the greeting taking place by the door, but a tall, immaculately dressed and booted gentleman, who gripped Le Guinec's hand in turn, and then lifted his head to look out at the moor, before ushering them both into the house. Recognition was instantaneous: this was Captain Yeo, the naval officer who had dined at Chittesleigh some months ago, the so-called family friend of the Wentworth's under whose command Justin's brother had died at sea. He too was known to her father, and a visitor at Alverscombe. There was no mistaking him, but she found herself wishing earnestly that there was, because it was yet more bewilderment, which she had begun to fear in a way that she had never felt fear before.

It was in this state of total disturbance with her pulse racing uncontrollably that she heard Andrew drawing up alongside, his habitual good sense accepting the unexplained anxiety that had sent her off without explanation, admittedly on territory of which he had no reason to be apprehensive. He looked at her, but all he said almost inaudibly was 'Ma'am', the term he used habitually when they were riding together because he had found that she preferred it. That much was normal, at least. She could not confront the farmhouse and what it contained. That would have to wait. They turned their horses' heads, and in this instance she followed Andrew as they made their way back to the grey antiquity of the stone cross, and then on home to Alverscombe, her head spinning.

CHAPTER IX: ESCAPE FROM JOSSELIN

The day was warming, with only a light breeze to cool it, and his breath came in long, harsh gasps. His legs were sore and painful. He could not remember the last time that he had run like this; perhaps at the university, that ridiculous bet, along the river, just like this. Nothing in Canada, for all its wild urgency, had been so relentless. He cursed rivers, English and Breton, the Cam and the Oust, because they were the witnesses of his torment, and they stretched away remorselessly, offering no hiding place or escape. His only consolation, in the heat of his effort, was that the blues did not have horses, or so he chose to believe. The idea of Republican cavalry seemed absurd, since the nobility alone knew how to ride, and they had emigrated. The same was true for the French navy, with many of its officers now in hardship in London with their families. Quite why these thoughts now ran through his mind he was unsure, although he had intuitively been listening for the sound of hooves behind him, another kind of madness, with the ground soft in many places.

He had kept from the road, taking a cut past the mills at Josselin, after pushing through angry and confused workmen on the bridge, shaken by the sound of muskets, some women holding children back, others themselves in working clothes and clogs. No one had paid any attention to him beyond the passing glance, the shrewd eyes momentarily taking in his well-dressed appearance. Others were making their way up from the riverside, disappearing into the alleys of the quartier Sainte-Croix, so he was not alone in going at first that way, although he had then cut left into Saint Laurent and the smells of fleece and hides.

But that run! He was just as apprehensive at first that he would be seen from across the river as that he would be caught, and tempted as he was to throw off his jacket, his backwoods skills told him not to leave anything behind. There were paths and tracks, and thankfully there was no one on them, and he recalled the safety plan that Yann had told him, to fall back on the clog-maker's cottage at Plumelec. But the directions he had for that village were by the main road south out of Josselin, not by this escape route.

The church spire emerged from behind the trees at the point when he felt he could run no more, and he collapsed into a ditch with a low hedge above it, lying first on his back to catch his breath, lifting his knees slightly to ease the ache in his thighs and calves. The sky held its usual beauty, white and grey broken by slashes of blue wonder, and the air was sweet and refreshing as he gulped it in. If he was to go into this village — and that he must do — he should look calm and collected, not like an outlaw or a fugitive, and although he knew they would think he looked strange, he hoped he had an answer for that. He swung his legs back and forth gently, massaging the backs of his thighs and calves, and then sat still and listened. The breeze was more or less behind him, light but enough to carry sound, and he could hear the call of a water bird, the treetops moving slightly. But there was nothing else.

In the end, he chose the larger village of the two, judging by the more massive tower of the church over the small spire of the chapel. He skirted around the smaller village and away from the river, and by the time he came in on the rough road to the first of the houses, he was cooler, his clothing shaken out, and he knew what he would say. If necessary, he would have to walk, but he must know in what direction, and he would rather not walk. He heard a shutter creak, and saw an old woman's face behind it in the shadow of the room, but chose to walk on. He passed the crossroads in the centre, with a brief surge of annoyance that there were only lanes leading out to the south and the east, as if back to the river, which was no good at all. But he followed the narrow road that led to the church, which stood in open ground at the end, carried on up to the door, and into the interior. It was cool, and by now sure that there would be eyes on him, he went forward to light a candle, knelt and was silent. A side door creaked, and he caught movement in one of the archways, the rustle of what his almost instinctive vision told him was a black dress.

He did not stay long; there was need for that. He had done all he had to do. And as he emerged, he saw two figures outside the precinct across the open space, standing as if in conversation. He allowed himself a smile, and it broadened as he crossed over to them.

'God be with you. I came to pay honour to the saint. I have walked from Josselin. I have to be in Plumelec for my trade. I have need of a pony.'

He spoke in Breton, and watched their faces as he did. It was the Breton of the central hills and forests of the Landes, close in intonation to their own, and as in Josselin earlier it released them from suspicion. A hand came out to his arm from the older of the two men.

'You have eaten?' he asked.

'I have.'

'Then a mug of cider? You must have a thirst after that walk. It is a good way.'

If they had heard the musket shots on the wind, they did not ask about them, nor about his business. The older man turned his head slightly, and shouted over his shoulder. 'Nolwen, a pitcher, two mugs, quickly, girl.' This to a child who had appeared at a doorway just back down the narrow lane, and was staring while pulling the ends of her hair.

'Tudual here has a cousin who has a pony. He goes to the woods for kindling for the ovens. Gorse is best.' He paused. 'He might spare it for a day...'

The younger man nodded, all the while keeping his eyes on Justin's face.

'I can pay,' said Justin. 'I have coins.'

The girl came to them shyly, holding a clay pitcher and two wooden mugs, while the younger man set off around the side of the church. She poured into one of them, and then spilled the cider, so Justin took both the mugs and bent down. It was more successful this time. They raised the mugs to each other in a slight gesture.

'To the saint, and to your journey.' He realised how thirsty he was, achingly thirsty, and the older man watched as he filled, and then re-filled.

'To the saint,' he said.

The pony lurched, and Justin felt some sympathy for it, because behind him was the boy, snuffling from time to time for no particular reason. It was a load, but the pony had its way of working, swinging from side to side as it advanced, used to a burden pulling down on its back. In the heat of the day the boy smelled strongly of sweat and the pigsty, but he came with the pony, to bring it back, and he knew the way. They made an odd picture, he thought, and at that moment Amelia came to mind, with sketchbook and laughter, and his mother at her shoulder. This was Cervantes, she would say, Don Quixote on Rocinante with Sancho Panza, but apart from his clothes there was truly nothing much out of the ordinary about either of them. He had been right; they had had to track back out of the village in order to pick up the road to Plumelec.

Apart from the clip of the hooves and the creak of the harness, the day was silent, the air now relatively still. They made fair progress, passing no one on the road. They saw some lads working in a field a little way off, who stopped to stare at them, but the boy shouted a greeting in a guttural voice, with someone's name in it and part of a coarse joke that Justin picked out of the sound. If the boy himself had a name, Justin did not know it, since Tudual's cousin had just told him curtly, 'The boy goes with you.' He had been generous, and the cousin had pulled at his beard and set the harness, adding an oily felt cloth for a saddle for both of them.

At times, the journey seemed eerie, as when they gradually drew alongside and past the elaborate closed gates of a small chateau, clearly visible from the road but with its windows shuttered, no sign of life at all, grass growing already on parts of the gravel driveway. The hamlet that followed it on the road was also eerily quiet, with just the sound of chopping wood coming from a yard at the back of the ancient houses. The chopping stopped briefly as they passed, and then resumed.

It had been a long day, and he was worried now that they were bound to be getting close. He ached all over, and had had nothing to eat all day, so the cider had now gone to his head. Added to that was the renewed fear that surely, at some point, they would run across a detachment of soldiers, not necessarily in pursuit but ranging the countryside. He might talk his way out of that, but it could be very risky. He also feared for the boy, who was now whistling, and loudly at that. All he knew about Plumelec was to find the clog-maker's cottage. He could either risk asking the boy, or try himself, on the ground. But it was getting late, and he was tired. So he swung round, startling the boy, who stopped whistling and stared at him open-mouthed, and disturbing the pony too, who came to an abrupt halt. Justin decided that few words were best.

'Plumelec. The clog-maker. His cottage.'

For a moment, the boy seemed not to have heard. But then he raised one arm and pointed. 'Plumelec.'

Justin could see nothing, but the boy might be right. They were in woodland, after all. 'How far? Close?'

'Not far.'

'The clog-maker.'

'Yes, the clog-maker.'

'You know his cottage?'

At that the boy laughed and pointed to his feet, on which were a disgusting, stained and battered pair of clogs. And as the pony moved forward again, and from then on, he heard the boy muttering to himself and laughing, with the word 'clogs' mixed up in whatever he had to say to himself.

It was the spire that gave notice of the village, and Justin shifted on the pony's back, sore and strained in his joints, apprehensive of negotiating another set of curious inhabitants, all or any of whom might pass on the word to those who came asking. Who could tell where loyalties really lay, which tradesman or burgher might incline, despite appearances, to the Republic? Had it been possible, in another world, he would have liked to have talked to them; but he had no doubt about keeping his head on his neck, and the bullets out of his heart. He bolted awake with alarm from this reverie as a hand grabbed the worn halter of the pony, and a large head and broad shoulders began to run alongside, part crushing his leg. The boy was laughing, as ever, and there was a gruff exchange as they trotted and bounced aside sharply off the lane into a narrow yard, with the gate held open by a grinning Yann. He slammed it behind them, picked up a clog and waved it in Justin's face, before pulling him off the pony to embrace him unceremoniously, the boy laughing all the while, and having his head clipped affectionately by the clog-maker.

The food was by now welcome, and relief spread through Justin's body like the gentle warmth of a strong wine, or in this case the *lambig*, which burned its way down his throat and began to reach even his sore joints. The boy missed all of this, since he was sent away home with the pony and a good chunk of buckwheat cake, grumbling all the while despite the small coins that Justin pressed into his hand, and which he looked at suspiciously before putting them in his mouth.

'So you are sore, Baron? By Saint Arzhel, we had to run! But you found a war-horse. Not since the time of pennants and men of arms was there such a beast! And your page! Of the best family, I do not doubt, but I would rather dip him in the Oust.'

'Yet here I am. I am not sure if I owe that to Saint Servant in his church or Saint Gobrien in his chapel, but they both have my thanks. I went on my knees in front of Saint Servant, that is for certain, and as in the old stories came out of the church to my salvation. But now I would ask you, or Perig here, for a place to put my head.'

Perig ran his large, scarred hand through his curls. 'Well, master, I would dearly love to offer you what I have, but Yann has other plans…'

Justin looked up at the light framed by the door, which was already fading. As he did so a figure stepped into the frame, dark in the half-light, gave a greeting with his hand, and stood silently just inside the door.

Yann stood, stretched, and crammed his hat on his head. 'You must go with Maelig. We cannot stay; it is dangerous here. We must be gone before dark, not be here tomorrow morning at any price. I am sorry, Baron. Who knows who may have seen and said?'

Justin stood up. 'Do I keep these clothes?'

'You cannot leave them.'

'Where do you go?'

Yann held up his hand regretfully, and Justin accepted the gesture.

'Ah, you cannot say. But you know where I am going? And Maelig will lead me there, through the Landes? And you know who I am expecting to meet? But you do not know where the meeting-place is, or rather you will not tell me now? But some other will know? Am I right?'

'You are right, Baron. May Mary the mother of God and all the saints preserve you.'

Justin had heard of Maelig, the man of the woods who was occasionally glimpsed over many years by children like himself, who brought down charcoal and led villagers to timber that he had cut, who took food and necessities in exchange, and looking at him in the dim light from the yard it did seem as if he was ageless. In Cornwall he would be called a pisky, no doubt, here perhaps a *korrigan*, but in truth he was too large for that. Sinew and almost shining muscle, a face as wrinkled as an aged piece of oak, a finger on his left hand missing at the joint as he rubbed his bald head and replaced his crumpled cap. He smelt of woodsmoke and charcoal, and also of leaves, of the leaf-mould that stained his tunic and breeches, themselves the colour of earth. It was said that he never spoke.

Perig passed Justin a scrip with biscuit and cake, which he showed to him before folding them inside, and a strap to sling around him. Justin stood, placed his hand on Perig's shoulder, turned to grasp Yann's hand briefly, and ducked out through the door. He was followed closely by Maelig.

CHAPTER X: RENDEZVOUS IN THE DOLMEN

Babette looked up from her work. She had caught a movement at the edge of the woods. The sun was climbing to her right, but she squinted again. Where the track led out there were two figures dimly visible, both of the same height, not in uniform, nothing glinting, dressed darkly. She put the bowl on the ground, brushed her hair out of her eyes, and waited. Yes, they were coming out of the wood and walking towards her. The figures began to take shape, and she recognised the woodsman, Maelig, walking close to the other figure, another man. She waited again, just to be sure, and then picked up her bowl and went back to shelling the beans. She had sat outside to this end, as she had when she could over the past weeks. Now she was sure. He had come.

Justin felt the sun on the side of his face and rejoiced in it. The woods had been comforting and secure, and the two of them had trod lightly, watching deer as they flitted through the shadows, listening to the chatter of squirrels annoyed by their progress, hearing the rattle of woodpeckers, always in the middle distance, never seen. He had spent the night under the stars, without need of a bivouac, lying on his back and remembering his childhood as well as Canada, how he had been in these same woods as a boy as well as a young man. His woods, although he rarely exercised the right except over the deer, which would otherwise be shot and sold for money, so hard for many to find by other means.

Ahead of him he saw the cottages, and a pang gripped him, because the sight and even the smells were so familiar. The people would be too, although how they would receive him he did not know. He could already see that some were gathering around a seated figure, and one at least was pointing. Maelig grunted beside him, as if to acknowledge that his job was done, but Justin paid no attention, his eyes fixed on what lay ahead.

Suddenly a young lad came bursting out of one of the cottages and ran like lightning towards him, shouting, '*M'seigneur, m'seigneur!*' He flung himself on the ground at Justin's feet, grabbing his knees and then his right hand, which he kissed, laying his cheek against it. 'You have come, *m'seigneur.* I told Babette that you would come, but she never listens to me. She called me a fool, and other things I cannot say to you, but she has been waiting herself. Come, come, you must come!'

Justin lent over and pulled the boy gently to his feet, resistant though he was. 'Gilles, you do not need to tell me to come. I am coming, as you see. Now you must not pull me around so.'

And, indeed, Gilles was now tugging at his arm to make him speed up, and was surprisingly strong, so Justin almost stumbled on his way, laughing, towards the small group. By now the men had gathered in front of the women, the few children with their mothers, and there was forehead-touching and cap-doffing, one old man, Loïc, down on his knees mumbling a prayer of thanks, only Grosjean standing back, smiling a little, but his eyes wary. But Gilles pushed past them, opening a passage for Justin, and he saw Yaelle, who had once worked at the manor, and behind her the figure sitting on a stool. At that moment he remembered Maelig, and pushed back through the men to find him; but Maelig had gone, vanishing into the trees. Justin stood and gazed after him, and then Gilles was back again, dragging him unceremoniously to

Babette, who had put aside her bowl of beans and risen from her stool.

'Baron.'

Justin looked in her eyes, but could read nothing there. 'The boy is well. You have looked after him.'

'I did. You wouldn't have me leave him out for the badgers. Gilles, you little weasel, stop pulling the Baron.' Then to the rest of the men: 'Why are you standing there? Is there nothing to do except stamping like cattle? Away with you. The Baron is tired. I shall feed him. Now. But just him, mind. He is well, that is all we need to know.'

The voices confirmed that this was so, and the men shuffled off, leaving the women talking, gradually turning away to their tasks now the excitement was over. Justin followed the boy as Babette ducked into the cottage in front of them. The interior was dark and cool, the smoke from the fire stinging, but the smell was good. Gilles pulled up a bench and sat down, pointing to a place for Justin, who moved the bowls and spoons, and sat down holding them. Babette bent over the pot hanging over the fire, and added some of the beans.

'They are fine fresh,' she said to no one in particular. 'It has rabbit, and has been stewing since dawn.'

Justin, who was playing five fingers with the boy, furrowed his brow. 'Since dawn?'

She glanced across at him. 'Ay, we heard about Josselin. It was only a matter of time.' She sensed readily enough that he was worried. They had known each other for a long time, and needed little to bring their thoughts together. 'There was word. Passed along. Only to those who were … close. Who would keep their mouths shut. It had to be, or we could not help you. It will be different now, no avoiding that, and we must act quickly. Here, hold those bowls, and keep them steady, Gilles, or you'll be the one who is scalded, and serve you right for the mad boy that you are.'

Gilles did keep still, taking the bowls from Justin and bringing them back, steaming, delicious to a hungry man. He burnt his tongue. It was worth it. She watched them both, a little more at ease now, perhaps loving both.

Babette had nothing herself. After a while, she came behind Gilles and grabbed his ear. 'Now, you, out. I have to talk to *m'seigneur.*' And as he protested, 'No, out you go, now.' She led him a short way and then shoved him out of the door. She remained by it for a while.

Justin felt the stubble on his chin. Some different clothes would make him less conspicuous, but he might talk his way out of trouble better if he looked respectable. So a razor, if they had one here.

'They killed Guareg. Took him behind the cottages and shot him. He'd been wounded. Yaelle went out of her mind.'

Justin broke out of his concern for razors. 'Soldiers? They have been here? When? How many?'

Babette turned round. 'Does it matter how many? Enough to kill a man with a wounded leg. They'd been off in the Landes, picking off the blues, Grosjean and the others. They call themselves Chouans. One day they'll be the death of us all.'

'Just once?' said Justin.

'Just once. I told Grosjean not to piss on his own patch, and they've been further away. The Vannes road. The soldiers like the towns; their officers want them in the woods and fields.'

'Does Gilles know?'

Babette came and stood over him. 'Know what? He knows his mother died, and he knows he's not really my brother. The other children tell him often enough, taunt him, sometimes. No father, no mother.'

'Does he —' and here he looked squarely in her eyes — 'know who his father is?'

'It may be he thinks he knows.' She held his searching look and shrugged. 'But he says nothing to me. And I nothing to him. So that is that, and will remain like that. It is what we agreed, a long time ago.' She took the bowl from him. 'You had better get ready. We must leave soon. This place cannot be safe; they could be back at any time. That captain was a sharp devil. They may have been at the manor too.'

Justin stood, but did not move far. Everything was coming at him far too quickly. 'At the manor?'

'What did you expect? They will want to take it, and Yaelle who works at times for Le Guinec brings us news.'

Justin felt like a fool. He knew nothing of this. 'Le Guinec? Who is Le Guinec?'

Babette came up to him, and made as if to shake him disrespectfully by the lapels of his coat. 'Ah, Baron, the world moves on and you are left behind. Le Guinec is the new steward. Do not look at me like that. It is not of my doing.'

'But where is Mael? I did not appoint Le Guinec.'

'No, he is your cousin's man, or perhaps that should be your mother's cousin. Mael has gone. They say he was ill. So then we have Le Guinec. He comes and goes, and the government men have been and gone, taking with them some of what is stored, and Yaelle has also seen soldiers.'

'So, Laurent and Le Guinec. I have not heard the name before.'

'But we heard Le Guinec had gone to England and returned. Perhaps he did and missed you. What does it matter? The government will steal it all anyway. You are an *émigré*; you can do nothing. Or they will have your head. You should not be here.'

Justin's face was set. 'You say we must leave. You have been told of the meeting.' It was a statement, not a question. 'Is there a razor in any of the houses? Who sharpens the tools here?'

Babette looked at him again. 'You are right. It is not much of a beard, and it would give you away, neither one thing or another.' She went to hang a smaller pot over the fire, which she kicked into life. 'I shall fetch you a razor. Watch that pot, *m'seigneur*, if you please. It has a little water in it, and will boil away.' She turned at the door and answered his unspoken question, with that sense of each other that they had. 'Yes, I am going with you. A woman and a man, dressed as you are, will be safer than that great bear Grosjean or any of the others. I know where to go. It is in the forest. Yann is no fool; he sent his message to me.'

'But not to me?'

'How could he? You might be caught. They would have no pity for you. They are used to making men talk. Now, that pot, and the razor, and I shall tell Yaelle to look out for Gilles while I am gone.'

And she was through the door, leaving Justin feeling vulnerable in every way, ignorant of what was going on around him. Why had he agreed to do this? Would it prove to be worthwhile? He looked after her, forgetting the pot and her instructions. She was a beautiful woman, just as she had been when she was a girl.

She led him at first through parts of the woodland they had known so long ago, above the manor, places which, although he had lived there and visited infrequently afterwards, he had never been to again. There was the 'devil's crag', as they had called it, the 'mountain' — another outcrop of rock — and the spring bubbling out at its side. She said nothing, walking ahead as if he needed a guide on his own land and through his own memory. After that, the woodland became scrub, the track gradually unfamiliar and then completely unknown, glimpses occasionally of a cottage or a shelter, small clearings soon swallowed up again. Once he heard a twig crack, and once or twice he thought he saw the hint of a figure, perhaps just the glimpse of an arm or the side of a head, but at a great distance, and it was gone. If they were being tracked, there was nothing he could do about it, and nothing that he should, because no Republican soldier could move that silently in this alien world.

He felt her presence, and the renewed conviction that she was bound to him; but he remained uncertain whether this was a thing of the past, or enduring. It was so long ago, and since that time she had willingly cared for Gilles, childless herself, taking the boy from his dying mother, loving him as her own. That Gilles was now nearly grown might have aged her, but despite being Justin's age, or close to it, she was still a young woman. He had no impression whether there was a man in her life.

The trees thinned out, leaving gorse and bramble thickets, and a winding path into them, and then there was no doubt, because an armed man suddenly stood out on the path ahead with the red and white flash of a Chouan brigade on his jacket. Others appeared to the side, so Babette came to a halt easily and put her hands on her hips. She had her hair up, and was wearing a cap but no coat, because even in the shade it was warm. The man on the path had his gun over his arm, and he was chewing, scrutinising both the woman and the man, taking in what he saw. One of the men to the side whistled, and the man in front beckoned to them and led the way on.

They emerged into an open space, totally surrounded by the scrub and the woodland, at the centre of which was a dolmen, a massive granite tomb from ancient times. The blocks of which it was built were immense, the capstone impossibly lifted up on standing stones, creating a passage with a low, wide entrance. Babette stood to one side at the edge of the clearing, and sat on a boulder, looking out and away into the woods. All around the clearing and in the scrub were men set as guards or lookouts, a good twenty or more. At the entrance to the tomb stood another Chouan, this one with a sword in his scabbard, wearing a broad-rimmed black hat, and the same red and white flash. He walked forward with his hand still on his sword hilt and stood in front of Justin, then tilted his head, inviting him to follow. He ducked in under the massive lintel, and Justin kept his head clear of the granite roof all along the passage. At the end, as he came out into a chamber, he found his arms gripped and held behind his back by two men to either side of the entrance. He could stand, but he was not free.

The chamber was lit by candles and oil-wick lamps, some placed in crevices in the walls, and some on the floor, and although the smell of grease and oil was strong, the air was refreshed by means of the gaps between the stones. At the back of the chamber three men were seated behind a small table, with a pen and ink and what looked like a map of some sort in front of them. One of the men was young, and what Justin would have called 'dashing' to his sister in other circumstances, with short black hair, a white neckerchief, and a white jacket, sporting the Chouan flash. He had his hand on the table, and the other resting on his thigh, his right leg stretched out to the side. He looked at Justin with great disapproval. On the other side, there was an older man, bare-headed also, who was wearing a priest's collar, and who was looking at the ground. In the centre was a large man, nearly as young as the man to his right, but with a square face and a powerful neck buried in a high collar. It was he who spoke.

'I think we know who you are. But tell us. Let us hear you speak.'

'I accept that you will have heard of me by now. The incident at Josselin was unfortunate. I am the Baron of Kergohan, one Justin Wentworth by name.'

'Indeed.' There was nothing else said.

'I will presume that you believe me. And if so, perhaps you would tell your men to let go of my arms. To be held like this is painful. I am unarmed, and I am sure they have weapons.'

The man in the centre looked at the priest, who nodded. The young man on his right said nothing, and continued to stare at Justin.

'I believe your speech. It is from this region, and we have other testimonies on which we can rely.' He raised his finger and moved it from side to side, indicating to the guards to let Justin go, which they did. 'But you will continue to stand there.'

The priest now spoke. 'There has been much expectation that has formed around your despatch and arrival. We have our channels, of course — there are many *émigrés* in Britain, and some venture here still. But there have also been many disappointments. It would be true to say that there is much distrust of Mr Pitt and his ministers, of the good will of the admiralty and the military in general. So, what is it that you have come all this way to tell us? Or is it to ask?'

The man in the middle nodded, and pushed his chin up out of his collar, leaning back against the stone with broad shoulders. The priest waited.

'Do you have a letter? We might expect a letter, and perhaps place trust in it.'

Justin had begun to feel more at ease. This was the moment, and he was well prepared, although he could not be sure of his reception. 'There is no letter. It was thought to be too dangerous, too prejudicial to the mission. You have heard rumours of an expedition, I am convinced. Those rumours are correct and justified. There will be an expedition, and it will be departing soon. It will not come to the north coast, as some have wished, but to the south, as you may have guessed by my difficult progress here. I did not land in the south, because had I been captured it might have given too much away. It was decided to make the expedition to Brittany because of the strength of feeling in your uprising, despite the capitulation by some in Rennes in April of this year.'

He paused here for breath, but also to assess how this had been so far received. The young man appeared to be more interested, and the bullish figure in the centre had looked very sour at the mention of Rennes.

'You, sir, will surely be Georges Cadoudal. The British government is firm on relying on you.' There was no reply. 'Am I correct here?'

Cadoudal blinked and said nothing, but no one denied it. So the journey and the peril had not been totally in vain: he was at least with the man he had come to find. He decided it was time to add more.

'I shall be brief. The expedition will come to Morbihan, and it is imperative that you be there to receive it, in as much force as possible. There will be an *émigré* army, led by Puisaye, whom you may trust, as does the British government.' Here was silence. He coughed, and took the risk of spreading his arms as he spoke. 'Is this satisfactory? Acceptable to you?'

The silence was broken by the men across the table shifting slightly on their seats. Cadoudal pulled his ear, and the priest put a finger on his lower lip. Nothing else happened.

'Where?' The young man had spoken.

Justin took a deep breath. 'Quiberon. I am authorised to tell you. There will be landings at Carnac. The British ships will control the waters. There is no apprehension about the Republican navy.'

'When?' the young man continued.

'In this month. They have sailed. At the end of this month they will occupy Quiberon town, take the fort on the peninsula, and land at Carnac. They want you to be there before them. There, you have it all.'

Cadoudal now spoke, and his tone was a mixture of patience and pragmatism. The government had judged their man well, Justin thought.

'What do they bring with them for us, Baron? You and they must have known we would ask that?'

'Apart from an *émigré* army, there are transports with provisions for thousands for three months or more, uniforms for thousands, tens of thousands of pairs of shoes, similar for muskets, six hundred boxes of ammunition, I was told, and cash.'

'Uniforms, but no army,' the young man scoffed.

'The British are bearing gifts, I see,' added the priest drily.

Cadoudal tapped the map lightly. He looked right and left, and seemed to get what he wanted from his companions. 'It will do. It is better than we have had, and better than it might have been. We will be there. You can tell Puisaye that we will take Carnac, and wait for him. Just before the end of the month. He can put his flag on the top of the Mont at the back of the town. But if we have to wait too long…'

'I shall send to Puisaye at sea if I can. If not, we must trust that they will keep to their time.'

Cadoudal stood. 'Your servant, Baron.' The two other men leant forward to speak to each other, ignoring Justin. One of the guards at his back pulled at his arm to tell him to leave, and the other pressed his head down to avoid a careless scalping on the lintel.

Justin and Babette left the clearing in silence, the Chouan captain with the sword gazing after them, but there were no ribald jokes among the lookouts, who kept facing out, vigilant. The sun was declining, and they walked back in silence. Justin struggled with the sense of relief at a commission performed while he contemplated the violence of the battles that must follow.

When they were close to home, in the ground where they had spent those many hours together, Babette drew alongside him. They were by what they liked to call the 'sacred oak', which time had barely altered.

'Do you recall,' she said in almost a whisper, 'you once were so close to taking me here. We had reached the age when we should have stayed apart. And I was close to letting you do so.'

He was astounded, but he did remember.

'I kept from you after that. I would not open myself to my own ruin and shame. And I am glad that I pushed you to the ground, and ran, and ran. Better the mother that I am not than that.'

Before he could think of what to say, she had left him. They walked back through the edge of the woodland to the cottages, one behind the other.

CHAPTER XI: DESOLATION OF THE MANOR

It had rained hard all night, but Justin had been dry in the straw above the stall where the pigs were shut in at dark, with just enough cracks in the roof timbers to provide him with some fresh air. The pigs' noises were comforting rather than disturbing, but he would have slept soundly in any case, exhausted as he was and also relieved, in part, by what had been achieved. He had washed in the yard without any interruption, even from Gilles, no doubt because Babette had given strict orders on privacy. After that initial welcome, which had been warm, the tenants had hardly approached him, out of respect, but perhaps also because they would not have known what to say to him, nor he to them. He was not aware of having been severe, nor of his grandfather being so; but a few words were often enough, although he would talk through work or a problem at length with any individual.

Babette had been considerate, as always, brushing down his clothes and boots before he had risen. She had left him biscuits by the hearth in the cottage, and a rare beaker of wine, which she must have been keeping somewhere for a special occasion. But she was nowhere to be seen, until he put on his hat and came through the door, setting out on the path to the manor. At that point, she appeared with Gilles, who ran to him again, but in this instance just took his hand and kissed it, saying nothing.

Today, there was more of the young man visible in him rather than the boy, and Justin realised that Babette was keeping him as a boy for as long as she could, rather against the pull of nature. Seeing them both together, she was aware that there was little to choose between them in height, the boy lacking weight and width in the shoulders, but strong enough for all that. Sensing that today was different, Justin took his hand and shook it gravely, closing his left hand over their clasp. He was tempted to add something commonplace, such as 'You will take care of Babette', to confirm the impression of growing maturity, but he was conscious that she would laugh at that idea, and so break the moment.

'*Kenavo*, Gilles.'

'*Kenavo, m'seigneur.*'

'*Kenavo*, Baron.' Babette's voice was even, and her eyes gave nothing away. 'Come, Gilles, the Baron must leave. It is dangerous for him. We are fortunate to have had him as our guest.' She smiled to make it easy for all, and it was a release.

So he had marched off along the edge of the woods, putting memory and worry behind him, content that the boy was well, that he had stayed with her, that she remained resolute on whatever course she had chosen, but also aware that the boy had taken her youth. Something else had taken his, and it might have been duty, an attempt to make things work through hardship for what he thought was the best, although now his belief in that was shaken. Which brought him to Amelia, to whom he was devoted, and how she was no longer a child and must soon leave him. And where would he be then? He was his mother's son, but she missed George as well as his father, and there was nothing he could do to repair that loss.

In that frame of mind, he found himself already in the copses that stood above the manor, leading down to the south and the sun, but he came to a halt, shocked to see open ground to his left, or rather a clearing of stumps and brushwood. It was extensive, and it looked as if the clearance was spreading up the slope, although to the left the broken woodlands were still intact. Below him stood the manor, Kergohan, with its orchard to one side and the stables behind, the pressing house with its cellar nearest to him, at the back of the orchard, the timber yard back from the stables.

His suspicions were now aroused, since this felling was unprecedented, something that his steward Mael would never had allowed. So it had to be this man Le Guinec, or worse, someone else taking the timber unauthorised. That must mean the Republicans, in some shape or form, backed up by soldiers. He crouched while he surveyed the panorama. There was nothing on the horizon to the south, and he sensed that there had been nothing in the forest. He scanned the outbuildings, and then the house itself for any sign of movement, allowing his peripheral vision to register even the slightest flicker.

There was nothing. He had not expected to find his house like a grave, but he recalled the chateau he had passed, with its ornamental iron gates locked, its driveway patchy with weeds. It did not take long for things to fall silent. He took the timber yard first, crossing from the felled ground, finding stumps of what had been chestnut, oak and hazel of mixed age, a young grove by and large, but still a grove. There was little cover here, but he had little to fear. There were deep ruts leading away, brushwood still on the ground, discarded as worthless, which it was not. The local people had plainly not dared to come and pick it up. Some was fresh cut, other patches older, but not by much. He crouched again to look and listen, and then ran lightly down to the timber yard, to which the ruts ran. He edged around the buildings cautiously. The carts were there, but he had heard no horses, nothing drifting up from the stables. The long saws were hanging as they should be, oiled, perhaps freshly, but when he came to the saw-pit the evidence was all around, and deep in the pit itself: sawdust in heaps, and trodden down to a brown mush. Bark and offcuts had been thrown into a pile. The cart-tracks led off from a blur of dried ruts and dust down and around to the driveway of the manor.

There was nothing more to do here without someone trustworthy to ask about it, and so sentiment drew him to the house itself. Mael would have kept it locked and clean, as he always had done, but he and the other staff had gone. Justin decided to try the door by the kitchen, from the yard into the buttery and the washhouse, and to his surprise it was slightly ajar. He put his head to the gap, but nothing stirred. All was as it had been, slightly stale but untouched here. He trod quietly, stopping at every turn, along the serving corridor from the kitchen, past the dining-room towards the salon. As he approached the door he heard a cough, and for the first time a sound of movement, what seemed to be a brush. This could not be Le Guinec, here by himself. And there was no one else in the grounds, he was sure of that. So he resolved to confront whoever it was, and find out what he could before leaving promptly.

As he stepped through the door his first impression was one of shock. The room was virtually empty, the Aubusson carpet, the walnut furniture, the Ormolu mantle clock that his mother had loved and his grandfather had hated, the blue Sèvres porcelain, the long drapes, all gone. He had never imagined such desolation, the room that was so much a repository of his memories stripped bare, leaving only an echo of the past. Some instinct had allowed him to ignore the man who was staring at him, one hand resting on his wide broom, his other running idly through his hair. His face expressed recognition and warmth, but his manner showed reservation and hesitancy. He was of middle years, and when Justin's gaze finally rested on him, he bowed his head.

'I know this must be a surprise to you. You know who I am, I can see. I may have met you. Forgive me that I do not recall…'

'Yaelle's uncle, Baron. I used to work in the stables, help out, from time to time.'

Justin had returned to looking at the room. 'What has happened? Is this the work of the new steward, Le Guinec? Or is it depredation, by the soldiers? Come, there must be some explanation? Is the dining-room the same?'

The man looked embarrassed, awkward, as if he had been caught in the act of stripping the room instead of cleaning it. He rubbed his hand through his hair again, and dared to speak. 'Well, sir, rightly both, I s'pose. They come wi' carts and took it away, some that was soldiers, in the main men from town. Dinin'-room is as 'twas. There are one or two rooms above…'

'What about Mael? Where is he? What happened to him?'

'He's been gone nigh on two year now. They said he took ill, went off to be with his cousin.'

'They? Who were they?'

'New steward, sir. We ain't heard nothing from him after.'

Why this room? Was it the wealth of it, its value? Justin supposed so, as with the rooms upstairs, no doubt the women's rooms. Or perhaps just some kind of safeguard, the show of wealth being dangerous, a liability beyond its worth? Perhaps a mixture of both, if a man was canny enough, and Justin began to think he might know who that man was. In an abstracted mood, he walked across the empty room to the windows, staring out at the familiar landscape that now seemed very blank to him. As he did so, he caught sight of a movement at the end of the avenue of elm trees that delineated the drive. Instinctively he stepped back behind a pilaster that stood to the side of the salon windows, and watched as the indistinct group began to substantiate itself. There was plainly a carriage, but also horsemen, and he was convinced he could see blue bobbing amongst the darker colours, possibly the glint of metal.

'Are you expecting anyone?'

'Not that I know, sir. Mebbe it's more for the timber, Baron. They have taken timber, and at any season, not that they…'

'This does not look like a felling party. There is only one vehicle, and it is not a cart.' For the first time, Justin smiled and put his hand on the man's shoulder. 'I must go. They must not find me here. And take care: they must not know that I have been here. Not a word. The village will know, but they will keep silent about it. One day, perhaps…'

'Perhaps, sir, God willing.'

'I must go. No word, now. You have not seen me, not seen anyone.'

The man nodded, and resumed his sweeping.

Justin left the same way that he had come in, without looking around elsewhere, despite his strong urge to do so. It would, in any case, only have angered and distressed him further, and so distracted him. He would make his way up around the other side of the manor, through the orchard and up past the pressing-house; there was plenty of time. But once in the orchard he was tempted to linger. Unless he was mistaken, they would not be looking for him there, and he was intensely curious, since chance had come his way, to find out more, whatever those scraps of information might prove to be.

The group was now rapidly approaching the manor, the vehicle and horses scuffing and grinding along the driveway, raising dust. There was a high hedge that shielded the orchard from the approach to the house, a formal feature that had never been removed, and it was now overgrown. Its arc bordered the turning circle of the driveway in front of the main entrance to the house, and Justin felt secure, with the orchard behind him in which to vanish. So he waited.

The carriage that pulled to a halt in front of the house was plain, but well-ordered enough, and the lad sitting next to the driver jumped down and stood at the head of the horses. Waiting to see who stepped out of it was intriguing enough, but with a soldier's instinct Justin was looking at the uniforms first. There were only three of them, and they were all mounted, which rather put paid to his careless assumption that the Republic could not stretch to cavalry. Confiscated horses, no doubt, but they sat them well enough, which also knocked aside his prejudice about town recruits. He was particularly taken by the one with the tricorne hat and the braid on his uniform, a sharp-eyed, close-shaven captain, he would guess, young, younger than him. These three kept to their mounts while the door of the carriage was flung back, the step unfolded, and a young woman's voice declined to climb down.

With some remonstrance from a male voice inside, two men climbed out in quick succession. The first was dressed in brown and black, with a white neckerchief at the top of his coat, and was unknown to Justin. His hair was striking, being thick and wavy, and beginning to grey. But he was quickly followed by the all too familiar face of the man whom Justin had used to call cousin, Laurent, in fact his mother's cousin.

This was Laurent Guèvremont, and in that case there could be little doubt that in the other man Justin was looking at Laurent's steward, Le Guinec. Laurent rubbed his hands together briefly, and then spoke back into the carriage.

'We shall be walking up towards the timber yard, Joséphine. This will not take long. I am sure that Captain Leroux will entertain you. If the caretaker is about, he may let you into the house to look around. Leroux, you may look around outside. As I have said, this may need guarding; you would be advised to keep a presence here. There is ample accommodation in the stables for a few men, and the locality will easily afford sustenance.'

With that, he and Le Guinec set off at a brisk pace to the side of the manor in the direction he had indicated. They would be gone up the hill, Justin estimated. The horses scuffled about for a moment as the captain watched them go, and then he sprang down lightly, and handed his bridle to one of the others, who had dismounted with him. He seemed uncertain what to do, when the young woman's voice came again from the carriage. Would this be Guèvremont's daughter, now grown up?

'Leroux, a gentleman would hand me down, if you would be so gracious.'

Leroux did not immediately reply, but spoke to his men. 'Take the horses to the stables, and have a look at the quarters. I shall join you there. Report on anything of note.'

'Leroux!'

The captain walked to the carriage door and held out his hand, as if on parade. Justin then saw the young woman descend, who must surely be Joséphine Guèvremont, no longer the girl he had known, but elegant and self-possessed.

'I thank you, Captain. Graciously done, but you kept me waiting. It is clearly yet another missing element of your education. Still, you hand me down well. I feel secure. So, what do you think of our family estate? Or at least, of our manor?'

'The porch is fine,' Leroux replied, 'and I admire the windows. You are fortunate here in the provinces that they remain intact.'

She had kept holding his hand for the while, but now released it, brushing her glove. 'The dust sticks to you, Captain. You do not pay enough attention to things of this sort.' She swung her arm round to indicate the extent of the manor and the estate. 'And what do you say to the probability that one day I shall be the mistress of all that we see? In contrast, as a man dedicated to the military life, what can you hope for? A billet, and a ghastly garret with a camp bed and a broken chair when you retire from service with your wounds?' Here she laughed. 'And, of course, a landlady, with no doubt a scullery maid to bring you your bowl of gruel.'

'I have my principles, *mademoiselle* Guèvremont, and my duty. The rest is not in my power, or, I will admit, in my sight. But it gives you pleasure to mock me.'

Joséphine at this moment seemed to relent, and there was a pause. 'Of course, when I am mistress, I may do as I choose. My father has always admired the military, particularly the upper ranks … as I do myself.'

Leroux bowed to her. 'Come, let us go into the house. One never knows, it may provide you with an idea of the life to which you might, with the favour of fortune, aspire. You may not hold my arm, however, with those oafs of yours close by.'

Leroux bowed again, and they proceeded up into the house, which the caretaker had opened for them. There was nothing more for Justin, and during the last exchange he had felt too much like a voyeur in a comedy to be entirely comfortable. But what he had heard had begun to consolidate an understanding that made him deeply apprehensive. He made his way carefully through the orchard, confident that no one was watching him, and decided on a whim to look into the pressing-house. The massive cider press was still in place, and judging by the smell there were full barrels of cider along the walls. He slipped down the staircase to the cellar, and his face set hard as he saw that they had removed all the bottles of *lambig*, and then had no doubt that the smaller cellar in the house itself had been denuded of its wine and brandy.

He was coming up the stairs when he heard the sound of someone cursing as he made his way through the orchard. There was only one entrance to the pressing house, and Justin ran to the blind side of the door, first grabbing the long wooden lever by which the screw of the cider press was turned, but then discarding it for one of the chocks that levelled it off. He held it in both hands, flattened himself against the wall, and threw an old bolt that he found on the floor against one of the barrels opposite. The soldier thrust through the door, and Justin clipped him around the head soundly enough to lay him flat on his face on the floor, dazed and groaning. That was enough, and he stepped over him and kept on running up the hillside as he heard more voices and a shout from the bottom of the orchard. He would not stop now until he reached the safety of Quiberon, where he expected to find the British fleet anchored offshore, and the simple certainties of his own military uniform waiting for him.

The caretaker had timed his run up through the orchard well. He could see that the soldier was slowly coming round into consciousness, and went back out of the door to shout down the hill. The captain and his other man climbed up the slope after him, and Yaelle's uncle found some water in a trough and soaked the concussed man, who was sitting up and cursing roundly. Captain Leroux told him to be silent, and listened outside. The forest and the orchard were making their calm summer sounds, undisturbed by the noises of a man in flight. Leroux came back inside.

'Get him upright. Slap his face. Shut up, man. Hebert, that's an order.'

'Yes, sir.'

'Did you see him?'

'I saw him in the orchard. Or I saw his back. We were coming back from the stables…'

'Never mind that. What did he look like? Young, old?'

'He was of middling height, sir. Not old or young, as you'd say…'

'And of middling complexion, neither brown nor blond, nor a Christian nor a Jew, I'll bet my horse. Hebert, you are a fool from a stinking farm in a squalid corner of Picardy. I'll put you on discipline when we are back. Vincent, did you see anything of this individual?'

'No, sir. We were coming back from the stables, as Hebert says…'

'I do not want to hear any more about those damned stables. Take him back down, and see that he is fit enough to ride.'

The two men lurched down the hill. Captain Leroux now noticed the caretaker, who had let him into the house.

'What do you want?' he asked angrily. 'Get down to your duties.'

Yaelle's uncle ran his hand through his hair, looked at the ground, and looked back up again.

'Well? Have you got something to say? Get on with it, man. And make sure that you speak in a French that I can understand.'

'Surely, sir. I saw him as he was running. I was first here, after the soldier was hit. He looked back over his shoulder. He was older than they say, wild-looking, ragged, bare feet, a ruffian. I have seen him hanging around before, prowling about. He may think there is drink to be had, empty house…'

'A ruffian, eh? Get back down, and be vigilant. Are you armed? I thought not. Go on, get you gone.' Leroux knew there was nothing to drink in the cellar, and nothing in the house either. Anyone who had been watching the house would know that. Guèvremont had removed it all, and much of it had been auctioned for the Republic. The man could be lying. These Bretons would lie as soon as look at you. And if he was lying… He continued, talking aloud but in a low voice to himself.

'My nose tells me you are one and the same, and I will have you by the tail before I am finished. But why are you here? I catch a scent of you in Josselin, and in Kergohan, and rumour has it that you have spoken to Cadoudal, whom I shall also have by the ears one day. There is something in the air, I am sure of it; I can smell it, but I cannot see it. But it will answer to musket and shot, and the forces of reason and justice will crush it.'

There was a rustle, and a waft of powder and perfume on the summer breeze.

'Quite the little orator, aren't we? But you must be aware that talking to yourself is not a good sign, Captain. There are those who do so that end up in the asylum. Come, my father is waiting. You are fortunate that I came to look for you myself. His temper may have settled by the time we descend. You may take my arm, but you must not be so heated. I deplore it absolutely, unless it is about me, which I fear it is not. Never mind, it will be soon. My arm, Leroux.'

The captain began the long walk down the hill, and Joséphine chattered artfully to him, musing all the while to herself why it was that she was willing to admire the line of his jaw.

CHAPTER XII: A DECEITFUL PROPOSAL

Although Amelia had visited the Wollastons at Alverscombe Hall, as the spring turned into summer it was Arabella who stayed more at Chittesleigh, taking an interest in the village and its inhabitants and accompanying Amelia, and occasionally Sempronie, on visits. Some of these included tenants on the outlying farms, with Sempronie leading when they called on a young wife who was with child, but in general it was the village that took most of their attention. There had also been other trips to Okehampton, and despite persuading her friend once at least to call in at the White Hart, Arabella had not seen anything of either man again. But she did manage to engage Altringham in making a duplicate for her riding coat, and was tolerably satisfied with the results.

The highlight, at least as Amelia viewed it, had been the unexpected attention of two young officers from the militia that had gathered in Okehampton, who came to Chittesleigh to pay their respects. The younger of the two, who reminded Arabella unaccountably of a lurcher puppy, sported brave mustachios of which he was evidently if rather naively proud, and she noted wryly the good impression these made on her dear friend. At least, Amelia was notably more responsive to this ensign than she was to the older lieutenant, and since their uniforms were very similar, something in his manner or appearance must account for that. They received them in the drawing room, and the gentlemen were greeted with a decanter of wine from which they drank sparingly, commenting with some gravity on its quality, although they mistook a Bordeaux for a Burgundy.

The ensign, whose name was Tregothen, came back to the leading question. 'And so, Miss Wentworth, we find your brother away from home.' He was standing close to her, and conscious of his profile, which he could just study in the wall mirror. Amelia looked briefly across to Arabella, but she was engaging in polite yet cool conversation with the lieutenant, both standing with their backs to the mirror.

'Sadly so, Mr Tregothen, or no doubt he would be keen to join you.'

'E'gad he would,' said the older officer, who had seemingly been caught by this strand of conversation, because he had brought Arabella over to join the other two. 'Fine soldier, good experience, and inclined to the infantry, which deters many of the gentry, it must be said. Yes, Wentworth would be a gain to us, no doubt, and a credit to the company. Be demm'd, in fact, if he might not have served as a colonel.'

Mallingham, for so he was called, was a thick-set, rolling kind of man, whom Arabella mentally compared to a Red Ruby bull.

'My father was a military man himself in his time, sir, and not known to despise an infantry colonel in the field, or off it.'

'You could surely without blame grace me with the use of my first name, Miss Wollaston, if you will. I should be honoured...'

'But that would imply familiarity, sir, and I abhor the too casual use of first names. I am, I assure you, most protective of my own.' And at that Arabella strolled over to the half-empty decanter on the tray in her most casual manner, turned to smile back at Lieutenant Mallingham, picked up a glass and poured herself some wine. 'Your health, Lieutenant, of which I am sure we have need for the defence of our country.' She raised her glass and drank gaily, although sparingly.

The ensign showed wisdom greater than either his years or his experience of society, for he came in quickly to pursue his former subject as much as to spare his companion further embarrassment. 'But, Miss Wentworth, we cannot be deprived of the squire for long. Your brother will surely…'

Amelia placed her forefinger delicately, and perhaps beguilingly, on her lips, which were already the subject of Tregothen's admiration, and appeared to ponder. She had, as she wished, the ensign's full attention, and even a little from the disgruntled lieutenant.

'My brother is, I believe — and Miss Wollaston, please correct me from your memory — on a tour of the outposts to the west of the city of Plymouth, on behalf of the Admiralty, although perhaps my attention was failing me at that point.'

'I am sure it did no such thing,' Tregothen came in gallantly. 'It is worthy of you, Miss Wentworth, to recall details that many would regard as irrelevant once they were sure of the location, and the extent of stay, of their loved one.'

'Indeed,' said Mallingham, who was beginning to expose his inferiority in almost every respect to his younger companion of lesser rank, Arabella observed. But he surprised her. 'Yet it is a puzzling line of duty that you mention,' he went on, going himself to recharge his glass at the decanter, and appearing to think for the first time. There was no response to his comment, and the young women as if in concert smiled back at him when he turned to face them. Since that schoolboy Tregothen, who had been assigned to him, seemed to be about to intervene, he continued. 'Yes, quite puzzling, but our superiors are so, are they not, Tregothen? A tour of that kind is a charge one might more readily expect to be placed in the hands of a naval man, wouldn't you say, Miss Wollaston?'

Now that was a clever move, a kind of feint that could be derived from playing chess, or perhaps, in a less elevated way, from turning the tables on an Oxford chum. No, not Oxford, Arabella thought — or not at least for very long. She decided to respond. 'Sadly I have no intimate knowledge of the plans of our ministries for the defence of the realm, Lieutenant Mallingham, and I am sure that Miss Wentworth shares with me the habitual willingness of our sex to defer to the authorities in such matters. Indeed, I hardly know what may lie to the other side of Plymouth, because I fear I have never been there in my life. I hear it is scarcely civil in parts.'

'Which may, we might surmise, be quite the reason that my brother has been called to survey its roughness, and exposure to the winds that blow from France. When he departed, he spoke of Cornwall.'

Amelia was well-satisfied that this much at least was true enough. The two friends linked arms in a charming way, as if to convey visually to these nascent infantry officers that they could not be caught in a flanking manoeuvre — for all that Amelia might, on another occasion, be inclined to encourage those mustachios.

It may be that fate intervened, or it was more probable that Thomas had a good estimation of the quantity of wine that two gentlemen pleased with their new uniforms might consume, and how long it would take them to do so. There was a discreet tap at the door, and Thomas appeared after a bright call to advance. He walked up to the table, carrying with some deportment another decanter, which if they again called it Burgundy he might be tempted to substitute for a thin and tasteless Val de Loire on a subsequent occasion. Mr

Wentworth, like his father, had always served claret, and this taste for Burgundy during daylight hours was a thing for London and its more disreputable clubs.

In view of carrying the new decanter, and removing the old, Thomas had against his usual practice left the door momentarily ajar, and as Arabella moved considerately across to place her glass on the table her eye was caught by the figure of Andrew standing in the relative shadow of the hall. When the groom saw his mistress, he took a step towards the door, as if to indicate his urgency, but stopped out of confusion about how to proceed further without encountering the wrath of Thomas.

Arabella decided to put him out of his misery. 'You will excuse me,' she said, and provided the military men with just the slightest of curtseys before sweeping out in front of Thomas. This swirl of garments renewed Mallingham's flagging interest, but despite himself he determined to give his attention to the other chit, whose hair was far too dark for his taste, but who spoke to him with a degree of interest.

'But surely you must ride to camp, or do you go by carriage? Even infantrymen cannot walk everywhere, and besides, the officer must be distinguished…'

Out in the hallway, the sound of Amelia's distraction of the officers was cut off with the closing of the drawing-room door, and Thomas crossed disdainfully past the lady and her manservant, considering to himself how the manners of the aristocracy might fall short of those of the gentry. Speaking to grooms in the hallway was, for Thomas, an unconscionable species of conversation with passers-by. He shut the door leading to the kitchens firmly behind him.

The voices from the drawing room were muted, the light in the hall dim, the age of the house darkening its entrance.

Andrew spoke in a whisper. 'You'll forgive me, ma'am, stepping into the house here under the eye of Thomas, but you…'

Arabella was indulgent, but she interrupted him. 'Yes, but what is it?'

'He has ridden off, ma'am, the man you've seen sneaking about in the house, as you said, and in the town besides. I've been helping at the stables, as you suggested, and what better for me to do, truly…'

'I know, Andrew, we had agreed, apart from exercising the horses and that trip to Hatherleigh for the stirrup, which was mended. We do not need to detail your duties, since we both know them. Quickly, now. When did he ride off?'

'Why, only just now, ma'am, although I'd reckon he'd been shaping for it for some time, messin' about down there and talking to Jem and the lad, and before you know it he talked his way into exe'cisin' some of Mr Wentworth's horses, rightly like my duties an' all, an' I spoke to Jem an' he's done it afore, so off he goes…'

Arabella was making for the stairs. 'Where, Andrew? Where was he heading?'

Andrew came towards the staircase, still keeping his voice low. 'There mayn't be anythin' in it, ma'am. He's rode off before, as I said, but off to the north, I'd say, and so says Jem.'

Arabella gripped the banister. If she could trust Andrew implicitly, as she did, she could afford to be patient. 'You say "but", Andrew. Which direction did he take this time?' Patient she might be, but her voice was strained, and she could hear it.

'Why, ma'am, begging your pardon, but that's why I'm here. T'other direction, to the moor, or leastways to the side on it…'

'To the farmhouse we saw on our previous ride? In that direction?' And before Andrew could answer, she was away up the stairs. 'Saddle our horses, and the roan for Miss Wentworth,' she instructed over her shoulder.

The horses were stamping, and Jem held Miss Wentworth's roan contentedly while he watched Andrew manoeuvre Miss Wollaston's chestnut mare and his own Black Diamond, its blazon magnificently clear, spirited but not above nudging its master in the back to gain his attention back from the mare. The cobbles rang with the stamping, and those mounts left in the stalls were restless, occasionally kicking the doors to provoke a shout from Jem, who knew the offenders without looking round.

It had been Arabella's intention to come round to the stables in such an eventuality, so as not to occasion notice in the house, and so it was that she came through the tack-room already attired, the older green jacket preferred to the newer, and a pair of sturdy calf-skin boots that were as good off the horse as on it. Andrew held out the bridle to her, and Jem touched his forehead, not altogether comfortable with quality in his yard, although Miss Wollaston was no stranger to stabling. But he was astonished to see Andrew cup his hands together, and the lady step on them like a trooper to sit up tight on the side-saddle. Black Diamond bucked his head at this, impatient to be seated and off himself, but Arabella rode and turned the chestnut, holding it on a tight rein for the instant.

'I want you to wait for Miss Wentworth, Andrew. Do you hear? Do not follow me until you have her with you. Do not tell Miss Wentworth anything more than I have written in my note to her. But I do want you within hailing distance of the farmhouse. If he is not there, then we have missed our purpose, and shall have to take advantage of the exercise alone.

And Jem, you are mum, d'you hear? None of this to anyone, short of the ladies of the household taking a ride with their groom.'

Jem nodded his agreement, deeming it right not to speak, and looking to Andrew, who said nothing. Once his mistress took command, he was content with few words.

'You understand, Andrew? I have left my note with Thomas, to take to Miss Wentworth after a short interval. The officers will leave for Exeter; that is their intention. Their horses are in the village, and they will walk there comfortably. They are infantry, after all.'

The last comment was delivered mostly to herself as she tapped the chestnut with her heel and cracked out of the gateway in good order, as Andrew observed to his satisfaction. The only creature left disappointed in the yard was Black Diamond, who snorted as he was led to a tethering ring on a post, and had to be content with a thwack on his flank from Andrew, and a ruffle of his mane, which he shook to show he was not yet pleased.

The chestnut mare found her way to the farmhouse without the least difficulty, because Arabella had let her rides out with Amelia or on her own with Andrew drift across to that part of the pasture on the edge of the moor. They clipped the edge of the fields that must belong to the farm and avoided scrutiny from its door or outbuildings. But as she drew near, the impetuous spirit in which she had determined on this course of action began to dissipate, in favour of calmer reflection on what precisely she had in mind to do, and how she should conduct it. She had no fear. The sneaking man from the house was for better or worse in the employ of the manor, and she would be as safe with him as with her father's retainer, of whom she had seen no trace since that once at the White Hart. Nor would Le Guinec be a threat to her, had he returned secretly to England, which she doubted. As for the naval captain, Yeo, he was a gentleman, known to her and her father, and closely bound to the family at the manor.

Nonetheless, she was a woman and she sensed her vulnerability, although in this instance that vulnerability was intangible. Did she fear that her father would aim to restrict her freedoms, if she committed an indiscretion by forcing her way into an encounter that she was not meant to witness? She shifted in the saddle. It was almost an instinct running through her veins that told her she was about to break a vessel of thin and delicate glass, once she chose to step through that door and challenge those inside. And yet another instinct, or perhaps an intuition, told her that something was badly wrong, that whatever intrigue was in progress was at best misconceived, at worst threatening. But to whom? To her friends, surely, and beyond that to one whose back was turned… Shame on them. Her face was burning, and she brushed away a tear with a gloved hand. The horse was urged forward, and as she passed the hawthorn she felt herself becoming calm. She would need to tether the mare somewhere round the side of the house, preferably away from the stable, and get to the front door of the farmhouse undetected, or all would be lost.

Her decision was to approach the building from the side, which was easy, because the green lane ran down and then alongside the farmhouse, picking up one or two tracks from its yards, one of which led to the rear. She kept to the saddle, partly for comfort over the ruts, and partly to be able to turn away and ride off casually if anyone came out of the doors. There were no windows on the side she had chosen, just the cob wall above a grounding of stone and below the thatch, and just in front of it the circular stone wall of a well, with the housing above it for the pulley. There was a bucket on the ground, which had water in it, and Arabella slid to the ground just next to it, hitching the reins to the pulley-handle and allowing the horse to drink. So far it had not been greeted by the horses she knew to be around the far side in the outbuildings, and she was satisfied with her calculation that the wind was responsible for that, blowing towards her across the front of the building.

She could hear absolutely nothing, and all her apprehensions suddenly surged to the surface, making her grip her riding whip all the more tightly. It was plain that she had to approach the front, since snooping was out of the question here, and would bring no rewards. Those would lie in confrontation, and her ability to gather what she could from surprised reactions and expressions, and hopefully from some unguarded statements. She tucked the whip away in a fold of the harness to have both hands free, and picked her way carefully to the point that she must pass a window in the front wall. This she did at a pace, and reached the porch of the farmhouse without a cry coming from inside, although she did just catch the sound of voices.

She had made up her mind that she would knock and then enter, in the hope of disturbing something that might, momentarily at least, be revealing. She was acquainted with farmhouses from visits on her father's land and with Amelia to some of the manor's tenants, although she had never been inside here. Her quick eye saw that the latch was a heavy but simple mechanism, with a solid handle on it which she gripped resolutely. It might stick, in which case all would collapse in awkwardness and embarrassment. The door opened inwards, as the jamb confirmed to her, which suited her purpose well. A solid, curved iron knocker was within reach of her left hand as she gripped the latch, and as she raised the knocker she heard laughter and what she took to be the clunk of crockery. It was the ideal moment, and she did not hesitate.

The first thing she sensed was the cool of the room compared to the warmth of the day as she stepped smartly across the threshold and let her eyes adjust as quickly as possible to the duller light. She had prepared her opening speech, because she did not want to be distracted by fumbling for words. In the event, her confrontation was even simpler than she had expected, because across the room was none other than Captain Yeo, quite as her relentless suspicions had led her to expect. His face was a picture of astonishment, which he struggled to replace with a welcoming and benign smile as he put the flagon he was holding down on the trestle table that occupied the centre of this large, homely room. Not so composed but just as familiar was the figure to his left, the servant from the manor, who had had his back to the door, but who had swung round at the sound and then appeared completely disconcerted. He glanced at the captain for some kind of prompt, and then over to a tall, thin man who was standing in a doorway that led to the back of the house with a tray in his hand. This must be the tenant of the farmhouse. His face was the hardest of all, unyielding and just short of hostile, and he came forward with a gait that Arabella likened to an animal defending its territory.

'Well, ma'am…' The farmer could get no further, because Captain Yeo took charge of the general confusion, and came to her side with a hand part raised to be of assistance.

'Miss Arabella, Miss Wollaston, of course, what brings you here? No mischance, I hope? You are well, you are walking. Has your horse gone lame? We must be of assistance. George, call your wife, if you please. Miss Wollaston has more need of female support and attention than of our witless selves.'

It was an accomplished display on his part, very much the officer, and mayhap to him she was a little akin to a boarding party, she thought wryly to herself as she said: 'Captain Yeo, I believe. How astonishing!' And she took his outstretched hand in hers briefly, to acknowledge his deference, but removed it before he might feel relieved at her complacency. She turned to the farmer's wife, who had appeared at the inner doorway, and was as round as her husband was thin. 'I should be grateful for a glass of water, provided that it has come from your well, my good woman, and you will forgive my intrusion.' The woman bobbed, but stepped on the toes of her husband, who was standing behind her and still looking off-and-on to the captain for inspiration, as it seemed to Arabella.

'Yes, of course, you must be seated, Miss Wollaston. I am forgetting myself.' Captain Yeo made a show of brushing a seat clean on a chair that looked as though it might accommodate her, and ushered her towards it. He was clearly intending to stand over her, but she was having none of it and instead walked over to the hearthplace, which was ample in the Devon way, but of Dartmoor granite and without a mantle. This allowed her to pass the flustered man whom she clearly recognised as the man she had set out to follow here, and she seized her opportunity without demur.

'Do I not know you, my man?' She swung round to face him after gaining his attention. 'I can assure myself that you are known to me from my time at the manor. I confess it is a surprise to me to see you here, and away from what must be your duties.'

It was a resolute attack, and only interrupted by the farmer's wife bringing the water across to Arabella, in a glass no doubt handed down as an heirloom, and as clean as anyone might wish. Arabella took it, thanked her with a nod, and raised it in a gloved hand, but he was not going to escape.

'Well, my man? What brings you here? I am sure that Mrs Wentworth, or her steward, would wish you to account for your absence.' That much was exaggerated and unlikely, as Yeo might surmise, but it would do to scare the man a little and provoke some response.

The man shifted uncomfortably under that stern gaze, and looked briefly to Captain Yeo, but the captain's attention was elsewhere and no help was forthcoming. The man cleared his throat, and the answer when it came was firm and confident. 'Yes, ma'am, but I been doin' this for a while now, takin' one o' the horses out on exe'cise, which Jem will know, when all else be done in the house, beggin' your pardon, ma'am.'

Arabella did now take a drink from her glass, because she wanted to keep him on a hook. 'Ah, indeed, a thoroughly practical point. But it does not altogether explain your presence here.' She sipped again, raising an eyebrow over the glass, which she then lowered as she set her chin at him. It was plain that he would not escape. The man brightened visibly and looked to the inner doorway, where to his relief he saw the thin farmer lounging, perhaps rather insolently, although it was his dwelling.

'Well, ma'am, happen that I do from time to time call in for summat to wet my throat, it bein' dry work riding in the summer, as you have found yourself, with respect, and George here, or his missus, bein' a cousin of mine back home, so's I can allus get a welcome, as you can see, ma'am.'

'Indeed,' said Arabella, and motioned to the farmer to take her glass, looking hard at his face as he came up, which remained inscrutable. The man from the manor saw his chance and set off for the door, shielded by the husband of his wife's cousin, or whatever other fictional relationship he might dream up, Arabella thought.

'And now wi' respect, ma'am, I'll be leavin' and gettin' back 'fore they be lookin' for me at the manor.' And he made a gesture of touching his brow, before hurrying out of the front door, which he slammed behind him.

Arabella looked across at Captain Yeo, whose dress on this occasion was that of a gentleman and not an officer, with both jacket and breeches of a good cut, and the shirt underneath of excellent linen. She moved a pace or two towards him, and then stopped and raised an eyebrow.

'You too may leave us now, George, and shut the door behind you.' Yeo spoke to the farmer without turning round, and his voice had the ring of command. 'Miss Wollaston…' He tailed off. Outside, a horse clattered away on some cobbles.

'Captain Yeo?' she replied, amicably enough, but offering him no hope of a reprieve.

'This is a strange circumstance, and I suppose the philosophers have something to say about it, to do with coincidence. I am not sure which of us is more surprised, and you must be wondering quite what brings me here.'

If she was wondering, then he did nothing to enlighten her, because he was evidently completely at a loss to explain his presence in an obscure farmhouse on the edge of Dartmoor, in the domain of his friend's family. Or was he? He looked up, and Arabella misdoubted the look in eyes.

'Miss Wollaston, Arabella … I find myself somewhat at a loss for words. We have so often met in circumstances … in company, in the company of others…'

Arabella was having nothing of this presumed familiarity. 'Often, sir? I fear you do exaggerate. Why, I do not precisely recall the occasions, but I think "often" exceeds the case.' She had decided the hearth was good ground to hold, and held it.

Captain Yeo was either inspired, or too cunning to accept this repulse. He virtually marched to the table, as if in agitation, and then grasped its edge with both hands, resting the back of his well-cut breeches against it. He once again attempted to fix her with his eyes. 'I think, Miss Wollaston, you mistake my intent. I have been unable to converse privately with you before now, which has run counter to the tenor of my feelings.' Here he put one hand to his face, but removed it almost immediately. He appeared to come to a resolve, because he then strode across towards her, and grasped her right hand in his. 'I admire you, Miss Wollaston, I admire you greatly and would beg this chance to express myself to you with the fervour…'

Had he regarded the object of his profession rather than the granite of the lintel as he was speaking, he would have seen a sudden change as the flush of anger rose to her cheeks. As it was, he felt her withdraw her hand from his in an urgent gesture as she pushed past him to the centre of the room, standing still for a moment to calm her raised heartbeat, to cool herself. She was initially at a loss for words, because she suspected dishonesty, and not just pretended presumption, which fuelled her anger to a point almost beyond her control at this moment. There was silence.

'I see you are dismayed. I may have spoken too soon, too abruptly. Miss Wollaston, I believe I should relieve you of my presence, which must be burdensome.' He gathered his gloves from the table and called for George, who was suspiciously not far away. 'My horse, George, to the front, quickly now.'

Arabella was both insulted and affronted, debating whether he had treated her heart or her intelligence with more contempt. She was inclined to the latter conclusion: it was most unlikely that he would credit her with much intelligence. She refused to face him.

He went to the door. 'Miss Wentworth, your servant. I hope that despite all, I may be allowed the opportunity…'

Whatever the opportunity that he had in mind, and however acerbically Arabella might have dismissed it, he was interrupted by a female voice that he was not expecting.

'Bella, I… Captain Yeo! Oh, I fear I am … I had no idea, dear Arabella. I must leave you. Forgive me.'

The voice was Amelia's, the tone one of complete shock, mitigated by a dawning sense of intrigue and of something that might be hopeful, something to be treated with delicacy. At the sight of Amelia, whom she had been expecting perhaps even sooner, Arabella broke from her reverie and ran forward to grasp her arm, so preventing Amelia from executing her about-face, and providing the officer in an instant with a more formidable problem than he had faced so far.

Captain Yeo paused, because the doorway was now blocked to him, and bowed to Amelia. 'Miss Wentworth, your humble servant.' He passed his gloves to his left hand and rested his right on his hip, because it was plain to him that he had nowhere to go. This was equally plain to Arabella, who had come to the view that nothing was too bad for him after that shameful manoeuvre. There was now a sparkle in her eyes, which he noticed with apprehension.

'Is it not a strange chance, Amelia, my love, that Captain Yeo should be here in the very house of one of your tenants to which I just happen to turn for a summer refreshment? And stranger still that he has given no explanation of that remarkable fact. I believe him to be a man of mystery.'

If Yeo was a man of mystery, then at that moment Arabella was a young woman of mischief. Amelia had taken some steps into the room to acknowledge the officer's bow, and was at a loss to know what was in progress between the two of them. Was this a rendezvous which they had both wished to conceal, as well they might? Would such a rendezvous account for Bella's repeated visits to the manor over spring and now summer, a ruse to escape the notice of her father in a liaison with an officer he might well deem to be beneath her rank or her proper expectations? But why now invite her here if that were so? The written summons from Arabella she had just now been given by Thomas had explained little. It all seemed most unlikely, if not precisely impossible. But if it were not the case, what would account for her friend's perplexing behaviour?

The captain, in the manner of those who are guilty or feel themselves to be so, had mistaken her puzzled silence for a brooding calculation of his possible misdemeanours, and he decided that instead of embarrassing Miss Wollaston further, he would offer some part of the truth. 'Miss Wentworth, I know not quite how to explain this to you.' Despite all propriety, he went to the table and sat on the chair he had earlier prepared for Arabella, who returned to her favoured place by the solidity of the granite hearth. Outside, a horse whinnied impatiently, and voices spoke quietly to it.

'You alarm me, sir, unless it is that you are declaring an affair of the heart, which, if it is as I suspect it to be, could never alarm me.' At this she glanced across affectionately towards Arabella, who was as immovable as the stone against which she was standing. To Amelia, this was very odd indeed.

'An affair of the heart I might wish it to be, but I do not speak of that.' He contrived to look in difficulty, almost as if in pain, and once again made that gesture of passing his hand across his face.

Maybe it was a naval mannerism, Arabella considered acidly, adopted when officers were sending men to their deaths. She suspected another pretence, but found herself rather too thoroughly disarmed by what immediately followed.

'The truth is, Miss Wentworth, that there is fear for your brother. No, please listen to me further, and you will be put for the most part at your ease. I myself, under the charge of Miss Wollaston's father, have undertaken to keep watch over his affairs. I have a man in the household to that end, who is a loyal and honest man, who serves his country as well as the family. He is to be trusted, and not questioned. He reports to me, and I to Miss Wollaston's father.' He gestured in Arabella's direction, not meeting her eyes.

Another silence followed this second and bewilderingly different tale.

'Forgive me for offering you a shock, Amelia, as an old family friend. There has to be some subterfuge. There are those, you see, who have regarded your brother as a man of shall we say radical views, from a family known to be of an enlightened turn of mind. The atmosphere in the nation is disturbed; there have been laws passed and prosecutions conducted, and suspicions fall easily when encouraged. We have undertaken to mount a guard on the family and on your brother's reputation while he is away on a mission of which I do know a little. We must bear in mind that there are those who would contrive to ruin a man just for speaking his mind innocently.'

Amelia had taken herself to the hearthplace alongside her friend, who took her hand surreptitiously and squeezed it. 'Captain Yeo, it would be hard to receive such information with equanimity. I am sure that I speak for both of us when I say that. My brother is both an honourable man and a patriot, but if he is threatened then I can only say that he and my family owe you a considerable debt of gratitude for the actions you have taken. As we must also be indebted to Sir Francis Wollaston, in this as in many former ways. But you must forgive me if, as you say, I am shocked. I must return to the manor. This is not as I expected. Bella —' and here she returned to her opening assumption, which was now quite deeply undermined — 'will you be accompanying me, or do you wish…?'

'I shall most certainly accompany you. Captain Yeo previously announced his departure, and there was in any case nothing here to detain me. Perhaps you would be kind enough, Captain, to allow us to take charge of our horses before you?'

The captain had little need to assent, because Arabella led her friend through the door, where the reassuring figure of Andrew could be seen, standing by Black Diamond with the bridles of the two mares loosely in his grip. Close to him was George, who was holding a fine grey with an elaborate military harness that had taken to stamping with impatience. There was a granite mounting block in the yard, and the young women rode smartly away, with Andrew following discreetly.

Captain Yeo stayed inside the house for some time, then passed his hand abruptly through his hair and across his face, transferred his gloves from his left to his right hand, and slapped them carelessly and distractedly on his left palm. The resolution then came to him, and he stood and marched to the door, flinging it open and taking the air while he drew his gloves over his fingers.

'For God's sake, George, what do you think you are doing, man? Leaving a horse to stamp like that. Bring it to me.'

This was no sooner said than done, since George for his part had no patience with this kind of horseflesh, and never rode if he could walk.

The captain swung easily into the saddle for a naval man, and brought the horse's head round. A few scuffles and it was peaceful, waiting for the off. The rider breathed deeply and leant forward to stroke its ears, before urging it to the south. It was, at least, not too far from the truth, and as such a kindness to the women. But it had been a close shave, and he would not want to see another like it.

CHAPTER XIII: AT THE SIGN OF THE LITTLE PIG

Justin went down and stood on the beach in Quiberon as the British fleet arrived, a growing mass of darkened wood and canvas, ensigns flying high and confident in the stiff breeze. The troop transports, along with the ships of the line, rolled in the swell, and the townspeople of Quiberon gathered on the shoreline with excited talk. There was a Republican garrison firmly in place in the fort at the neck of the isthmus, and Justin had no doubt that there were those who crept away to them, although from where they were on the ramparts the soldiers could see the extent of the threat to them clearly enough. This was a divided town, but for the time being those who favoured the Republic had to lie low and keep their opinions to themselves.

He had had several duties that fell on him. The first boat that came ashore carried a lieutenant with rowers and marines. It was a strange sight to see the red uniforms bobbing on the waves, the lieutenant standing high in the stern of the pinnace, to be clearly visible from the shore. The leading men of the town, whatever their sympathies, had come together on the beach, and when the pinnace came in the lieutenant showed his courtesies punctiliously to all who were there, keeping them occupied with greetings, and a letter from Commodore Warren. A second boat brought a purser and clerks to begin to arrange the billeting, who gathered behind the lieutenant and the group on the beach.

Justin slipped into the second boat that came to shore, and greeted the midshipman from the *Pomone*, the Commodore's frigate, before it pulled off unnoticed to make its way back to the fleet. It was a matter then of meeting Warren, and sitting in conference in his quarters with him and with those who were leading the *émigré* force, Puisaye and the other commanders of regiments of French royalists. The rendezvous with Cadoudal had now been confirmed by *émigré* officers, put ashore the day before from the frigate *Galatea*, and the liaison with the Chouans secured for the moment. The rush was now on to get supplies and munitions to Cadoudal, who had taken Carnac, and was in control of the beach that ran for over a mile around the belly of the Bay of Quiberon.

Justin had decided to throw his weight in with those landings, which were quickly followed by the disembarkation of the first *émigré* regiments from the transports, boat after boat thrusting fully loaded onto the beaches and pulling back empty. Cadoudal had sent men and carts to collect the guns and ammunition, and it became chaotic for a while when Republicans attacked to the north of Carnac. But they were beaten back. Despite the exhaustion, much made its way to the right places, and Justin collapsed back on board confident that the first stages of the expedition had been successful.

For a time there was a lull. Along with most of those who were not sailors, Justin came ashore to find a room in the town, cheek by jowl with some British military men and many, many *émigrés*, not all of whom, he found, agreed about anything at all. At night and even during the day there were arguments and altercations, but all seemed to subside into a sense that now was the moment. The streets of Quiberon ebbed and flowed with optimism and rancour in almost equal proportions, mixed in with the views and hopes of Chouans, captains and men, and some of their women and children. The town was overrun, overflowing with an impassioned humanity. Fortunately, there were ample provisions from the expeditionary fleet and its transports, meant for campaigning but capable for the time being of supplying the needs of an excess population. There was also drink, not just the local varieties, which were far too coarse for those of refined taste, but the wines and spirits that the *émigrés* had taken care to lay up for their own consumption, and had now brought on shore. There were those who saw this seething influx as a God-given opportunity, mostly landlords and entrepreneurs who let out all the rooms they had, while cramming their own families into a basement for the time being, and keeping what they trusted was a close guard on their women. Cooks and tavern-keepers cooked and poured as fast as their arms could lift and clean, and the narrow *ruelles* carried as many fine odours of fish and enticing cuisine emanating from kitchens as they did the evidence on their paving of over-indulgence, and the stench in some doorways of stale cider.

All of this was relaxing in its way, a far cry from the harsh inadequacy of most military life, the ruthless discomfort which had been the norm for Justin years before in the backwoods of Canada. But who could tell what the future would hold? The expedition was in its infancy, and his own involvement with it was uncertain. What he had was a uniform, that of a captain of infantry, the commission he had taken when he had accepted this posting, on which, indeed, he had insisted as a condition of acceptance. At some point, he might wear it. For now, it was folded neatly in a box, the sword in its scabbard, with frog and white cross-belt, hanging from a nail on the door. It seemed to him like a guarantee of something, although if he entered into combat he would be an officer without an army.

The *émigrés* and the Chouans had been brought red British uniforms to mark them out, but they would hardly take his orders, or be in his chain of command.

For now he should drink, and eat, and sleep, and prepare for something, an involvement that he could not anticipate. Caught up by the excitement, he had even taken up smoking again. The fleet had brought tobacco with it in barrels, and pipes were everywhere, sold on street corners because of the abundance. But he had ended up choking, broken the pipe, and thrown it into the empty hearth. He was kicking his heels. Relaxation was all very well, but it could so readily lapse into fatigue and indolence. That midshipman from the *Pomone* had looked so like his lost brother George, the same age or thereabouts. Or perhaps that was sentimental fantasy. Either way, it was damned depressing if he dwelled on it. He pushed back his chair, grabbed his hat, and strolled out to find a fellow officer, to listen with amusement to the pretensions of the *émigré* captains, and observe the nuances of their fateful incompatibility with their allies, the Chouans of Brittany.

Captain Leroux had not been involved in the recent battles, although it was true that he was now entering the lion's den. After working his way through southern Brittany flushing out rebels wherever he could find them — which had not been that often, he reluctantly admitted — and losing men from time to time to their barbarity, he had been posted to the fort on the Quiberon peninsula. He had always disliked garrison duty, and this was not made any less dull by re-naming the fort Sans Culotte in honour of the Parisian revolutionaries. He had had some of those revolutionaries in his unit, and could hardly be inspired by recalling their pantaloons.

He did not intend to stay at the fort. Because the Chouans were everywhere on the peninsula, he had come in to his posting at the fort by boat, under cover of dark, a long and miserable journey during which he had been sick. The owner of the boat was happy enough with the coins he was offered. At sea he could hardly betray a Republican to anyone, and in any case, he calculated, who could guess which way the wind would blow? The captain had in many respects been a messenger, who had seen the British fleet arrive and who was primed to speak words of encouragement to the garrison, and reassure them that the army of the Republic would soon sweep all before it in an advance into the peninsula. The men had heard such reassurances before, and received this unlikely news in complete silence.

Leroux could not sit and wait for things to happen. He was not impetuous, but he saw what needed to be done by doing the first part of it, and now he was determined to find out what he could of the enemy's plans. He realised that was a grandiose description of what he might hope to achieve, but it inspired him and prompted him on a course of action. He had managed to compel the fisherman who owned the boat to stow it and himself in a small bay just to the south of the fort, giving him money and provisions for a few days. He might well walk into the lion's den that now was Quiberon, but he would not do so by walking out in the light of day from the gates of the fort. So, as he had intended, he sent word to the fisherman, and arranged to meet him in the early evening. There was just enough dusk to make their movements inconspicuous, had anyone hostile been watching that side of the fort, and they slipped away down the *côte sauvage*, the wind making it difficult, the fisherman preferring to keep out at first and then come close in.

By the time they made landfall it was getting dark, and the daring of his pilot struck home to the landsman that Leroux was. He had been less sick this time, but the sight of the bright surf under the moon on the jagged, granite margin of the peninsula was terrifying, the approach seemingly beyond any skill of man, better for a bird, or better not at all. As they came closer, the boat pitched at a reef and Leroux grabbed at the gunwale, but the fisherman had judged the wave, and the boat slewed again, away from the reef and miraculously into the gravel that formed a tiny beach between sharp headlands. It was totally concealed, and Leroux did not even get his feet wet as he jumped over the side at the front, and helped to pull the boat a little further onto the shore.

The fisherman told him that he would fish that night and in the first part of the morning, and would come back to that cove and rest until the late afternoon to wait for the captain. That agreement for a rendezvous was in the money that Leroux had given him, and the further sum that he had promised him, and with the fish it was more than enough to make the trip worthwhile. But after dusk on the day following, Leroux would be on his own. To repeat the landing too often would be to risk discovery, and to be sure the fish would not keep, as the fisherman said with a grin. The captain had better not lose his wallet, or he would lose his fare.

Leroux thanked him, wishing his grin at the devil, climbed up the narrow gulley without much difficulty, and began to walk. He knew he would have to sleep rough, but that would add to the savour of his clothes, which he had taken from those stripped from prisoners at the fort. They were coarse but not filthy, and he had allowed his beard to grow, against his firm inclination. The hat was crumpled, ordinary but respectable enough, and above all should hide his features from any prying gaze. He had bargained on there being accents from all around France gathered now in Quiberon, and most of the *émigrés* would not be acquainted with more than a few from their own locality, as with the first days of any army. But he would have to sharpen his habitual Parisian slur; not many came from that direction.

He could see lights in the town, some moving as those holding the lamps lighted their way to lodgings and billets in the suburbs, if that was what you might call the hamlets that backed some way up the peninsula. There was nothing for him to do in the town after dark, and here was as good as anywhere. He had bread in his wallet too, and some good cheese, which he had had the sense to bring with him to the fort, and guard well. Wine in a small bottle, which he could throw away. What else could he want?

Babette took care to keep well away from the fort, which loured over the narrow neck of dunes and scrub linking Quiberon to the country from which she had come. She had never been this far down onto the coast before, almost into the sea, and she was terrified by the sight of the ships in the bay. People were passing her, back and forth, and from time to time a cart rumbled by, piled up with boxes, armed guards sitting on top. Her feet were sore, although she had on the boots that Grosjean had found for her and a pair of old stockings that one of the girls had picked up at the manor. They were not bad, but she had been walking for so long that the hard, old folds of the boots had begun to cut into her feet. She had no idea what was going on, although on the way down she heard the sound of muskets, snapping back and forth, and unlike the single shots she'd heard coming from the forest when men from the manor were hunting. Those shots had been in the distance, but now the cottages were increasing in number, and so were the people, rather like the outskirts of a village on a market day, when you knew you were getting close to the centre.

But she was not near the centre. She asked, and they told her this was the village of Saint Pierre, and the town of Quiberon itself was a long walk on. She could have asked for a ride in one of the carts returning empty from wherever it was they had been. But she had seen the looks that the guards, now relaxed, had been giving her, and it was the kind of welcome she could do without. Just outside Saint Pierre she was passed by an old man with an old thing on two wheels that stank of sour wine, with a mangy pony between the shafts, and she risked hailing him. He grinned toothlessly and gabbled something that showed that she could climb up, and pointed to some sacking that would cushion the rough ride. He then started talking back over his shoulder, but what with the rumble of the wheels and his speech over bare gums she could hardly make out a word, thinking it would do to shout back, 'Sure enough!' or 'You're right!' from time to time. It was a small effort for a good ride, and a rest for her sore feet. She even took some food out of her bag and swallowed it too fast, although she did have some of the well-water left in her old leather flask that still tasted sweet. What could she do, or hope to do? She had no real idea, but she could, she hoped, find the Baron, and he would know, surely enough.

But when they came towards the town, she was less and less sure of that. It was not so much the size of the town, which seemed in some way to be more a collection of villages than a large town such as Auray. It was the mass of people milling around, passing this way and that, standing in groups, dressed in all kinds of ways, some that she hardly recognised, uniforms and fine clothes, rough working tunics and breeches and jackets with the Chouan flash or a white cockade. It got worse and worse and they got closer, and when the old man asked where she was heading she could not make any sense of the names he mentioned, although she did hear the word 'beach', along with the word 'fishing'. Even in her confusion, it came to her in flash that if she was down by the sea she could work her way back into the town or along the shore or the coastline. So she shouted back 'beach' and 'fishing', and he nodded furiously, as if to say that he not only understood but that he thought that was a wise choice.

So the port it was, although quite which port she did not know. He seemed happy enough, and headed off for where the smell was strongest and the nets were spread. But she knew that her business was with the other kinds of boats, the parts where the soldiers were ashore or coming ashore from the ships. On her way down, from time to time, she had seen a kind of traffic of these smaller boats out in the bay heading off to the ships and coming back, but could not see them where she now was.

But, *diable*, the people there were pushing past her straight away, babbling, some in Breton, yes, but many in French, much of which she could barely follow. Nor had she ever seen so many weapons, swords and muskets and poniards, and what looked like daggers without a proper handle stuck in sheaths at their side. The uniforms were bewildering, white and red and even some blue, which at first made her wonder if she had stepped into a world where enemies walked the street together. And when she heard English she looked quickly into their faces, but he was not there, and why would he be speaking English? *Well, he might*, she answered herself, and then began to despair.

Justin made his way through the crowds to the tavern he liked best, and found himself ashamed to admit that was because it was more popular with the English. The *émigrés* got on his nerves, because their talk was wild, their hopes and aspirations to his mind unrealistic. More and more as he looked at this expedition, this army in the flesh, on the ground, he was confronted with the question of whether the revolution in France could be reversed, whether the nobles and gentlemen, the second estate as they were called, could by a titanic struggle put a people in arms back in their grim lodgings in the cities. It was not so much the numbers as the combination of rough violence with the money of the artisans, merchants and bankers who knew their own ability and had reason to doubt the good faith and the capabilities of those traditionally viewed as their superiors. In Britain, when the king had been executed, it had taken a generation to reverse it all, and to achieve it the second King Charles had been a ruthless man.

The door to the tavern was open, and a few looked up as Justin worked his way in, many in white uniforms, many with the royalist white cockade, some fine clothing and dress, some rough, some perfume even amongst the sweat. There were women and girls in there, most excited by this extraordinary pool of male arms and knees through which they swam, coming to rest in some cases, mixing a show of independence with a measured degree of insinuation. Some were wives, but these would be the wives of soldiers, used to this life, to towns they had not known, part of a circle of acquaintance that guarded its members fiercely from any unwelcome advances.

He shoved through to the back partition, where the light was even less, but where he could hear English voices, one in particular talking about horseflesh, boasting about his own back on his estate, another chipping in about racing and losing money. He saw his friend Eugene, who interpreted for the English naval commanders in meetings with the *émigré* generals, gatherings which could get by in either French or English for a time, but then collapsed and needed support from such as Eugene. He was from Tours, but he had taken a large part of his education in England, some of which was more in the pattern of learning from life, as Justin ironically put it, rather than from books.

Justin pushed in on the bench next to him, and heard the word 'Penthièvre' coming from the next table, *émigrés* who as usual spoke loudly and without concern for any secrecy. He picked up the flagon, and mockingly made as if to tip it into his mouth, provoking a loud protest from the whole table, then rinsed out a beaker onto the floor and filled it. The stuff they gave them here was not bad, but it had probably been sold to them by some sharp practice on the transports, so it had had a long journey across the Channel and back. Eugene, who was more than a little warm, rubbed his hand across Justin's head, and gave him a couple of slaps on the cheek. He then leant over and shouted in Justin's ear.

'Sleeping on your own again, Monseigneur Franglais? I have warned you about it. It makes you go blind.'

Justin winced, as much at the shouting in his ear as at the sentiments. It took him back; Franglais had been one his many names at school in England, along with traitor, of course. Boys, like men, were ruthless.

'Have you come across Antoinette? No? Many have. She's around here somewhere, probably with Aimé, the scoundrel. She's warm o'nights. You've heard about Penthièvre, the fort that the revolutionaries have renamed Sans Culotte?'

'You ask me? What would I know? I'm with munitions from now on; you're with Puisaye and the others. What are they saying?'

'It's of no consequence.' He put a drunken finger to his lips. 'All mum, as you English say, I believe.' He leant over to shout something at another colleague while keeping his arm round Justin's shoulder. Justin took the opportunity to look around the room, as well as anyone could, because the tobacco smoke from pipes was thickening the atmosphere, and dimming the effect of what few lamps and candlewicks there were.

There was a figure at the counter, some distance away, whose hat sat hard on his head over broad shoulders, standing indistinctly alongside a line of men and women, at least two deep, broken into groups and pairs and some individuals. He occasionally turned to face out into the room, and once or twice had walked away from the counter into one corner or another, looking as if he might be heading for a table, but turning back slowly and making his apologies as he squeezed past again back to his position at the counter.

There was something about his profile that had vaguely caught Justin's eye, in the odd intervals when Eugene was not shouting some absurdity into his ear, or one of the others was not asking him about the young sisters they hoped he had, or the horses, or his time at the racecourses in Bath or Brighton, to which there was a short answer which politeness padded out. But some figures did tend to catch his eye, as if he had picked up some of Amelia's powers of observation, which he much admired. It was also something of an instinct he had developed, that ability to catch something in the corner of one's eye, a movement or a shape that could be telling or even threaten fatality, a backwoodsman's life skill. You picked up the flicker of the motion, and adjusted what you were doing before you could work out what it was, or the animal or human being of which it was a part. It was what made deer bolt, rabbits run to ground, marksmen drop before they became the mark themselves.

His eyes then followed the young woman who had been pointed out to him as Antoinette, and despite himself he found that his gaze was resting on her hips. There was a young *émigré* in the doorway, a stylish man with a confident smile, whose own gaze was quite evidently taken up with admiring those parts of her body that confronted him. Antoinette came swaying up to him, fully aware of the other eyes on her, and kissed his cheek, to cries of horror from the other drinkers around, one of whom at least was pushed to the ground off his stool by the woman he was with, causing yet more drunken laughter and ructions.

Justin was disturbed by the pang of physical envy that he felt when he saw the young man running his hand down Antoinette's back, placing the other hand behind her neck as he kissed her lavishly, to roars of approval from the drinkers. As the pair left the tavern, and the attention of the those inside shifted back to their tables and companions, Justin suddenly caught a movement in the vacant doorway that was odd, incongruous in some alarming way, and he looked up and across again. At that same moment, Babette, who had heard that some of the English congregated in the Little Pig, and had gathered enough courage to get to the door after working her way through the puzzle and twists of stinking lanes, saw his face looking up at her from the darkened room. Her expression was one of astonished relief, one so strange that Justin immediately pushed back the bench, occasioning a protest from Eugene, and forced his way over to her. She started to come in, looked quickly over to the counter, and then backed outside, wiping a tear from her face.

Justin looked at her again, scrutinising her face. 'Come with me,' he said, and took her arm in his.

But Babette stood still, and then pulled him back from the doorway. 'The man in there. I think I know him. I cannot forget his face.'

'Which man? Why are you here? What on earth has brought you here, all this way? We must go to my lodgings.'

'No, I am sure. He is not why I am here, but he should not be here. He is the French captain, the one who came to the village. I will never forget his face. His men shot Yaelle's man like a deer, at the back of the cottages. Two shots. I looked him in the eye. I came to find you, but why is he here too?'

Throughout this short speech Justin watched her intently, following every word, trying to take stock of what he heard and to put aside his complete puzzlement about why she was here at all. His arm kept her behind the door jamb and out of sight, while he himself risked a glance around it into the crowded tavern. 'Which man, Babette? I think I know the one you mean. With the stubble. You saw him across the room?'

'At the counter. He has a hat over his eyes, but it is not enough to hide his face from me. He is a…'

Her expletive was lost on Justin, because two things happened at once. Through the smoke, a pair of eyes saw him looking from the door, and quickly turned away, their owner vanishing behind other bodies at the counter. Justin shouted to Eugene, who was closer, but Eugene did not hear him, although he looked up aimlessly for a moment. Quickly urging Babette to stay where she was, Justin began to shove his way through the mass of bodies, earning complaints and even the occasional threat as he did so. He knocked his shin on a stool and stumbled, falling into a corpulent *émigré*, who pushed him away with some sharp abuse. He looked up, but could not see the man, guessing that he had worked his way out through the back, which had the buckets that acted as a crude toilet alongside a few of the empty casks. At the back of that yard was a small gate that led into a filthy lane. By the time Justin reached the lane there was no sign of the man. Which way to go? Right or left? Into the town or down to the port? Would he opt for running away or hiding? Eugene had followed him out, and was perched uselessly against the gate.

'What is it, old man? I thought you had come out *aller pisser, mon ami*. Who is that woman you were with, you old dog? Where are you going?'

Eugene stood at a loss while Justin chose the way to the port. There was an even darker alley down at the bottom, and he had no weapon with him, so he edged up to the corner and looked around it, crouching on his knees, a good position from which to hit someone if you were unarmed. But again, there was no one in sight. He ran down the alley, and here faced a different problem: it opened into a street leading round the harbour, which was packed with men, women, children, and dogs; nets, hampers and fishing pots; carts and ponies; and boots, clogs, uniforms and rough tunics. There was every kind of movement, from boys running to people shuffling in the shade, and groups that shifted and changed their shape, individuals breaking free and then disappearing behind others.

Reluctantly, he made his way back. But with one urgent concern laid to rest, at least for the time being, there remained the other, so his pace picked up. He had cruelly left Babette out in the street. He need not have worried. For all his bravado, Eugene had proved the gentleman. He had gone outside, introduced himself to Babette as Justin's friend, and sobered up remarkably quickly, shielding her from any of the unwanted comments of those inside. When Justin came through, he had said 'Mademoiselle' in parting, and left them to it, whatever it was that held them together, which he sensed was not quite what one might expect. She raised her eyes to Justin's in a question, but he shook his head.

'The bastard,' she said.

Leroux now understood that he disliked this kind of skulking, this sneaking, dishonest work. Running for his life down murky alleyways, without a weapon he could use, without an enemy's face to confront, without a uniform that expressed his pride in what he did… Disgusting. Not shameful, because his purpose was intelligence, hopefully saving the lives of his soldiers and serving the Republic, but in some ways degrading. To be caught like that would be appalling, and he must never do it again. Never. The words came easily into his head because they kept time with the thumping of his heart from the running, and because they were a compensation for the inevitable surge of fear. Any one of these people would have put a blade through his belly without the slightest hesitation had they known, or put him up against a wall and shot him, as he had done himself.

As it was, he had stopped running once he was out of the alley, and walked on through the town, gradually cooling, occasioning only the odd glance from a girl or young woman, or someone loitering with time to stare. What he was wearing had made him unrecognisable, although what that cursed woman from the back of beyond had been doing in the tavern he could not imagine. He had caught her eye even when she was standing in the doorway, and had sensed that she would speak to the man who had gone to join her. He remembered her well enough. She was the one who had stood up to him and his sergeant in that pigswill village, and who in a disturbing way had attracted him. She was like an animal, of course, as these Breton peasants mostly were, but in her case that had been compelling. She hated him, inevitably. They all did. And as long as they stood in the way of progress and the revolution, he would hate them back.

As he did those so-called *émigrés*, whom he would rather call traitors and enemies to their country. He had listened to their vanities and arrogance in the taverns, as he searched for some snippets of information that might help him and his general, and despised their assumption that they could return and take back lands and titles. His grandparents had been dispossessed by them, his mother forced to go to the city, to work in squalor, and he and his parents had lived in poverty until his father found work with a merchant and his mother employment in the merchant's house. That man was respectable, a citizen, and he had paid for Leroux's education so that he might further himself, put his natural abilities to the best use to contribute to his society.

If that meant the army, then he would do what the army demanded. And now he had heard enough to justify undergoing this brief humiliation, because the aristocrats were fools, whose heads were best under the guillotine, not letting out what should be secrets and boasting about how the fort would be taken in the next day or so. It was not much, but it confirmed his suspicions, and to be forewarned was to be forearmed. The garrison might hold out, or be relieved, but he could report his information and then go on back to General Hoche, who was young, competent, and ruthless as he should be, and so had his firm respect.

His heartbeat and pulse had tempered by now, as he was walking through the outskirts of the town and past scattered cottages, hoping he could remember the way back. He headed for the coast, along tracks that led through the scrub away from signs of habitation, and across to the sandy paths along the top of the low cliffs of the *côte sauvage*. The afternoon sun was less intense, although the heat came in from the west and over the sea. He swore as he took in the inlets and coves: jagged rocks with no way down, nothing at the bottom except breakers, surf, flotsam crashing uselessly against the rocks. The rough path led along the headlands, and fortunately there was no one else wasting their time walking along it. He found himself thinking about that woman again, and idly comparing her to Joséphine, to whom he was also drawn, as she had surmised. He thought that Joséphine's neck was paler and more slender, but still…

He heard a call and looked down. He could see nothing. He was on his guard, and once again swore at the fact that he had no weapon. He would walk on, because wherever the call had come from it was not in front of him. But the shout came again, louder, and he heard one word: 'Captain'. And now he remembered that dreadful accent and the fisherman, and to his left he saw the inlet, the tiny beach, the fissure in the rocks up which he had climbed. He felt relief, he had to admit, but did not bother to reply. He glanced around to make sure that no one was following him, and scrambled down, scraping his ankles, to grab the edge of the boat and jump on board.

That man at the tavern, he thought. Who was he? Was that him? Was that a sight of him at last? What had he been doing in the countryside and now here? The boat lurched as the fisherman poled it away from the shore, and Leroux fell backwards into a basket of pilchards. The fisherman looked angry rather than amused, and pulled him out, muttering something in that barbaric language of theirs, and telling him in French to sit down in the bottom of the boat. 'Stinking boat, and stinking fish,' the captain muttered under his breath.

Babette had kept completely silent as they had walked the short distance from the tavern to Justin's lodgings. The landlady had given Babette a knowing look as they passed her at the foot of the stairs, but Babette had ignored her, while Justin had mouthed '*Bonsoir*'. They closed the door, and Justin sat on the bed, motioning to Babette to take the chair. She sat there quietly, looking at the floor, and when she spoke her cheeks were flushed.

'He has gone. Gilles. We don't know where he is. Just vanished. A week ago now, or nearly so. He's not in the woods, nor near the manor, as far as we can tell. The rest is anyone's guess.' She fell silent. It was a very long time since Justin had seen her so moved.

'And so you came to find me. At least you knew where I was, or could work it out.'

She nodded. He got up and went to the small window, which looked down on nothing better than a narrow, dank courtyard. There was a seagull on the tiles opposite, and it began to call raucously.

'But he could be anywhere, Babette.' He turned to face her, himself now working things out. 'You guessed that he had come to find me. Is that it? Am I right?'

She nodded again, but the tears were now falling fast. 'He is all I have. I have nothing else. And now you have come back, and he goes. What else can I think?' She looked up, wiped away her tears, and then said fiercely, 'You have always mattered to him more than you should. I will not say more

171

than you deserved. That is why he would follow you … perhaps to the end of the earth.'

'But not to Quiberon, Babette. I regret deeply that you are upset. But he has had the opportunity to come here to me, if he chose, and to find me. It is not difficult, as you yourself have discovered. He has not done so, nor have I heard word of him, until now.'

They both were silent now, and Justin sat down again on the bed, opposite her, but he did not lean forward to take her hand, nor would she have let him.

'What can we do?' He dared to look at her, to see if she would respond to the thought that had occurred to him and had almost immediately become a certainty. 'He has gone to join the army.'

She looked up sharply at this, as if to protest, then sank her head in defeat. He could see that she nodded ever so slightly.

'He is no longer a boy, Babette… Or, rather, he is a boy who thinks he is a man. It would not have happened if this had not happened. It is at his door. It is his great opportunity, or so he sees it. He does not know what he is doing, in truth. He will have joined the Chouans, and will have lost himself in them, hidden himself from us.'

'So he will be here,' said Babette.

'Here, or more likely at Carnac, with Cadoudal. Had he heard you talk of Cadoudal?'

'No, but he will have heard the others. Cadoudal is all they speak of, the great fools.'

'And it is common knowledge where he is. That is where he will be. With Cadoudal, in Carnac.'

'In Carnac,' she said abstractedly. 'I had thought of going to Carnac, from what I heard on my way here, but I came to you instead. That was a mistake.' She stood up and gathered her clothes about her. 'I must go to Carnac. If I set out now…'

He stayed sitting and looked at the fading light coming through the window. 'If you set out now, you will walk all the way in the dark. You have already walked too far. No.' He stood up. 'You must stay here, and in the morning come with me. My boats are ferrying munitions to Cadoudal, across the bay. It is the quickest way, and I can start to look with you.'

'What's in that box?' she said abruptly.

'My uniform. A British uniform. The Chouans have them too.'

'So are they now British too? What is it to be — French, or British, or Breton? What are you? And what is Gilles?'

'It is confusing,' was all he replied.

'Will you be wearing that uniform tomorrow?'

'Yes, I shall be wearing it.' Then he changed the subject. 'You shall take this room. I shall go and rest with Eugene on board his ship — he's the man you met at the tavern. I shall come back for you, and take you on board too, so we can go in one of the early boats to Carnac, with the ammunition and the muskets. Have you food with you? Good, but best to keep it. The landlady has more, and I shall speak to her. You will be quite safe here.' Justin went to the door and opened it.

'He thinks you are his father. You know that, don't you?'

Justin paused. 'Yes, I know that. Goodnight, Babette.' He closed the door, and she heard his footsteps going down the stairs.

CHAPTER XIV: FATHER AND DAUGHTER

The imposing grandeur of Alverscombe Hall, home to Sir Francis and Arabella Wollaston, had its rear set to the uncivilised mounds of the moor, and looked out placidly over the gentler lands of its estate. The Hall had been rebuilt by Arabella's grandfather, who was a notorious rakehell, womaniser, and ultimately drunkard. Yet despite his vices, which were both extensive and prolonged, he had managed in addition to be a success with money, not only marrying well — though that phrase concealed many sorrows — but investing even better in overseas enterprises that probably bore very little scrutiny. The result was a long portrait in the entrance hall that gave no impression of corruption in its smiling face and relaxed posture, one hand on the head of an admiring shooting dog, game hanging lifeless from a hook held by the other.

Outside, there was a neo-classical façade for the house that gave even less away, apart from the intended impression of immense wealth. The man's arrogance had insisted on a covered and columned *porte cochère* rather than an imposing stairway to the front door of the mansion. A small flight of steps did then lead up from that alighting spot for carriages to a pair of remarkable glassed doors, through which the entrance hall could be glimpsed, with its Adam brothers' ceiling, a triumph of curled plaster, and below it the black and white diamond-patterned floor.

Arabella stood with one foot on the lowest of these steps, looking up at the coffered ceiling of the *porte cochère* for no obvious reason except that it afforded a delay to entering the house itself. There should have been no occasion for her apprehension in that respect, for it had been her home since birth. Her father's marriage and her conception had followed quickly on the death of the old man, who had lived to see his house completed, and then gone on swiftly to meet his maker for what, Arabella surmised, may have been a difficult interview, from all that she had gathered about him. Alverscombe was her home, but it seemed like her father's house, and although she was attached to certain rooms — not just those of her playful childhood, but also others in which she remembered her mother — she felt that she had no hold on much of its interior. Outside, she was mistress of the rides and the edge of the moorland that was part of the estate, and her eye gave approval to the gradual transformation of the parkland from fresh planting under her grandfather's instruction to spreading trees under her father's unobtrusive management.

It was on this parkland that she had set out this morning to get away from the house, trailing her maid behind her, an unusual procedure for her, since she valued Grace's company and her discrimination. But this morning she needed to reflect and ponder in anticipation of the interview with her father which she had requested. The walk had done her no good at all, and if anything she returned rather more agitated than when she had set out. That in itself annoyed her, and she was glad that she did not have to say anything to Grace. Grace measured her mistress's feelings with an unnoticed but attentive assessment, and quietly left her to take the parasol around to the back of the house. It had seemed a wise precaution at the start, but the bright early morning sun had now clouded over, dulling the light but not the gradually increasing summer warmth.

It became clear to Arabella that she had needed this last moment of solitude. She stepped back down into the *porte cochère*, and found that her breathing had slowed. She dwelled on the image she held of her father, but how well did she know him? He had been devoted to her, the more so after her mother's death, for whom he had what Arabella might now recognise as a passion. Curiously, she blushed at that thought, but it endeared him to her, despite his sternness which had increased with age, or perhaps with her years and his increased responsibilities. Sir Francis knew Pitt and Windham, and others whose names were less current, but he inclined to the harsher strain of old Tory politicking, Arabella felt. After serving in a rather desultory way as a colonel, he was too much an associate in latter years of military and naval officers, and eminences of the Admiralty, such as Lord Haworth. These were either bluff or shrewd men, in her view, and she pictured them as ruddy and jowled, or hawk-faced and still bewigged, their strange, parchment-like skin tanned and tightened over their cheekbones. She might wish that he kept less hardened company, although thankfully he drank only socially and in moderation even then, scarred as he had been by the most intemperate of fathers. All in all, he was a dear man, dear to her, but she wished he allowed himself to be diverted more by the kind of company that Amelia's brother brought to Chittesleigh, although that did at times include Captain Yeo.

Captain Yeo had recently been a visitor at Alverscombe far too frequently for her preference. Her eyes narrowed, and she began to realise that she would indeed need courage to face her father with what she had discovered in Okehampton and Chittesleigh, and what she suspected, although she knew that she would be dependent on him for its full and proper interpretation. Might she trust him? It must be the case that she could. She had never confronted him like this before, and prayed that her suspicions would be laid to rest by a reassuring explanation, or by a sincere declaration of ignorance.

A sound came to her from beyond the polished doors, perhaps a distant bell being rung or a door shutting. As she turned to walk up the steps, the front door swung back to reveal Grace, who bobbed to her, holding it open. Arabella smiled in acknowledgement of the timing, which showed concern for her evident mood. But she walked past, intent on finding her father before her purpose dissipated. Grace stood back and calculated that she would do well to prepare a dish of tea, and perhaps even secrete something stronger into Miss Wollaston's bedchamber, since it would be there that she would retire after this interview with her father. They separated in the entrance hall, Grace passing quietly towards the dining room and beyond to the kitchens, but recording with complete accuracy as she went the sure steps of her mistress across the hall, the pause at the door of the study, and the light knock upon it.

Sir Francis Wollaston, like many men of his age and rank, could only with reluctance leave the state of the nation alone. But when he did so, it was to look at his daughter with what he believed to be indulgence, and comment on how she was the image of her mother, which she was not. Arabella's blond hair came from what had been his own fair crop, now grizzled and too thin to be assessed accurately; but her mother's had been neither blond nor dark, and was finer rather than thicker. He was alarmingly like his own father in looks, but not in temperament, having witnessed the rule of licentiousness and its tempers throughout his youth, and so early foreswearing excess with admirable determination in one still of an age to be forgiven some lapses. He had kept to his promises, and when his sweet wife had mysteriously collapsed while out riding he had not forsaken them either in grief and mourning, or in subsequent loneliness. But as Arabella knew well enough, his kindness to his daughter was now suffused with a stern response to almost any challenge, and with regret she had found the best way to live was all too often to keep at a distance. This was in some part the role of Chittesleigh in her life, and her father by no means resented it, since he thought that he was allowing his daughter to live independently, and in safe keeping at the same time.

He had long since ceased to read books, and it was from the newspaper that she had drawn his attention, which he left on a side-table as he stood to greet her with a smile. He was unsure why she had chosen to interrupt him at one of his favourite times — when he was informing himself on matters of state in the morning, before spending the hours before dinner writing assertively to ministers and associates. Yet the morning had been her choice, and she had given him no hint of what was on her mind. He himself had his hopes, which were founded on very little, but he would if prompted bring forward what he had detected in the manner of these young people. It could indeed be the case that the initiation of a courtship might have disturbed her feelings. After all, he had reason to suspect that Yeo was warm to her, and he might just pass muster in what was proving to be a difficult time, although she should in truth do far better for herself. Courtship had been so much more forthright in his day, or at least in his case, which was truthfully all he knew of the matter. He held out his hand to grasp hers, lightly but with contained emotion. He did not kiss his daughter, but he had held her tightly when she was a child, and that would have to be enough.

Arabella was distracted, and she glanced at the pamphlets on his writing bureau, and at the several newspapers that lay on the table next to his winged chair. Some of the drapes were pulled across to shut out the sun, but from the gap in one pair she saw a drift of dust illuminated in a shaft of light. It gave her an odd opening to the interview, and letting her hand slip from his she walked across to the tall ranks of shelves.

'Father, your books are in need of dusting.'

'I dare say they are, my dear.'

'I shall not take one out and demonstrate to you, but you neglect them badly, in favour of newsprint.'

She took herself back a little towards him, trying to sense the best distance from which to conduct the conversation, coming up alongside the bureau on which the pamphlets lay scattered. On one she saw the words 'patriotism' and 'the nation' boldly printed, and her eye was unnervingly caught by 'treachery' and 'traitors' buried further down in the smaller type. Her father had begun to construe her implicit criticism of his reading habits, and he hastened to provide reassurance.

'I shall ask Mrs Rudd to arrange a cleaning party.' He looked across at her, and misinterpreting her silence and the slight flush on her face, he attempted to find excuses. 'Come, Arabella, you know how I value some of these volumes, and so many are becoming fragile. I have hesitated, my dear, to let people loose on them. One cannot always be present to watch over labour…'

'Indeed, Father,' Arabella said, mysteriously.

Once again, he cursed himself for his ineptitude in reading women's moods. What did the chit want? Was it books, dust, or his attention? Dammit, he had thought her happy with her absences at Chittesleigh, but perhaps he was wrong in that. 'But never mind books, m'dear, tell me about Chittesleigh, and young Miss Wentworth, and our dear friend Mrs Wentworth. How are they all keeping? And will you be standing while we talk, or shall I ring for a glass? What is it you like? I think they have lemonade since it is summer.'

'Madeira, Father — chocolate in the morning, tea at the daily festival that takes its name. Madeira at other times. But I shall have none.' This last was as her father reached for the bell-pull.

In exasperation he pulled it anyway, rather harder than was necessary. 'Well, I shall have some coffee. I like it at this time of day.'

A slight knock at the door introduced a sallow-faced young man, who bowed slightly and looked exclusively towards Sir Francis.

'Coffee, Nathaniel, a jug for me, with cream and Lisbon sugar.' The door closed behind him. 'I do like the sugar; it's my age, I think.' Sir Francis gripped the mantlepiece lightly with one hand, and turned amicably enough to face his daughter. 'Now, what is it you want to discuss with me, my dear girl? And will you come and sit with me? You cannot be needing money, surely? You are so frugal, and Mr Coleton tells me that your mother's estate is in good order. That is a blessing for you now you have come of age…'

'Father, I believe you have been deceiving me.' Arabella could see no other way of approaching the subject that was not itself devious, and she decided to rely on over twenty years of familial intimacy to negotiate the rough passage. Her face was set, and she knew her colour to be slightly heightened, but she stood her ground, one hand on the writing bureau on which the word 'traitor' stood in uncompromising print. There was a further knock at the door, which opened to a silver tray with a coffee pot and cup, a small jug and a sugar bowl, carried by the sallow-faced young man.

'Thank you, Nat. Set them there. That will be all.' The door shut, and there was no further sound. Sir Francis leant forward and poured himself some coffee. He left it on the tray. 'We are good friends, I hope? You have been away so much. I am at a loss…'

'Father, there is a man I have seen with you many times over the years. A stocky individual, I believe his name may be Garth or Gareth, or some such. I saw him in Okehampton, in the stable-yard, a month or two ago.'

'Yes, Garth it is. The man may have been in Okehampton, or anywhere else for that matter. I don't see…'

'In the stable-yard there, at the White Hart in the town, with another man whom I have seen at Chittesleigh, and who I believe now works there in some capacity. They were in conversation.'

'Stable-yard? My dear, what has this to do…?'

Arabella was not to be deflected. She made up her mind to hold unswervingly to her narrative, to let it do its work for her. What came at the end, when it was finished, would have to look after itself. 'There is a man called Le Guinec, who claims to be a steward on Mr Wentworth's estate in Brittany. He has been at Chittesleigh on business, which is not remarkable, but he has also been visiting a farmhouse on the Chittesleigh lands in Devon, which I find more remarkable.'

Here she looked hard at her father, who met her eyes without his own showing any kind of emotion, or even an expression of a process of thought.

'This man was welcomed to the farmhouse by Captain Yeo. On another occasion, I saw the man from the house at Chittesleigh at this same farmhouse, once again with Captain

Yeo, who seemed at a loss to explain his presence there, as did the man himself.' She paused, partly because the narrative on which she was relying had come to its obvious conclusion, and partly to catch her breath and wait for a response. Instead, her father cleared his throat and smiled at her. She felt herself flushing. She would not be patronised by him, but how to avoid it posed another question to her turbulent sentiments.

'What is your interest in this set of coincidences, Arabella? I fail to understand how it can appeal to you, nor even how it was that you came to collect what seem to be disparate incidents of no particular significance together. You and I both know Captain Yeo, and indeed he is also a close friend of the family at Chittesleigh…'

'That man Le Guinec is a scoundrel. Do not ask me to confirm that, or offer you evidence, but I am sure of it. And Captain Yeo attempted to deceive me. What business do Yeo and Le Guinec have in meeting clandestinely away from the manor at Chittesleigh? Besides, Father, I trace your hand in this. That man Garth hardly stirs without your instruction, has not done so for years, and yet I see him in conference with another who has his feet firmly under the servants' table in Justin's manor.' Her voice was rising, do what she might to keep it under control, and consequently her anger was showing.

'Justin is absent, of course.' Her father's expression remained still, as did the tone of his voice, although he tried to put the kindness he felt into it.

'Father, do not talk to me of coincidences. One or two I might dismiss, but I can plainly see threads crossing over, even if I cannot detect the weave. I can bear this no longer…'

'My dear.' Sir Francis picked up his coffee cup, paused, and then replaced it. 'Are you sure you won't sit down, Bella?' As she shook her head, he continued, 'I had hoped that none of this would come through to you. It does no good that it should. But it seems that you have either been exceptionally curious or observant, or that others have been too casual. Not that it matters in the long run…'

'Matters, sir? You mean to tell me that none of this matters? Then why is this web of intrigue or subterfuge set in place around Chittesleigh if it does not matter? You ask me to believe what is scarcely…'

'Miss, I have not asked you to do anything. I would wish you to moderate your tone to me as befits an exchange between father and daughter. You will not find me raising my voice to you, of that you can be assured.'

His voice was stern, but not intractable. She waited, silently but not subdued by his reproach.

'As I say, I would rather it had not come to your attention. The fact of the matter is that for various reasons some of his close friends have seen fit to protect Mr Wentworth, notably in his absence. For that reason, Captain Yeo and I…'

'Sir, I heard this cat's tail of nonsense from Captain Yeo, of suspicions arising from Justin's association with those of a radical persuasion, presumably in London, for there are none such of my acquaintance in Devon, no more than will o' the wisps. Even if this were the case, it gives you no reason…'

'Nonetheless, despite your scorn, we are keeping a watch on him and on his family, as I had gathered from Yeo himself that he has informed you. By so doing, we can absolutely exonerate Wentworth should anyone be so foolish as to raise plots and denunciations in London. They have been rife, as has been conspiracy against the crown and the institutions of parliament. Justin knows of this…'

'Do I hear you correctly, sir?' Arabella was not to be appeased. 'Do you tell me that Mr Wentworth is himself aware of this imposition, is party to it? What about his sister, and his mother? Are you saying that they too are aware of it?'

'My meaning is that Justin Wentworth is aware of the turmoil in London, and the arrests and the trials. Why, we have spoken about it together, he and I. But no, neither he nor his family could know about our devices for protecting him, because his complicity would ruin their standing with those authorities who might be faced with complaints against him. And I would urge you…' Sir Francis's voice was now strained, if not precisely raised against her.

Arabella herself was nearing the end of her patience, and she was strongly aware that her constitution was telling her that there was a limit to this interview. She came towards him and managed to smile, but as he relaxed a little and looked to embrace her, she raised her hand to prevent him. 'Father, it misgives me that a man like Le Guinec should be involved in what is, in this account, a strictly English affair. I can see all too readily the connection of your kindly intrigue with protection against the mindless application of the patriotic slogans shouting from such pamphlets as circulate even here. But Justin Wentworth is in France, in the king's service, and Le Guinec is from Brittany, and in whose service he is enlisted remains completely open to question. I conclude, then, this affair is not confined to Britain.'

'Arabella…'

But she had turned away from him, and gathered her feelings into one last passionate expression of loyalty. She stood with one hand on the door, and did not now feel the need to face her father. She spoke quietly, and not a little tremulously. 'Let me just say to you, Father, that I shall do whatever lies within my power to stand by Justin and his family. I shall not see him caught in a web of intrigue that may lie even beyond your powers of control. And as for Yeo —' and here she did turn her head to look at him — 'the man had the audacity to cover his false steps with a declaration, for which he has my utter contempt. I bid you good morning, Father.'

The door clicked behind her, leaving Sir Francis with food for thought, but also, he had to confess, astounded. He had never anticipated this consequence of his daughter spending so much time at Chittesleigh with that innocent girl, Amelia, and her delightful mother. He gazed down at the cooling coffee in his cup, the oil now forming on its surface, and reached up to ring the bell. His elbow rested on the mantlepiece, in a gesture that he had developed as an adolescent and which had never left him.

A gentle tap on the door. Sir Francis spoke without looking round. 'You may take this away, thank you.' Nathaniel came and went silently. The door clicked again. The dust was still drifting up in the rays of sunlight, and there was no sound between the walls of books, except perhaps the scratching of a mouse behind the skirting board.

What was Yeo doing proposing to her without so much as a by-your-leave, whatever his known inclinations? Either Arabella was mistaken, or the man must be mad, and he would speak to him forthrightly about it. It might have been a diversion, as she had averred, but it was a strange choice, perhaps an impulsive misjudgement. And was he right in detecting something more than loyalty in his daughter's feelings about the Chittesleigh family? He grimaced and admitted reluctantly that he should be prepared for this kind of complication. The chit was no longer a girl, but why that Wentworth lad, for heaven's sake, who was far too radical in his thinking for a man of property? *Because,* an inner voice answered him, *you have put him in her way thoughtlessly, and have taken no care to introduce her to others. She should be in town, but you have allowed yourself to rest here for the summer in comfort.*

He shrugged his shoulders, if only to loosen them, and looked across the room. He must speak to Yeo, of course, to ask him for an account of his dealings with Le Guinec, about which he was inadequately informed. It was, he reflected, quite certain that his daughter was confused. Nor did she understand the dangers that threatened. Wentworth had drifted all too close to the wrong set, and more fool him if he had written to them, or they to him. Writing was a danger, and had severed many heads from necks in the past, even if that was way beyond likelihood in the present case. There was nothing yet, but one had to keep an open mind in troubled times.

He sat down, and with some relief at last picked up his newspaper. Maybe Wentworth's actions in France would clear his name of any suspicions. Lord Haworth was certainly of that opinion, and was swayed by Justin's military record. Sir Francis congratulated himself that he was willing to maintain an open mind on the subject, but he was sure that he knew his duty, if it came to it. His thoughts began to drift towards the column he was reading, and his worried face became relaxed as he allowed his feelings to settle comfortingly on how dear his daughter was to him.

CHAPTER XV: THE DEAD AND THE LIVING

Babette and Justin sat silently, lost in thought, watching the shore at Carnac getting closer, caught from time to time by a light sea spray blown by the feathered oars. They were on a thwart in the stern of a large boat, a launch from one of the frigates, loaded with barrels of gunpowder, boxes of muskets, shot, and some provisions as well. The routine was that the munitions and supplies were unloaded on the beach, which was shallow enough, and then loaded back up on to carts, taken from trades and farms from all around. These were driven up into the centre of the town by the church, or off to either side, some further on to the north and west, facing Plouharnel, others closer to the farms and cottages to the east, north of the beach and island at Le Men Du. There was no telling where the attack might come from, and there were men in every bit of cover, in cottages, behind walls of stone, in copses of trees, even on the dunes in some places where they gave good protection.

It was early in the day, and that alone gave them hope. Neither of them had slept well, Justin unused to the sway of a ship and the constant creaking, Babette staring at the ceiling in the lodging, imagining every disaster that she could, every wound that the boy might take, even the worst, although that was something she forced out of her mind. She was aware of Justin now, sitting next to her in his red uniform, a strange and unnerving sight. She looked at the line of the shore, at the figures moving on the beach, and for a moment felt like an invader herself, and wondered if she should have a knife. After all, she might have to defend herself as much from those whose side of the battle line she would be on as from any enemy, and she was no stranger to the use of a knife. A man was no different from an animal; she could gut one as easily as the other. But then there would always be another behind the first, and she reckoned that her tongue was a better weapon, and maybe even her hand and arm, which had set more than one hopeful back on his heels before he had got started.

Justin had been close to her when they had boarded the launch, but he had been careful to show her no particular attention after that, so there were no looks. The men were tense anyway, sailors rather than marines, not keen on being stuck on land with gunfire around them, anxious to deliver and then get back to the safety of the ships. The launch steered clear of the jagged rocks, finding one of the open approaches, and seemed to speed up on to the beach. It would be easy to float it again once it was unloaded. It ground into the sand, and before Justin could climb the gunwale, Babette was swinging herself over into the strong arms of a grinning sailor, who put her down without a thought, and turned back to the barrels. She walked out of the warm, shallow water, and stood looking up over the low dunes, the breeze now gentle on her face. Something told her Gilles was out there, but where to start?

The carts were getting full, the launch emptying fast. There were planks laid down over the sand, rising up to the lane that led to the village inland, and right and left to the various outposts. There were other boats unloading at the same time and the officers had given up worrying about where precisely the munitions went, apart from ensuring that a good half of them headed for the centre, and the distribution by the church that Justin had helped to establish.

They decided to walk, following the sound of gunfire, walking towards it, not knowing what they would find.

The muskets crackled to Gilles's right, and he found once again that he could not tell whether they were close or far away. This town was bigger than he had thought, although some of the men called it a village. There were scattered cottages all the way down to the open beach, or at least to the salt marshes. That was odd. You could pick up the salt and taste it, put a handful in your bag, think of taking it back. He fought off the tears at the thought of going back. It made him picture Babette, how angry she would be with him, how upset she might be now. That was wrong, he told himself. She should think of him as a man doing what he should be doing, with the other men. There were boys here younger than him, he was sure, one who was so young they told him to go away, but then he made himself useful by carrying messages. They had found him later in a corner by the priest's house, crumpled under a wall, a great hole in his head. He was chucked on a cart and taken out into the marshes with the others.

Tudal grinned at him. 'This what you wanted, boy?' He wiped his mouth, handed Gilles his flask, and set his hat back on his head. 'Time we went down the road and joined the others.'

They were sitting by the church, right in the centre, with Gireg too, who had adopted him. They looked good in their uniforms, which they had got from the beach, but they had distributed the latest cartload of powder and cartridges to a throng of eager Chouans, and now sat idly for a moment. The musket fire rang out again.

'It's coming from the chapel, up on Mont St Michel. There are many of us up there, but they could always do with more.

Many hands make light work, boy, rolling barrels, pulling brushwood, killing soldiers. Me, I hate this colour.'

Gireg looked with disgust at the red and white of his uniform. 'As easy to see as a hind's tail in the dusk.'

Tudal grinned again. 'You'd better hope they don't shoot you up the arse.'

Gireg spat on the ground. 'It's likely, is it, that they'd catch me running away? We take our pellets in the front, or better not at all. Don't we, boy?'

Gilles thought of the boy with half his head blown away, and said nothing.

'You want a knife, boy? Tudal and me will shoot 'em, you can run up and finish them off. Slip it across their throat, like a pig. You ever fired a musket?'

Gilles nodded. He had fired a musket. A man at the manor had shown him, and it had knocked his shoulder badly. But they wouldn't give him one here. He did not know how to load it.

'Go on, take the knife. You can stick it in their backs, if you want. Aim just here, between the ribs and the arse, a good, strong, straight thrust. The good lord will forgive you, for them not believing in God, Mary or the saints, that lot.' He crossed himself, looking to the church door. 'Mind you don't cut yourself, though!' And they both laughed, grabbed their muskets and pouches, and headed on out from the centre as another cart came rolling in from the beach.

Babette led the way, pausing from time to time to let Justin catch up. He had taken a pistol from Eugene on the frigate, but it would be a one-off affair, and for the rest he would have to trust his sword. He was slow because he was watchful, trying as in the past to assess the shape of an engagement, and finding it difficult. The sounds of fighting had grown in intensity, and the groups of soldiers resting that they had passed had shaken their heads when asked about a boy, until they came across a Chouan officer, who with his bodyguard was urgently sweeping the south of the village. He came up to them, with his own pressing concerns.

'What have you seen, Captain?' he asked Justin. 'Where have you been? How are things to the east? Are we holding well there?'

'I cannot help you. We have only come from the beach, and that is untouched, or was when we left it an hour or so ago. We are looking for a boy…'

'A boy? What do you mean, a boy? What is that to me? Who are you with, in any case? Puisaye and the *émigrés*, or Cadoudal? I have not seen you before, have I?'

'You will have seen me, organising the munitions in front of the church. I have been bringing them ashore…'

'Holy Mary and the saints, the boy is my son! I am looking for my son! Do you not understand, *genaoueg*?' Babette shouted at the officer. 'He is a child. He cannot fire a gun. He should not be here.'

The officer looked at her coolly, and one or two of his men ceased their conversation and looked across, shifting uncomfortably. They were twisting paper cartridges.

'You are lucky we are Bretons, and not those *émigrés*, who are from anywhere. Where are you from, *gwreg*?'

'What does it matter? From Kergohan.'

A bare-headed man spat on the ground and said, 'I know that. It is just south of the forest, above Plumergat. There is a manor that is empty now. My *mamm-gozh* came from near there. My grandfather went courting to her…'

'Yes, yes, all a long time ago now.' The officer did not wish to offend the man, but he turned back to Babette. 'How would we know this boy? Is he with anyone?'

Another man shifted his musket onto his shoulder and said, 'There was that boy down by the wall. We saw them loading him on the cart. The only boy I've seen.'

'Where was that?'

'No matter where. They took him away.'

The officer looked at Babette, and then across to Justin. 'He will not be the only boy. There are many, some with their brothers, some with their fathers. If you come with us, that will be your best chance. We are covering all the ground, and making our way to the Mont. That is where most of us are. You can hear. It is getting hot up there.'

'Where did they take this boy?' Babette was insistent, impatient, her worst visions coming to rest on this one certainty in a mist of hopelessness.

'They take them down to the marshes. We have men there who dig. The ground is soft... It may not be him, *gwreg*. There are many...'

'Where are the marshes?'

'Down towards the coast,' said another of the men. 'Ask for the chapel of Saint Columban.'

Babette started to leave, and Justin stood away with her. 'I must go on to the centre. I shall ask there, and then go up to the Mont. I am sure he will be alive.'

She hardly heard him, but her hand lightly pushed him away. She could not have believed him, the way she felt now. He watched her for a moment, then gave a curt farewell to the officer and set off for the church at the centre of the village. The men shouldered their muskets, and fell in behind the officer. They trudged for a while in the dust, while the sounds of the fighting swept in from the north of the town — constant, loud, mixed with human shouts and cries. Not far away, they could hear the sound of feet rushing past, a loud, brusque order ringing out.

'That was not the only boy.' The bare-headed man spoke as if out of a dream, but it was clearly a memory that had surfaced. 'By the wall, on the corner. There was another boy, watching as they slung the other on the cart. He was with two of ours in uniform.' He spat on the ground again. 'I had forgotten. But what does it matter? They have gone now anyway.'

The officer told them to hurry up, and the faces faded from their minds.

Babette had no idea where she was going. At first, she had wandered too far towards the sea, her old boots raising dust around the folds of her skirt. Perhaps it was instinct, taking her further from the sound of muskets which crackled like a gorse fire to the north behind the village. But once she reached the edge of the dunes and saw the bustle of activity coming up from the boats, and heard the racket of the carts, packhorses and mules, and the shouts, whistles and commands, she came out of her reverie. This could not be right; she was back where she had started.

The tracks across to the west, which she thought might be towards Plouharnel, were at first much quieter. No one paid her any attention, although she passed an infant scrabbling in the dust in the doorway of a cottage, and paused to look at it. At that moment, while staring at her, it picked up a small pebble and made as if to put it in its mouth. She ran across and murmured warm words as she extracted the pebble from its tiny fist, kneeling down next to it. The child looked at her in astonishment, and then set up a wail that brought its mother to the door, who pushed Babette away with a stream of abuse, grabbed the child, and retreated indoors, calling out for her husband. Babette pushed her hair from her eyes and took a deep breath. She was gone before anyone had come out after her.

Elsewhere, there were excited dogs, who had formed something of a pack, and were running over the scrub. She picked up a branch and waved it at them when they came over, sweeping it round in a wide arc and back again, then she began to shout at them wildly. One of them, bolder than the rest, stood its ground and barked at her, but after a while it lost interest and ran off to follow the rest. Babette stood there holding the branch, her heart pounding, and she threw it to one side, collapsing onto a stone, her voice hoarse, tears rolling down her cheeks. She buried her face in the folds of her skirt. There was a strange silence around her, like a child breathing in sleep, and without alarm she felt a presence next to her. Out of one eye she saw the bare feet, and she did hear the breathing, which was soft but wheezing a little, the barest trace of a whistle at the back of the sound. As she began to look up, a hand came first to her shoulder, and then both hands gathered her face between them, lifting it to look into her eyes.

'What is with you, *gwreg*? What is your sorrow? Is it for now or of time past?'

The old woman had matted hair, long and grey, and her face was tanned and wrinkled. She had come out of nowhere, and brought with her the scent of the gorse and bracken mingled with the smoke of a brushwood fire. Her eyes were grey, and there was a scar on her left cheek that ran across to a broad nose above her stained lips. *Berries, perhaps*, thought Babette. She gently reached up and removed the hands from her face, but remained holding them in her own. 'I am a fool, mother. I weep before I know the answer.'

'You call me mother. My mother told me that we weep for ourselves.'

'That's as may be. I would rather it was for myself than for another.' Babette stood up. 'I must go on, to see if I must weep more. Would you be able to point me towards Saint Columban's house, mother? I will be lost without you.'

'Ah, it is the saint who is waiting for you. There will be something there for you, then. A man might not be trusted, but a saint will stay for you.' With that, she coughed, and coughed terribly, and there was a fleck of blood on her lips. She smiled, almost apologetically. 'Never mind me, *gwreg*. Say a prayer to the saint for me.' She pointed across the scrub. 'You see those trees? Well, there is a path. It crosses down by the big stones to the springs. The chapel is above there.'

'And where are the marshes?' Babette's voice was strained, and the old woman looked at her closely.

'What do you want with the marshes?'

'I have to see someone there.'

'Well, take the saint with you. They are over beyond the chapel.'

'Thank you, mother.' Babette bent to kiss her.

'You call me mother,' the old woman said again. 'But I think you are the mother. I never was. Let Mary, the mother of God be with you, as with all of us women, mothers or barren, like me. Tread safely, child.' She gestured vaguely about her. 'There are men killing each other today. Tread safely. They will be gone tomorrow, or the next day.'

The silence came again, and hung in the air. Then, for the first time, the roar of an explosion, away to the west, followed by another.

'Quickly now,' the old woman said.

After leaving Babette, Justin walked forward like an automaton, his steps taking him in the right direction, but his spirits distracted and disturbed, unsure at this point whether he should be doing his duty, or in some way providing protection to one who had sought it from him. He also felt that he might be wrong. Babette might not have come to him for protection, but for help. So his steps faltered, and he hardly heard the voice that shouted to him, until it was repeated several times, and the footsteps came running towards him. It was his adjutant, Trevelyan, and behind him at a distance he could see Eugene, waving.

'Sir, there is a crisis developing. Frankly, it is a bloody mess, and what with that damn garbled nonsense some of these rebels speak…' Trevelyan was gulping air at the same time as stuffing his hat back on his head, and the effect did not impress Justin.

'Trevelyan, do you speak French?'

'Well, sir, I did…'

'Answer the question, Trevelyan. Do you speak French? Yes or no?'

'Why, yes, sir. You know I do.'

'Then what in God's name are you talking about?'

'It's not the French, sir. It's the local dialect.'

'It's not a dialect, Trevelyan, it's a language. Its existence is partly why they are fighting with us rather than against us. And you would do better not to describe them as rebels. Now, what is the problem?'

'Well, sir, as I was saying, it's a bloody mess. We thought we were sending weapons forward, towards the Mont Saint Michel, which is a damn good place to hold the line in my book, but the message is coming down now to get them past Plouharnel and on to the village of Sainte Barbe, wherever that is. Mr Eugene is tearing out his hair…'

'And waving his hat, as I can see. Let's speak to him. And for God's sake, Trevelyan, look like a soldier, will you?'

'Yes, sir. Sorry, sir. I am so relieved to see you, Captain Wentworth. I was beginning to lose control up there in the church square.'

And so am I, thought Justin, *because I must search for the boy as well as order this properly. The soldiers will look after him, that is certain, but if there is a rout then it will be every man for himself and the boy will have to run and hide, as boys do. Heaven knows where that will be, but if fortune is with us they will not have let him have a weapon. He would as likely discharge it at them as at an enemy.*

'Justin, be damned, we had despaired of you. I have been holding the fort, and barking at people like there was no tomorrow, which there may not be if we do not switch direction. But I'll be damned myself if I know the best route to Sainte Barbe, and if we can get past Plouharnel.' Eugene was flustered, but he had not been a fool.

'Have you held them in the centre?'

'Come and see for yourself, man. It's jammed up, carts everywhere. You can hardly step around the horseshit, some of them have even got their nosebags on, and the bloody drivers have taken to gathering in groups and talking in that confounded lingo… Sorry, old man. Disrespectful, I know. But we are lost when we fall out of French. I suppose you could call it our *lingua franca*, if time and tide are not too late for a pun.' He fell silent. 'Justin? Penny for them?'

There was a bustle around them, and groups of Chouans were making their way from the eastern outposts through the centre, no doubt heading for Plouharnel.

'Who has said Sainte Barbe?'

'Cadoudal. Apparently, he thinks he can hold the peninsula from there. It's going badly.'

Trevelyan was shifting from one foot to the other, looking agitated and out of his depth. Justin kept searching the groups that were passing, desperately looking for what his eyes almost immediately told him was not there.

'Cadoudal has good judgment. Many of these will make their way south of Plouharnel to Sainte Barbe. Get some of the carts to go with them. The powder mostly. Offload some others and give the muskets to those that are coming through. Trevelyan, get down to the shore and try to get some of the boats to make their way up through the channel to the head of the bay. It's a short haul then to Sainte Barbe. And send word to the fleet that provisions will have to go by the western approach. It's another beach there, not a bay, but there may be carts by then in Sainte Barbe.'

Those that are not being used for barricades, he reflected. *It will come to that soon enough. But if they are all going to Plouharnel, or past it to Sainte Barbe, then I shall go there too. If he is dead, then I have failed him utterly. I should have seen this coming. If he is dead, there is nothing I can do. But if he is alive, he will be coming through with the steady stream of Chouans, and at Plouharnel I shall look for him as best I can, sift the columns on their way through to Sainte Barbe. But what about Babette?*

It was evident that women and children were also on the move. Word had spread, and these scared citizens of France's new Republic were fleeing from her troops, who were not yet visible, but whose anger could be heard in the vicious snapping of musketry and the ominous boom and thud of cannon. Justin could not be sure how the Republican soldiers would treat those who were vulnerable. Yet if Babette were with him she would surely be in greater danger, for he was a target, and would be treated with rough justice if a shot spared him.

He had seen the boy! Frantically, he pushed past a group of women with young children, some clutching babies, and into the middle of a rank of Chouans. He had seen Gilles, his mop of hair, his face. Was he hiding from him? He thrust his way through the Chouans, who were tired and irritable, some saying that he was a madman. He began to shout, 'Gilles! Gilles!' wildly, peering amongst them. The Chouans looked around and at each other, and then suddenly the boy was in front of him, and Justin grabbed him from behind. A soldier put his arm out to restrain him, but he swung the boy round, almost throwing him to the ground in his excitement.

The unfamiliar face of a girl stared back at him, shocked and fearful. Justin dropped his hands.

'I am sorry. I thought you were … someone else.' He took a step back, and wiped the sweat from his face. His chest heaved with guilt and anxiety. A father spoke angrily in his ear.

Babette's feet were sore, and her back was hurting. The clamour all around was confusing, since it seemed like a threat, but remained at a distance. It was hard to pick out distinct sounds, and none of them were familiar to her, as most were in the forest and the village. Yet despite the noise she saw very few people, one woman driving a cow who did not look at her, two young children running over a field in the distance. She stopped on a slight rise to catch her breath, and saw the top of a chapel on the hill above her, sitting in a group of stone houses. To her left, there was a fountain and a pool, and she wandered over to splash water on her face. She pushed her hair back off her face and stared at her reflection. The lines were there, deeper than when she had last looked, but what did that matter in any case? She sat down on a flat stone and began to take off her boots. They had done well, these boots, taken her where she needed to go, but by Anne mother of Mary, they cut into her feet despite the stockings, which maybe were worn through now.

At that moment she heard the rumble of a cart coming down the road, the wheels grinding the stones, the pony plodding slow and sure. She watched as it passed her, the man in front leading, the load unmistakeable. She felt a sudden urge to rush down and halt the cart, look at the bodies and the faces, and then was overwhelmed by the idea of chance. Why should she believe so strongly that Gilles was dead? Did she know how many had been killed? Why not search for the living instead of the dead? She re-tied her boots and got up. Because to search for the dead was to face the worst, perhaps, and after the worst there might be hope.

She walked slowly down to the road and turned along it, following the cart at a distance. She had seen wounds before, accidents that had occurred in the woods or with tools in the village, and the dead were part of life. They were washed and laid out, and she had played her part before now, first when she had been no more than a girl, then when her mother had died, not so long ago. They were all people she knew, some she had loved, but these in front of her were, God willing, those she had never met, nameless to her, struck down well away from their families. The cart rumbled on, the flat ground showing the water beyond it, until it came to a halt at a shouting distance in front of her. Another figure came to greet the man at the head of the pony, and between them they led the cart on, turning right into what seemed to be rough ground, where it came to a halt again. One of the men stuck a nosebag over the pony's head.

Babette drew closer. The two men began to take the bodies from the cart and lay them out, and then Babette realised that what she had taken to be rough ground were rows of bodies, and she suddenly caught the odour of death on the air. She quickened her pace, and wrapped a cloth around her mouth and nose. The men at the cart were too taken up with what they were doing to sense her approach from behind it, and she stood for a moment, looking for a smaller body. One of them saw her, and held himself bent over while he turned his face to her. His look told her that he knew why she was there, but was wondering what kind of emotion she might be bringing with her.

'I am looking for a boy, an older boy, almost a man. Have you … any boys?' she asked, feeling the weakness of the question, but determined to show no emotion to them.

The men stood up.

'There are none on here. There have been one or two, but it's been a few days now… One mother came for hers. It's not easy here, and no one's thinking much about…'

'Do you know where they are?'

'You'd do best just to walk along, if you'll not mind me saying that. Our hands are full, if you see.'

'What about over there?' Babette pointed to where, some distance away, two men were working, one digging dirt out of a hole in the ground, another standing at the edge. He was looking over towards them.

'Do walk the rows first, as I said. Then maybe…'

He ducked away from her glance, and the two of them reached for another body. Babette took care as she walked along the rows, swinging her head from side to side in advance, hastening where she could, avoiding the danger of tripping. The rows were not long, and almost all were men. She saw only one woman and one boy, who was far younger. She hoped in a dull way that they were mother and son, because that would be better than one having to live without the other. At the end she came to the pit. It was small, but hard enough to dig, no doubt, because like all such pits it had to be deep. The head of the man inside was just visible, and just then she heard a volley of musket shots from the copse away to the left, over the lane. Once again, she felt a sense of urgency, and she looked at the face of the digger.

'A boy?' Her voice was almost a whisper, and she looked down as he pointed reluctantly to the end of the pit, where three figures were lying face down. Close to her the pit was shallower, and she put her hands to its edge and slid down. The man above followed her round, and stood over the three bodies. Sure enough, one was shorter and slighter than the others, though not by much.

'His face, *gwreg*... His head, even. You won't...' It was a warning to her. Without looking she stepped across and bent down, avoiding the head, and pulled up his blouse. There should be a scar on his back — it was not there — and a large mole on his stomach. She pulled him over, panicking that her search had only just begun. At that moment she heard cries and sharper sounds of muskets. The man in the pit ducked his head, but the man above grunted and fell, the sharp stubble of his beard grazing her cheek as he collapsed onto her and knocked her down in a suffocating embrace. She pushed him away in order to breathe, dimly hearing the thud of running feet, and then watching as faces appeared at the edge of the pit, the blue of their uniforms striking, one or two of them pointing their muskets at the man who had been digging, who now had his hands on his head.

'Get out, mole. And don't give us any trouble. We'll have more work for you before the day is done. Shame about your friend there.'

Babette heard another voice.

'And who was the fool who shot him?' Some of the soldiers turned to look at the approaching voice, which took the form of a young soldier, perhaps an officer, who stood at the edge. 'No doubt you'll say you don't know who hit him, which means that any of you may take over his work.' He looked down. 'What's she doing in there? She looks alive to me.'

His soldiers were unsure if they should say anything, so they kept quiet.

'Well, get her out of there, then! You can ask the mole to help her. Go on, man, don't you understand good French? Help the woman out.'

Babette was shaking, despite herself, when she stood once again on the edge of the pit. She had taken the cloth from around her face, and was wiping her hands with it. The young man was an officer, but she had never heard an accent like his. The revolution brought people from all over to be where they ought not to be.

'So what are you doing, woman? Speak up. Have you thrown your tongue to the cat? These Breton peasants, they act as if they don't know French until it suits them.' He thrust his face close to Babette. 'Well, listen to me. I'm arresting you as a scavenger of dead bodies. If you don't like the sound of that, you'd better find something to say before you get to where we're taking you, which will probably be Auray.'

There was more musket fire, and shouts came from the direction of the chapel. They all looked across, and Babette could see a three-coloured flag flying from the top of the small tower.

Close up, the Mont Saint Michel at Carnac looked enormous, as high as a church tower but far longer than any church, at least any that Gilles had seen. It was like a huge mound, except that it was not round, more like a wall built by giants. Perched on top was a small chapel which he had seen from a long way off, but close up it was like a nightmare. For a start, there was the noise, which grew louder as they approached, and was unlike any noise he had ever heard, made up of the crackling of firearms, the shouts and cries of orders and pain, and the thud of what Gireg and Tudal had told him were cannon balls. Just once he saw an explosion of bodies thrown off the top of the mound with earth sprayed out all around, the thud followed by screams. As they got closer, they told him to keep by their side. They had been joined by a whole group of others, rushing from the centre to where the fighting was 'hot', as Gireg had told him, grinning. They were running for much of the time, although alarms were given once or twice at the approach of parties of blues, but nothing had come of that.

Gilles was young, he could run, but what else he should do he had no idea, now he was getting near the enemy. No one had taught him anything, and they had refused him a firearm. Just the knife, and they laughed about that as well. He was strong enough, but he had only ever fought a man hand to hand, wrestling, and that was in good humour, although the clouts were hard enough, as was the ground. It was not so much that he was scared, which he was willing to admit this close to death, but that he could no longer be as sure as he had been that he was in the right place, that he would be useful.

They passed wounded men from time to time, some hobbling and limping, others leaning on the shoulders of companions, one or two carried on rough beds, or dragged half upright on something like a sled. Some joked with those around him, one or two passed on advice or snatches of information about what was happening, still others were too far gone to say anything, their heads lolling. He had to look away from some of the wounds, although he had told himself he would not do that. It was their pain he feared, not for himself, but that they had come to this after such hope.

Gilles heard drums to the left on the road, and could just spy the blues beyond the end of the mound, one of their flags held high, some way off but closing. Gireg and Tudal shouted to him and ran forward to begin to climb the slope of the mound, passing wounded men who were sitting there dazed. On top there was fierce fighting, the smoke drifting across in patches and revealing men kneeling or rushing along. Gilles saw a man knocked back, his musket thrown out of his hand as he fell, and then the shot began to sing past and spit into the ground above them. Tudal pushed him down, flat on the ground, and he saw over Tudal's back that the firing was coming from where he had seen the Republican soldiers. But they had been quick, and were now advancing around the end of the mound. There were shouts from above, and Gireg grabbed him by his blouse and heaved him around, almost throwing him down and pointing away. They slid down the mound and headed over the dry ground, down the gradual slope at the other end.

Out of the corner of his eye Gilles could see that there were blues now on the top of the mound as well, the resistance to them fading, and he realised with his heart pounding that they could fire down on them if they chose. He swung in front of an old oak that sat at the bottom of the mound, and as he did so he heard a curse from Tudal, and a shout from Gireg. As he turned, he saw Tudal on his knees, his hand and eyes on his leg, and Gireg standing over him.

'Get up, man! Here, never mind that wound, put your arm round my shoulders. There. That's it, we'll get out of the firing line at least.' He then saw Gilles, who had not moved, and was staring at them.

'What are you doing, boy? Run, for God's sake, and pray to Sainte Barbe that she will save you from death. Run, boy! There is nothing you can do here.'

Here was what he had feared. To be of no use. But to stay was to risk catching a piece of shot, without having done anything at all, and that was worse still. So he ran, along the hedges, across the fields, scattering with the others, who often ran in groups, although many had headed for the centre, and he heard them passing the word about Plouharnel. He tried to follow them, but found that he had run ahead and got lost. There were banks as well as hedges, and getting out of the fields was impossible, so he ended up with no idea of any direction at all. The sound of fighting was behind him, so he put as much distance between himself and the noise as he could.

It was then that he heard the musket. It was a single shot, but it was very, very close. Gilles crouched down and waited. A small animal rustled nearby in the hedge, but there was no other sound. He waited, listened, and put his hand into his blouse and wrapped it round the hilt of the knife. Which way to go? He then flattened himself on the ground. He had heard movement, and it was careless, blundering, at the end of the field where two lines of hedgerow joined. It was pointless to run. He could now hear the breathing, and he parted the grasses to see better. It was a Chouan, that was obvious, and now he could see that he was hit in the arm.

Gilles thought of what he had seen earlier, how one man could support another by wrapping an arm round his shoulders and walking together. If he could do that, then they might get away together. He stood up and waved to the man to get his attention. The other saw him, and collapsed back down against the bank in front of the hedge.

'Here, I can help you.'

'How can you help me?' The man hardly bothered to look at him.

'I have seen them do it, and I am strong enough, you'll see.'

'To do what?' the Chouan asked.

'To help you along. We can walk together.'

'Walk together where?'

'Come on, you'll see. Here, I'll help you stand.' Gilles bent down and gently raised him up. He was indeed strong for his years and his stature, and lifted the man easily. The Chouan grimaced. Gilles took the man's neckerchief deftly with one hand, and reached across to tie it tightly around the wound on his left arm.

'Bleeding, but no bone broken,' the Chouan commented, acknowledging the help for the first time.

'You will live,' Gilles replied, with a solemn face.

'Come, boy, I can walk.'

'No, I will help you, it will be better like that.'

As he tried to put the man's arm around his shoulders, he saw blue uniforms emerging into the field at the far corner. There was a shout to them, the words indistinct through distance or accent. One of the soldiers stopped and levelled his musket, but another pushed it away and down. They began to walk across the field towards them, clearly talking to each other. Gilles looked around at the other corners of the field. They were too far away. He ran his tongue over his lips, and his mouth felt dry. The Chouan spat on the ground, and tore off a handful of hawthorn leaves to chew. He scratched his ear, tore off some more, and offered them to the boy. Gilles shook his head.

A movement behind them through the gap in the hedge, and a voice that spoke in clear French. 'Stay very still. Move and you are dead meat. There are four of us here.'

The Chouan cast his eyes round, and nodded to the boy. 'We are no trouble, soldier. I have a wound, as you can see, and this one here is no more than a boy. He is unarmed, as am I.'

The other blues ran across the last part of the field. One had a bayonet fixed to his musket. They gathered round, and as they came close one of them took Gilles's chin in his hand, tilted his face up, sniffed, and said, 'I can smell his mother's milk.' He squeezed his chin, and then cuffed him round the ear. 'Next time, stay at home, boy, and we'll come and visit your mother by ourselves.' He pushed him aside and spoke to the Chouan. 'What's with you, friend? Hurt yourself, have you?' He reached out a hand, and clamped it over the wound and the bandage.

The Chouan's face contorted, but he said nothing.

'How many of my friends have you shot at, you ugly Breton bastard?'

There was a sudden movement, and Gilles's hand came out with the knife. The soldier saw it instantly and put his hand out to protect himself, but as he did so another brought the butt of his musket down on Gilles's wrist, knocking the knife out of his hand. The first soldier hit him in the face with his fist, and then clutched his hand, which was bleeding from a small cut.

'I'll make you pay for that, you little rat. You'll come under the law, see if you will. Take arms against the Republic —' he licked his hand — 'and the Republic will see you shot.'

The munitions carts were rolling into the village of Sainte Barbe, where Cadoudal and his lieutenant Rohu had their Chouans hastily throwing up embankments against the coming Republican cannon fire. All day long the refugees crowded past, desperate to get out of Carnac, and indeed Plouharnel, with as much as they could carry. In some cases, carts that might have been transporting ammunition and gunpowder were now carrying all that a family could stack on to them, and the flow kept coming, leading to fears that those in flight would be caught up in the coming fight. The *émigré* regiments and their commanders had not been able to make up their minds where to take a stand, and the fort at the neck of the isthmus of Quiberon had its attractions for them, perhaps as a base for a counterattack. Justin could see their point of view, but detested their endless vacillations.

All of this passed in front of Justin as he stood on the road at Plouharnel, watching the Chouan and *émigré* soldiers come flooding past as well, tired and dusty, some of them wounded, but not as yet defeated in their looks or bearing. Cadoudal's other officers were there on the road with him, standing in the sun, directing the men on to Sainte Barbe, arguing with some who had homes in the villages that were being gradually taken by the blues. To the north of the village of Plouharnel the fighting was still intense, watched with concern by the Chouan captains on the road, with smoke rising up and drifting away on the light breeze.

Justin looked into all the faces, half expecting to see Babette and anxiously scrutinising the features of any boy who drew close. He had broken off his vigil for a while to go down to the shore. The tide was more of a problem here, with some landing places drained out at low water, but arms had come in until men were trying to unload them from the edge of the mud. At that point, lighter and smaller boats had come into use, and Justin had managed to pass the word out to load them with shoes, which were much in need with the large number of fighting men now gathering together.

As the sun began to sink lower in the sky, he had followed the last of the carts out to Sainte Barbe with a heavy heart. His hopes of seeing Gilles had been high, and they had been worn down over the hours. There had been no sign of Babette or those who knew her, such as Grosjean. What would become of the expedition now was hard to guess. He hoped that he had done his duty, in uniform and out of it, and that he might at least now get to serve in arms. His head was aching from standing in the sun, and he had had little to eat or drink, but for the rest he felt able enough.

At Sainte Barbe he was reunited with his adjutant Trevelyan, who seemed duly satisfied with what had been achieved. He caught the occasional glimpse of Cadoudal, and more of Rohu, a man he had only recently met but who had impressed him with his solid ability. Rohu nodded to him, but Cadoudal was preoccupied, knowing only that these British officers had been useful to him and his army. By agreement, Justin and Trevelyan held the munitions in sheltered places in and around Sainte Barbe, a barn here, an abandoned farmhouse there, and soldiers of all the regiments came to them in good order. It was as secure as it could be.

Those who had been holding Plouharnel were starting to come in, and were being congratulated by the Chouan officers who welcomed them. *At least they can now have stout shoes*, Justin thought. There were no boys among them though, he noted with resignation. The women and children had mostly passed on down the peninsula to Saint Pierre and Quiberon itself, and from the reports he had heard Carnac was virtually deserted, left to the Republicans, the tricolour flying from its principal buildings. And now Plouharnel too was falling into their hands, with the dead left for the enemy to bury.

It was too late when he heard it. It was always too late in battle. Someone had seen the cannon brought into position on a height in the dusk, the blue uniforms scuttling around it dimly visible. He heard the shout of warning, but he was looking in the opposite direction, towards the setting sun, wondering futilely where those who were dear to him were, those for whom he felt responsible. He was standing foolishly on one of the new, protective embankments when the cannon ball struck only yards away from him, sending a spray of loose soil and stones flying up and out in its deadly blast. He was immediately flung backwards, and down into the depths of blackness.

His last image was not of Babette or Gilles, but of his sister, sitting in the garden at Chittesleigh with her friend Arabella at her side. They were laughing, and he wanted desperately to know what they were laughing about, to listen to what they were saying. But he could not hear a word.

CHAPTER XVI: ROOMS AT THE WHITE HART

The dust from the horse's hooves rose over the hedge and was blown in fits and starts by the summer breeze. The tenants had been at the hedge with billhooks over the winter, but the growth had by now long overtaken what had been cut away. Arabella had heard the rider approaching along the lane for some time, and allowed her curiosity to place her behind a small stand of trees that bordered her walk, beyond the orchard at the back of the manor. She stood still, with that mixture of anger and apprehension that had come over her when she thought she knew who would be riding here at this time.

She wore a light summer walking dress with a muslin scarf to protect her neck and shoulders from the sun, and standing in the shade she trailed her decorated bonnet from her fingers. The smell of the leaves was still sweet, and she congratulated herself on leaving for a solitary walk on hearing that Captain Yeo was to visit this morning. The man seemed to be enamoured of his naval uniform, despite being, as Arabella sardonically commented to herself, often so many miles from the sea, and mounted on a horse besides. There he was, blissfully unaware of being observed, and she wondered what contrivance he was now enacting that led him to seek an audience with Mrs Wentworth and her daughter.

Whatever it was, it followed too soon on her confrontation with him at the farmhouse for her to wish to be included, and she had insisted on walking out on her own along familiar paths. She watched him draw near to the gates, and then turn his horse's head into the driveway, scattering stones as he approached the manor. She would give him an hour, maybe less, and hear an account from Amelia once he had gone, perhaps in the absence of Mrs Wentworth. She saw Yeo dismount and Jem come out to walk the horse round to the stables, then she replaced her bonnet and resumed her path.

Despite his apparent inattention, Yeo had glimpsed what he thought was a figure through the trees. It was no great surprise to him, apart from the fact that if his guess was correct, he would be spared the embarrassment for which he had come prepared. There was neither need nor purpose in reacting, and a greeting would be, he was sure, unwelcome to both; so he continued on his way, feeling relieved. He anticipated a difficult conversation with the Wentworths themselves, especially in the light of their personal history, but he had brought reports of this kind on occasion to other families in the past, and so the responsibility was not new to him.

He followed Jem into the stable-yard, and found himself nodding to his agent who was brushing down one of the mares, but paying him little attention in that setting. He took the opportunity to bend forward and look at his reflection in a water trough, to dust and pick one or two burrs off his coat and its braid, and fluff out his thinning hair. Since that was enough to depress a man's spirits, he stayed no longer, but bid good morning to Thomas, who was now standing stiffly in one of the back doorways to the manor, and walked past him into the shade of the house.

Amelia was sketching her mother in the shaded light of the drawing room, a composition that had Sempronie reading a book, looking calm and collected, but with the light subtly catching her face. It was a demanding subject, and it had

Amelia tutting to herself from time to time, the only other sounds being the scratching of the charcoal stick and the occasional rustle of a turning page from her mother's chair. They were both aware that they were passing the time before Captain Yeo's arrival, and were quietly intrigued.

Amelia had been disabused of the romantic interpretation of the scene at the farmhouse into which she had stepped some weeks back, and had with some misgivings been prepared to accept the disturbing explanation that had been given her. But there was still much that puzzled her, notably about Arabella's involvement. Arabella had been forthright in declaring that Yeo was not her choice of suitor, yet had declined or failed to enlighten her about that strange rendezvous, or what had brought it about. It was evident to Amelia's sharp perceptions that her friend had hoped to be able to make a revelation to her, but that in some way this had not come to pass, and so she must remain in the dark.

If Captain Yeo was not coming to take the opportunity of cultivating his acquaintance with Miss Wollaston, it remained unclear why he might be visiting, unless, as Arabella teasingly remarked to her, he had learnt a lesson from his naval life and was now going about onto another tack. This Amelia doubted, although even a limited experience of life and young men had taught her not to be surprised by very much at all. But from hints she had garnered from Bella's account, obscure as they were, she rather believed that this visit might be connected with an intrigue which had no romantic hue to it, but was possibly far more sinister.

When it came, the knock at the door still made both of them start. Sempronie put down her book, looked over to her daughter and assured herself that she was now ready for what might ensue, and called out clearly to the visitor to 'Enter'.

This arrangement had been agreed with Thomas, much to his suppressed disapproval, in order to get the occasion off to a less formal start, so hopefully putting all — barring Thomas — at ease.

Yeo was the picture of vigour and health as he came in, immaculate in dress and displaying what Amelia could afterwards only call a 'sprightly' manner. They made their greetings, as intended, with as little formality as possible, and the captain was initially invited to sit, which he rather solemnly declined to do. Sempronie therefore felt that there was nothing she could do but to stand also, and she and her daughter exchanged a look, since the tone seemed to have been set rather militarily for them.

'Madam, Miss Wentworth, I can hardly imagine that you have found it a comfortable passage of time since you last had news of your son, madam, your brother, Miss Wentworth. I can see both of you look at each other as I introduce this idea, and I can only express my complete admiration for the manner in which you have kept enquiries at arm's length over the course of some months. You need not fear that any indiscretion of yours has allowed me to become party to what has been, to all purposes, a secret. But whatever the history of this secret has been, I am able to declare to you here that it is now plain and public knowledge that there has been an engagement at Quiberon.'

Here Yeo paused to consider the effect on his listeners. Their faces were grave, and not a little paler than they had been, but they retained their composure admirably. In fact, despite her apprehensions, Sempronie felt her impressions confirmed that Yeo was a pompous man, while some of what Yeo had said declared to Amelia that her friend's suspicions of him could be well-founded. Yet even if they might defer them momentarily by thoughts of this kind, they could not suppress their feelings of dread.

For his part, the captain took their continued silence as a sign that he had opened well. He had convinced himself, as on so many occasions in the past, that he ought to set the tone and take charge of the situation, and in this quietly elegant room he assumed that he presented a figure of authority. He decided that he should take up his position next to the hearth, which required passing between the two women, who had to adjust their stance and turn their faces towards him again. At this moment, he judged it suitable to hold up his hand before speaking, which he had often found to produce a good effect. The effect was only marginally diminished by the fact that those concerned were already completely silent.

'I am sure that you will be pleased to hear that Captain Wentworth has been engaged in distinguished service. I have this on authority of a naval source on whom I can rely absolutely. The actions in the vicinity of Quiberon have continued.'

Here Captain Yeo suddenly found himself at a loss for words. Nonetheless, this unplanned interruption in his control of the scene became a cue for the dialogue he had anticipated. As was fitting, it was the mother who spoke first, and he found himself pulling down the cuffs of his coat, a mannerism he had long despised in others. Her voice was barely perceptible.

'Poor souls.'

'I beg your pardon, madam? I do not quite understand…'

'My mother is thinking of the "continuing actions" that you mentioned, Captain Yeo. It is not difficult for us to imagine the loss of life in a region that is close to our family.'

Yeo felt uncomfortable, although he did not know why. He considered taking charge of the conversation again, and searched for the right words, but he was not quick enough.

'You spoke of my son, Captain Yeo, and I am sure that you came here to bring us news of him personally. We were aware, it is true, of his engagement abroad, but the details he kept from us. It was not hard to imagine that it would be in France, and quite probably in the region to which our family is attached through birthright and property.'

If Mrs Wentworth was now prepared for more to be declared, she was destined to be disappointed. Yeo had found his voice again, but apparently he had little to offer. 'I am afraid that is where my information comes to an end, madam. My source was aware of his involvement…'

'What kind of involvement, Captain?' This was the daughter, on the other side of him.

'Well, I know that ultimately he was serving in uniform, and he may have mentioned to you that he had been commissioned…'

'He was commissioned before he left the country, sir. I would rather you told me something that I did not know.' Amelia's eyes were slightly brighter, and he was sure that her nose was more pinched than it had been. There was no doubt she was an attractive young woman, perhaps the more so when her emotions began to rule her countenance. He thought it only natural for her to be upset, but he failed to recognise the symptoms of growing anger.

'Yes, of course, it is likely that he would have informed you. There would be no great disclosure in that. It was a great honour…'

'Captain Yeo, I believe you are concealing something from us, perhaps something you believe to be distressing, and I do not think this interview can continue if that remains the case.' Mrs Wentworth spoke up from his right. 'If you are not prepared to tell us more, then I believe I shall have to bid you good morning.'

With that, she moved gracefully past him to reach for the bell, and if only to stop her he blurted out, 'He is wounded. That is, not seriously…'

'How badly, sir?' The daughter spoke for both.

'I, well, my source … the matter of it is that we do not know the full extent…'

'Where is he?'

'That too remains unclear.' He felt himself getting hot under the collar, but it was not to be helped.

Mrs Wentworth walked past him steadily, and sat down in her accustomed chair. Her daughter moved slightly to stand by her. Both looked fixedly at him without speaking.

'He is in safe hands. You may be convinced of that. He is, according to an unconfirmed report, with Breton insurgents, because he is believed to have been fighting with them against the enemy.' He felt this to be reassuring, given what he knew of the family, and then added, 'He was in uniform, madam, his British uniform, in His Majesty's service, and proud to be so.'

Sempronie spoke quietly but distinctly. 'I had another son in uniform, and in His Majesty's service, Captain Yeo, and we may reflect on what happened to him. How much does this country demand of my children?'

'Mrs Wentworth, I cannot repeat often enough to you my sorrow at George's death in action. He was one of the finest young men under my command…'

It was the inevitable and incurable source of tension between them all, and once again palliative words would never be enough to heal the wound, despite the man's lack of personal guilt. But Amelia had detected something in his attitude to Justin which began to jar, and to substantiate the suspicions of her friend.

'My brother, Captain Yeo, has already served his country honourably and perilously in Canada. He emerged with credit then. Are you suggesting that he is in need of acquiring more? If so, perhaps you could explain yourself, since you appear to be unable to explain where my brother is or even whether he is still alive and in His Majesty's service.'

It was a little stilted as a speech, and it was clear from her reaction that her mother was puzzled by some parts of it, and unhappy about the growing possibility of a confrontation that could not help her son. She rose from her chair, momentarily placing her hand in that of her daughter. 'My dear, your brother will survive. You must not let fear for his well-being lead to harsh words to Captain Yeo, who is, after all, our friend and our guest.'

'Mrs Wentworth, I have stayed too long. You can be assured that as soon as I have more and hopefully better news, I shall bring it to you.'

Sempronie offered her hand to Yeo, who kissed it lightly. 'We owe you a debt of gratitude for bringing the news that you had to us in person. It was an act of great kindness. May we wish you a safe homeward journey?'

'Thank you, ma'am. Your servant, Miss Wentworth.' He bowed towards her, bringing his boot-heels together, and left the room. There was another silence.

'Amélie, I shall retire. Would you send my maid to me in my room? I shall feel restored, no doubt, after a little rest.'

'Yes, mother.' Amelia had not moved. 'I myself shall take some air.'

Sempronie paused by the door as a thought occurred to her. 'Oh, and to cap it all, that man Le Guinec has returned. Or is on his way, I think. He sent ahead. He wishes to see us tomorrow.'

Amelia broke from her reverie. 'Le Guinec? The new Kergohan steward? Why is he here? What does he want? Where is he staying?'

'My dear, *je suis fatiguée*. All these questions about a man we hardly know. I can answer your last, because it is fixed in my mind. He wrote that he will be tonight in Okehampton, at the White Hart. I doubt that he will have better news of Justin. Please make my apologies to Arabella. I shall, I am sure, see her later this afternoon.'

'Mother, you should go up. I shall send Betty to you.' The door clicked behind Sempronie, and Amelia went to the bell and rang it. She walked across to the sketching table and looked at her drawing, becoming aware of some residual charcoal on her fingertips. There was a knock, and the door opened, revealing the housemaid in a bob cap.

'Miss Wollaston, miss. She is just now removing her boots.'

'Thank you, Harriet. Would you send Betty up to my mother in her room? Oh, and do we have any orgeat, Hattie? Miss Wollaston will doubtless be parched after her walk. Please send it into the library, with two glasses and fresh water from the spring.'

Amelia placed the sketch in her portfolio, dusted her hands with a cloth, and tried to dismiss her misgivings about Yeo. She walked briskly through the intervening door to the library, which was cooler. It had a northern aspect, an advantage in this season. Not a large room, it nonetheless needed a fire from early autumn until late spring, but her brother loved its peace and quiet, and spent many restful hours here. For herself, if she wanted a book, she would take it with her into the drawing room, which was also her mother's preference, although from time to time she had sat with her brother, comforted by his company.

That thought brought a tear to her eye, and while she told herself not to be so foolish the sentiment was enhanced by the sight of his desk, which she herself had tidied earlier in the summer, replacing the books he had been reading on the shelves. In that mournful reverie, she heard voices outside talking gaily, and the door from the hall opened to reveal Arabella, in an animated mood, and Hattie with a tray of refreshments. On seeing Amelia, Arabella's lively expression gave way to one of concern. She came quickly into the library, and asking Hattie to place the tray down and thanking her, she occupied herself with pouring two glasses of orgeat, until the door finally closed. Without lifting the drinks, she then spoke gently to Amelia.

'What's amiss, my dearest heart? Come, you should drink this. It will restore you.'

Amelia impulsively clasped Arabella to her, and Arabella kissed the top of her head, a gesture she had learnt brought some solace when Amelia's spirits collapsed. Arabella held her at arm's length, scrutinising her face, and then reached for the two glasses.

'Come, like the men in their clubs, we must drink, drink, drink!'

Amelia laughed uncertainly, but declared that it was just what she had needed. They laughed again, this time together.

'There, listen to us, for all the world like a pair of old periwigs from Whitehall or Pall Mall, who have just staggered out of their coaches!' Arabella paused here, and decided not to leave it any longer. 'What did Yeo have to say, Melia? I saw him depart, looking as complacent as ever.'

Amelia held her glass in both hands like a child, but then placed it on the tray. She spoke away from Arabella, her head bowed. 'Justin has been wounded, Bella. We do not know how badly, nor where he is, except that as we surmised, it is in Brittany, and indeed not some great distance from Kergohan.'

It was Arabella's turn to flinch, and although she turned pale, she did not falter. Her feelings were of no account to anyone but herself. In truth, she had feared worse. 'My dear, I am so sorry. Your poor mother. How is she? Harriet told me that she had retired to her room. Is she bearing up? Are you?'

'Yes, I am bearing up,' Amelia answered in a small voice.

'And Sempronie?'

'Mother has had her share of sorrow, of terrible news brought to her, in times past. This was perhaps mild by comparison.'

It was a point that Arabella could appreciate, recalling George's death at sea, and one that she also understood herself, remembering that dreadful day when her mother was brought back to the house, after her mare had returned to the stables on its own.

Amelia now looked at her friend, as if the worst was over. 'She is rarely overwhelmed. She will recover herself.'

Arabella's face still showed concern, but she made an effort to soften her features. 'I am sure that she will. I have the greatest admiration for your mother.'

Amelia studied her friend's face. 'You know, Bella, I do not trust that man. But I think he is telling us what he knows. He makes too much of patriotism and service to leave me comfortable about Justin, wound or no wound. He will bring more news, when there is some.'

Arabella felt awkward. This was hardly the moment, and even so she had kept most of her suspicions to herself, because she could not substantiate them, nor would she repeat outright to members of this household the more disturbing picture that had begun to emerge during the conversation with her father at Alverscombe. But fortunately she was interrupted in these thoughts by something that proved to be a sudden prompt to action.

'Oh, and talking of men one does not trust, Mother says that man Le Guinec, the new Kergohan steward, is visiting us again. Now why would he be doing that?'

'Him? Again? When?'

'Why, tomorrow, Mother said. What is the matter, Bella?'

'Where is he staying, Melia? Has he yet arrived?'

Amelia looked at her friend, puzzled. 'Tonight, in Okehampton, at the White Hart, if I recall my mother correctly. But, again, what is the matter, Bella? You seem oddly more concerned with this steward than you are with the condition of my brother.'

A tight little smile from Miss Wollaston. 'If you will have faith in me, my dear Melia, they are more closely connected than you perceive. And the one I can do little about, whate'er I would. What else was there?' She had paced to one of the windows.

'Why, precious little. The naval dispatches are delayed, of course. What they convey is now a week past.'

Arabella remained staring out of the window. 'I mean of Le Guinec, my love. Will you forgive me asking if he gave a pretext, call it a reason, for his call on you tomorrow morning?'

'None. He sent ahead, and will put up at Okehampton. That is all. Unless my mother knows more.'

'So, at the White Hart. It will do. No doubt he will be assuming the manner of an *émigré*, and it may be that he has a pass with him. But that itself is of little importance.' She swung round, decisive in manner and in looks. 'Quickly, Amelia, we have little time. We must prepare to leave.'

'Leave?'

'Your mother must be informed … that you are coming with me to Alverscombe for a few days. It will do you good.'

Amelia was at a loss to explain her friend's sudden enthusiasm, and disturbed by her odd choice of diversion from the news they had heard of Justin. But she spoke gently, unwilling to offend. 'Bella, you must forgive me for saying that you seem to be neglectful of my own feelings, and those of my mother. Disruption may not be…'

'We shall take the small chariot in which I came here. Andrew will put up bags behind for both of us. We can see your mother when she comes down, Amelia, and I am sure she will give her approval to us.'

Amelia decided to stand her ground, since her friend was clearly unsettled, more worried than she was willing to display, without doubt about Justin. 'But I do not want to go to Alverscombe, Bella, not at this minute.'

Miss Wollaston walked across and put her hands lightly on Amelia's shoulders, as she had seen Amelia's brother do, and as her father did to her. 'You are not going to Alverscombe, my sweetest bird. You are going to the White Hart in Okehampton. Pray say nothing more. This is in your brother's interest. I shall explain all to you on the journey, as far as I am able. But for now, we should expect your mother, and remember, we are going to Alverscombe!'

Amelia disengaged herself gently, but noticed that Arabella's tense look remained, her hand closing and opening distractedly. She spoke brightly, and with a light touch. 'Should I end up on the ramparts of one of Ann Radcliffe's Sicilian castles by moonlight, I shall hardly be more surprised! There, there, Bella, you may relax that fist you are making. I shall do what you say, that is —' and here she smiled openly at her friend — 'if I can remember all of it.'

Their room was relatively small, and the upholstery had seen better days, but it would serve perfectly well, and Arabella registered her satisfaction with a nod. There were two beds for the two friends, and a small closet with a truckle bed for Grace, not that she would be troubling it if all went according to plan.

Grace had arranged everything with the chambermaid. She set the two bags on the small trestle in the room and left to go downstairs to join Andrew, or at least to allow herself to be seen to converse with him modestly. As the door closed, Amelia brushed out her walking dress, and wrinkled her nose slightly at the musty smell that hung in the air. She also removed her out-of-fashion bonnet, part of the rather dowdy outfit she had assumed in order to drift past any unwelcome attention downstairs, where she might just possibly be recognised. Not that she had called in at the White Hart before this day, according to her memory, but she might well have been seen in the street visiting shops.

Amelia placed her bonnet on top of the bags, and sat down primly on one of the easy chairs, conquering her fear of fleas. She folded her hands in her lap and put on her best schoolgirl face, looking up at Arabella in expectation of enlightenment. The game amused them both.

'Now, if you please, Miss…'

Arabella laughed roundly. 'Yes, you do deserve an explanation of my mad schemes.'

'Ah, so you do admit that they are mad. I find that an encouraging start. I had begun to wonder…'

'Perhaps why Andrew and Grace, and indeed Jem, know what I am about and you do not. You are in the right of it.' Arabella sat down on one of the beds. 'I had intended to lay it all out to you on the journey, but found I could not until I was sure of the ground here. The upshot of it all is that we shall discover what the good *Monsieur* Le Guinec believes he has in his possession —' and here she frowned slightly — 'that is worth crossing the Channel for, again. And there you have it.'

'Have what, precisely?'

'I…'

There was a double tap at the door, and the handle turned slowly. Arabella stood up sharply, while motioning to Amelia to stay seated.

'Yes, you may come in.'

The door opened to reveal Grace, who came in quietly and closed it behind her. Arabella said nothing, but raised an eyebrow in an expression that Amelia had not seen before. This was proving to be a day for surprises.

'Miss Wentworth, Miss Wollaston, I have spoken to Andrew. We stepped out for a while, as if man and maid. No one would think anything of it. He told me of what he had done.'

'Which is?'

'It is as you wished. The steward from France will have the large room across the corridor, which has a closet next to it, miss, just as here. And the chambermaid will leave the closet door unlocked. That is, she will unlock the door to the corridor once the gentleman is in, and has gone for his supper.'

Arabella clapped her hands, and clasped them in front of her. Amelia was beginning to look apprehensive.

'This was well done. Did Andrew say how he had secured this slightly shady agreement?'

Grace looked away briefly to Miss Wentworth, and then back to Miss Wollaston, and she blushed. 'He…'

'He flirted, Grace, I shall say the word for you, with the maid — that is it, isn't it? So much I had expected. And what was his story?'

'He told me that he said to her that he was charged with making the arrangement for a visitor to the foreign gentleman in his rooms, a visitor that none should know about. I think she liked the mystery, ma'am. He also told me that he let her think what she might, that it might be business or something … something of another kind. That the visitor would come in by a side door of the hotel or the back, but would be quite respectable … he would vouch for that.'

'Capital. Thank you, Grace. You may do best to take a dish of tea downstairs, and remember that you answer to any enquiries that we are travelling to London. You may use my name, but not that of Miss Wentworth, who is … what are you, Melia?'

Amelia was by this stage transfixed. 'Miss Edgeworth, I think. She will not mind. I believe she is in Ireland.' She did not add that she might wish to be there herself, since Grace was still in the room.

'Miss Edgeworth it is. I am sure I have heard that name somewhere. Be very careful, Grace. And remember, when the French gentleman has arrived, and placed his bags in his room, and when supper is laid for him, you will bring us that news. Both Andrew and Jem are looking out for him, and Andrew will tell you when.'

'Yes, miss. As you say. I shall be attentive. It is almost evening now, miss, so it may be that we do not have long to wait.' She bobbed again. 'Miss Wentworth —' and, as Arabella held up a finger — 'that is, Miss Edgeworth. Miss.' She left.

'And now, my dear, I trust you have a book with you, for we have to wait.'

Amelia had found it very hard to read, and time was ticking by very slowly. She looked up from her book at her friend's profile, and wondered once again if she might persuade her against this rash adventure. Arabella was standing at the small window, which looked out over a narrow court, but let in sufficient light to the room.

'My love, you did not fully explain...'

Arabella swung round, fully attentive, and by no means in the dream that Amelia had supposed. 'You are right, I did not.' But she said no more.

'You have said to me, with some assurance, that Le Guinec will be bringing something with him from Brittany. That is to be expected. But why cannot we wait to have it shown to us, as he did last time? There is such a risk involved...'

'Unless I am much mistaken, Amelia, he will be bringing with him something that incriminates your brother in some way. The very last thing he would do would be to show it to us.'

'My brother? *Incriminates* my brother, you say? But my brother is his master...' She was incredulous.

'No, Melia, your mother's cousin is his master. And Le Guinec is in league with Yeo.'

'Arabella, you amaze me. In league? What will you say next?'

'Something that you will again repeat, I dare say. No, my dear, I am sorry, that is too sharp, and I must not be so, least of all to you. Yeo and Le Guinec. I have seen them together, at a rendezvous, at the farmhouse to which you came, in most suspicious circumstances. And now Le Guinec has returned, and we know that we cannot trust Yeo. It is my firm belief that the steward will be bringing something to show him.'

'But there may be other reasons why he has seen Captain Yeo. I do not like either man, but…'

'You always said to me, Melia, that your mother's cousin was envious of Justin's inheritance of Kergohan, and thought the manor and the estate ought to come to him. Well, now is his chance, and there are those here on this side of the Channel, as you have heard, who may themselves have raised suspicions scurrilously against your brother. Of the company he kept, of those with whom he conversed, some of whom were imprisoned, of the books that he read. This is tinder, and all it needs is a match.'

'What will it be that Le Guinec is bringing with him?' Amelia spoke coldly, although her emotions were stirred, and her mind was racing in a struggle to distinguish between what was truly possible, and what she felt that her friend might well be imagining. Arabella walked away from her, as if sensing her disapproval, and realising her own weakness.

'That I do not know, I cannot, as yet. It will be something to do with the manor, with Kergohan, surely, some false title deeds, some documents… No, that would never pass.' She looked back at her friend ruefully. 'I confess I do not know, Amelia.'

'But why are we here?' Amelia remained even in tone, if cool, although she was unsure whether she was more annoyed or upset by her friend's imperious interference.

'To look in his folder, the one he had with him last time.' Arabella paused, and for the first time she looked dejected, and she spoke bitterly. 'I can see that you, even you, do not believe me. You do not trust me, or this endeavour.'

There was a long silence, with neither woman knowing what to say. It was broken by a light tap at the door, followed quickly by another, and Grace slipped into the room without waiting to be called.

'Miss Wentworth, miss, he has come, and left his bags. They were not many. The man had the porter carry them up for him and bring him down the key to his door, on his instruction. They are serving him supper. Andrew was just now persuading the chambermaid to come and unlock the closet door, which I think she has done. I saw her coming down the back stairs. She is a bold girl, that one, who might likely lose her place if…'

'She will invent a story, if she has need. It has been done before, although —' and Arabella was kind here, and smiled — 'I do not suspect it of you, Grace.'

'No, miss, perish the thought I should be so disloyal.'

'Indeed. You will go down again now, and watch with Andrew. We must be warned of anything unexpected. And then we shall try the door opposite.' She picked up her knotting bag from the bed, and waited for Grace to leave. She waited for a minute, then stepped across to the door. 'Are we ready? You will come, Amelia?'

The corridor was quiet, the faint sounds of Grace going down the far stairs, the summer warmth outside suggesting a lazy mood in the town, the smell of food drifting up from below. Arabella waited for Amelia to shut their own door, and then tried the handle of the door opposite. She had forgotten to ask precisely which room was the closet, and to her frustration the door in front of her was plainly locked. Amelia was acutely uncomfortable, and conscious of how the floorboards would creak when one was moving only slightly, as she was. Arabella looked at the door to her right, and moved swiftly down the corridor to try that handle.

The door opened, to Amelia's astonishment without a creak, and with the gravest reluctance she followed her friend into the room. It was certainly a closet, very similar in size and furnishings to the one attached to their own room. Arabella shut the door softly behind her, and edged across the room to another door. She looked round at her friend, put her head close to the frame of the door, and listened. Amelia could hear the sound of her own breathing, and her thoughts were still racing with prohibitions, an inner voice telling her that the sense of reliving adolescent mischief was seriously misplaced here and now. Now there was all of the fear and none of the delight, and she prayed inwardly for these few minutes to be gone.

It was evident that Arabella had heard nothing from the room beyond. If she was right, there would be no movement because the door to the room itself was the one along the corridor that she had tried, and that was locked, presumably from the outside. She took a breath, and then as if recalling an idea previously conceived, spoke over her shoulder to Amelia in a whisper.

'Remember, we have mistook our way to our own apartment. It will be enough.'

She opened the door as the thump of Amelia's heart now drowned out the insistent inner voice.

'There is no one here. And it is his room!' Arabella hissed these words back to her, passed into the room and out of sight, and almost immediately came back again. 'Come, I have found the folder. He has so little here. A travelling bag, and the folder beneath it. Just the same ribbons securing it as we saw before, but we may be sure its contents are not the same.'

In her excitement Arabella returned to the adjoining room without waiting for Amelia, who calmed her fears for the moment and followed her friend. This bed chamber was similar to their own, but much larger, a wide room at the front of the building and overlooking the main street. It had one bed, an easy chair towards the window, a trestle for baggage, and a small straight-legged table with an old-fashioned chair set under it. There was nothing on the table, but a coat had been hung from the chair, and a hat had been placed on the bed. The window was open to allow the air to pass through the room.

'Here is best.' Arabella laid out the folder on the small table and untied the ribbons. She rapidly turned over the contents, which were relatively few, and then spoke to herself under her breath. 'Bella Wollaston, you are an addle-brained ninny. Where is your school learning?' And then, more loudly: 'Amelia, my love, come and sit down here. I'll be damned if my French is quick enough for this.'

Amelia did as she was told, and fortunately felt her curiosity now rising to displace her agitation, at least temporarily. What she saw in front of her were letters, all dated to the year past, relatively short, and written in French. To her astonishment, she saw that they were signed 'M. Sarzou' at Kergohan, and her eye was caught by the words 'Commissioners' and 'Republic'. She read as fast as she could, initially with calm, but her frown increased, and she paused with her finger on the page.

'What is there, my love? Melia, what is in it? You must tell me.'

'These are letters from Sarzou, our old steward, dating from last year. In this one he says that he has had requests from the new Republic to buy fodder, foodstuffs, and the like from the estate. He is, it seems, seeking my brother's approval for supplying the Republican soldiers.'

'The devil he is. And the other letters?'

'This second is also like that. And this third … is from Justin. There is his signature. It is short, and … it gives his approval for what is written by Sarzou in the dated letters, here enclosed with his reply, as he writes.' Her hand was now shaking, and her face was pale and drawn. 'What do you think, Bella? Oh, what can we make of this? There must be something wrong. It looks so like his handwriting, but…'

Arabella was herself looking very shaken, but she became resolute. 'Whatever we make of it, he cannot be allowed to pass these on.' She leant over and gathered the letters together to put back in the folder, but she found her arm held by Amelia, whose grip was hard and firm. Her voice was low and tremulous.

'He never writes in French.'

Arabella looked at her. 'What do you mean, never writes in French?'

'Sarzou never writes to my brother in French.' She quickly fingered the letters again, and her voice became excited. 'He writes in Breton. And my brother writes back to him in Breton. It's something they adopted some years back when the troubles commenced in France, a kind of security. I remember Justin laughing about it to me. And —' she shuffled the letters — 'Sarzou always signed himself "Mael" to Justin, not Sarzou.'

'Are you sure?'

'I am completely sure. I have seen letters from him to Justin, and seen Justin writing to him over many years. But this is Justin's signature, or a very close likeness, so what do we do?'

'These are forgeries. Never mind Justin's letter and signature. It is somehow a forgery too. I shall fetch my bag. Tie up the folder, Melia.'

Arabella swept into the adjoining room, and Amelia gathered the letters together. At her back there was a soft click, and a light draught of air passed across her from the window into the room. She looked round, expecting Grace or Andrew, and instead saw Le Guinec, standing by the door with a smile on his face, one hand brushing his hair from his forehead.

'Miss Wentworth, perhaps I am in error? I may have mistaken my room.' He made a pretence of turning to go, and then pointed to his bag. 'But, no, that is my bag, I am sure. Perhaps the error is yours. It is so easy to be mistaken.'

Amelia had stood, with her back to the table and the folder held in both hands behind her back. Le Guinec stayed where he was, but he held out his hand. His voice was now less pleasant.

'You may pass my portfolio to me. Or perhaps I must ask you to place it on the table. And then you will leave, *mademoiselle*. There is the small matter of a reputation to consider, and I mean yours, of course, not mine.'

Amelia stood still for a moment, and then to Le Guinec's satisfaction laid the folder on the table behind her. She took a step forward, but then a voice came from the doorway to the closet.

'Stay where you are, Amelia. You will leave us, Le Guinec, to avoid the shame and disgrace that justly await you, and we shall keep possession of what we know to be forgeries.' Arabella's profile was outlined in the frame of the door to the closet, although she remained partly obscured by it. Her knotting bag hung loosely from her right arm.

Le Guinec, as a Frenchman, and a Breton to boot, considered himself a comfortable match even for two English ladies, and was quick to change language in addressing Amelia, whom he viewed as the more influential of the pair. '*Mademoiselle*,' he said, 'there is evidently some confusion, but I do not understand your friend completely, for which my apologies are due. But it is quite certain that it is best for you both to withdraw, and we shall accept that this is all a mistake.' The steward stepped forward, bowed slightly, and swept his arm around to indicate the door, smiling all the while.

Arabella's voice cut through his pretensions. 'Amelia, please pick up the folder, and come with me. We shall leave by this door. And you may tell this man, if he pretends not to understand plain English, that he will be well advised to return whence he came.'

Le Guinec's face hardened at this, and he made a move to prevent Amelia from crossing the room. But before he had taken a pace forward, Arabella brought herself fully into the frame of the closet door. Her right hand still held her knotting-bag, but in her left hand was a small, decorated pistol, which was levelled at the steward.

'You will stay there, Le Guinec, quite still. You are a scoundrel. You insult both our intelligence and our sex, but you should never underestimate a woman's resolve.'

Amelia remained speechless. Le Guinec felt a wave of anger and contempt surge over him. '*Imbécile*,' he muttered, and in acute irritation at the ridiculous arrogance of this interfering aristocrat he turned swiftly on his heel, and made a grab for his coat and his folder.

'Damn you!' Arabella shouted and pulled the trigger of her pistol. Le Guinec staggered and fell against the far wall of the room, knocking over both the chair and the table. Amelia put a hand to her mouth to stifle a scream which could not possibly have been heard, because the noise of the pistol was deafening in the confined space.

There was a sound of feet pounding along the corridor, and Andrew came bursting into the room. Outside in the street voices were raised, and a loud shout went up, answered by another, and more running feet. Doors slammed below in the hotel, and there behind Andrew in the doorway was the blustering landlord, partly restrained by Jem. Grace wove determinedly through all of the men, and went straight to Amelia at a sign from her mistress. Almost immediately, an officer in uniform also pushed through the obstructing bodies into the room, followed by two militia soldiers. He was red in the face and out of breath.

'Ma'am, Miss Wollaston, and, dammit, Miss Wentworth too! I mean…'

'This man is a villain. You may take him into custody and then to a Justice of the Peace. My father, Sir Francis Wollaston, will do. He may be injured. In fact, he appears to be. I shall give an account to my father of what has happened. We will now withdraw. Andrew, would you assure our host that he will be recompensed by me for any damage?' She turned to Amelia. 'Come, my dear, and remember to bring your belongings with you. Grace, please accompany Miss Wentworth. I wish you good evening, Lieutenant Mallingham.'

With that, Arabella placed her pistol calmly in her knotting-bag and pulled the strings tight, and they swept out of the main room and through the closet, Amelia taking the hint and bringing the folder with her, leaving the lieutenant staring at what was left. He took a breath, and then spoke brusquely to the two serving men standing behind him.

'Get rid of that blethering innkeeper downstairs before I lose my patience, and make sure he takes his wife with him. Get him to put a shot of his own spirits down his throat. That should settle his nerves.' Then, to his soldiers, 'Well, pick him up, you fools! Don't just stand there gawping. Take him to a surgeon. He's winged but not mortal, as far as I can see.

Sounds as if he's a foreigner, besides. That should condemn him, if nothing else does. Go on, then, get on with it!'

The soldiers lifted Le Guinec, who was conscious but in considerable pain, one of them slinging the steward's good arm around his shoulders, and took him out of the room. The smell of burnt powder still hung in the air, and there was a hole in the plaster of the wall where the ball had lodged. On the floor by the wall there was some blood, but the lieutenant had seen far worse. He was unconcerned. He scratched his ear, and blew air out through his mouth.

'Well, I'll be damned.' He sniffed, cleared his throat, and walked out of the room.

CHAPTER XVII: THE PRISONS OF AURAY

Justin screwed up his eyes in the glare of the sun, and then stepped into the shadow of one of the tall houses that lined the street. The overhang offered shade; the granite of the doorway was cool to lean against. A strange face on the end of the projecting beam just above caught his eye, carved when the house was young, now weathered and worn. *Like many of us*, an inner voice said plainly.

He still suffered from the blow he had received in the explosion at Sainte Barbe, and he could remember nothing of what had followed: the retreat, and the re-embarkation of many of the *émigrés*. Because he was hardly conscious, he had remained with Cadoudal's regiment, carried at first away from Sainte Barbe in a cart with others. After he had come round, he had chosen to stay with Cadoudal, desperate to work his way round to Kergohan again, to hear news of Gilles and Babette.

So he could recall sailing up the gulf of Morbihan to Sarzeau, the water calm and the coastline glowing in the sunshine, mockingly peaceful. But as they moved north on land beyond Vannes, he had left their company, and left his uniform behind him. There was nothing for him to do there anymore, nothing at all, and Cadoudal barely noticed him. He had made the journey through the forest, alternately telling himself he was feeling stronger, and then suffering from a bout of feebleness. Finally walking into the village again, and seeing Babette's look of desolation when he shook his head, had increased his weariness. But when Grosjean brought the news that Gilles was in Auray, both he and Babette had felt newly animated, and had argued passionately over who should go to plead the case.

He knew where to go. That would be simple enough in any case, but who he would find waiting for him was another matter. He had had his feelings stirred when he heard from Babette the account of her ordeal. She had been examined briefly by a committee of citizens in front of a military officer, whom she had recognised in Quiberon as the man who had been to her village and had Guareg shot by his soldiers. Justin was aware of his name from what he had overheard at Kergohan, and knew that the man was connected to his mother's cousin Laurent Guèvremont, to the daughter Joséphine, who seemed to be on familiar terms with him, and probably to the new steward of the estate.

Babette had stood in a line of Breton women in front of this committee, all of them tired and haggard after capture, detention, and incarceration, but defiant still, and taciturn by intention. Actually, it had been more of a sermon than an interrogation, she said, since the committee had realised that they would hear nothing to their advantage from these mute and obstinate figures, nothing that would remotely advance the campaign. Instead, the citizens had informed them of the clemency extended by the Convention — which one of the committee had explained as 'a pardon' — and insisted on the need to return to their villages and resume normal life. The military man for his part had made it clear that they should not engage in any further activities against the Republic, armed insurrection being the worst of these, and that leniency could not be expected on a subsequent offence. Had Babette not been indoors, she would have spat on the ground. Their names had been taken, and their place of residence, although how many of these were false only the women themselves knew.

So it was to Leroux that Justin would go to appeal for Gilles. Despite his own standing, wrapped around by centuries of deference to the nobility, he had had to argue for hours with Babette as to who should go. She asserted her greater security as a woman, but he kept insisting that he would have the authority to be believed in what needed to be said about parentage to gain the release of Gilles. In the end, she gave way to him, resentful and grudging, but fully understanding why what he had to say might prove to be decisive; and that was all that mattered in the end.

The prison was down a narrow lane off the centre of Auray. Walled and grim, it was newly built, ironically on the orders of a king who had himself been arrested, and then brutally executed. Justin had prepared his case, but was aware of the risks. From what he had heard, Gilles had struck out at a soldier, and despite his age that would go against him. As the day went on, the heat was mounting, and the stench in the town was overbearing in parts. Prisoners, both *émigrés* and Chouans and those suspected of being either, were crammed into various temporary gaols or places of confinement, as no doubt they were officially called. The town also supported a garrison, and the inevitable influx of human and animal life and fodder that went with that. The soldiers could at times be on a short fuse, because of what they had experienced in the campaign so far rather than as a result of any immediate military threat, and Justin could well believe that arrests were arbitrary at times, when so many were already imprisoned. It was as well not to offend the blue uniforms.

Justin both edged and sauntered his way through the centre, watchful but aiming to go unnoticed, a part of the flow of people going about ordinary business. Outside one fine house, he passed a small group of burghers talking earnestly, and realised abruptly that these were the new citizens with the most influence, no doubt the more so if they had lawyers to put their cases about property, assets, or even life and death. He wondered what that would be like in England, and found it hard to imagine the consequences. Yet he himself had said that the rising industrial class of factory owners in Britain would not be ignored. Not for the first time in recent years, he found himself perplexed. It was perhaps natural that his apprehensions about what he was doing, the meeting that he was edging towards along what was now the correct street, should be pushed to the back of his mind by other, imponderable concerns. He could see soldiers going in and coming out of the gates to the prison, and Justin waited until the gatekeeper had a moment of quiet before strolling easily up to him. His best guess was that this man would be local, and would have become used to orders coming to him in harsh French, so he spoke mildly in Breton.

'My friend, is this where I would find Captain Leroux? I have matters to discuss with him, information to bring to his attention.'

The soldiers sitting in the guard-room looked up at him briefly, said something in a low voice to each other about the language, and went back to their cards. The gaoler was initially unimpressed, but was taking in the look of the man with an experienced eye.

'So, it's Leroux, is it? And what would be your business with the captain? He does not like to be interrupted, and can be rough with time-wasters. And you won't be able to speak our language to him, *keneil*.'

The tone was kinder, and Justin suspected that the gaoler had been confronted by this kind of mission regularly enough over the last weeks. 'I wish to speak to him about a prisoner. A young boy, hardly yet a man.'

'There are some like that, but thanks be to the saints not many. The rest are ruffians, mind you, whom you wouldn't trust with an old bucket. You'll find Leroux in his cabinet, that's to the left inside. Don't mind the uniforms. Once you're in, keep to your business. The doors in there lock on one side only, so take care.'

He spoke through the grill and opened the gate, which swung easily on its hinges. An indefinable smell came from the building as Justin crossed the courtyard and approached the front door of the prison, fetid and depressing. There was a group of gaolers inside, sitting on benches, uninterested in him, men without sentiment or compassion when inside the walls, but no doubt with wives and children at home. A short passage led into the heart of the building and to another intervening door, this one again with a grill and evidence of a large lock. But Justin could see what must be the cabinet to the left, and heard the sound of voices. He stood back slightly, and at that moment the door to the cabinet opened, and a well-dressed man stood in the doorway, talking back to the occupant.

'What I say, Leroux, is not as weak as one man's opinion. Take note of that. There is anger, and it has a strong voice. Citizens will see justice done, and if there is a heavy penalty, then those who are guilty should be made to pay it. And that would be sooner rather than later.'

'Yes, indeed, Citizen Soulogne. I have heard all that you have said…' The voice came from inside the room, firm, clipped, but polite. But the other man was impetuous, and kept going.

'It is a hydra, Leroux, and like Hercules we must cut off all its heads. Not just the *émigrés*, but those beneath them who have never left, but stay seething in our countryside, unruly and murderous…'

'As I have stated, Soulogne, I have heard your opinion, and you can be sure that it will be considered.' The voice from inside had adopted a harder tone. 'Now, if you'll forgive me, citizen…'

'I shall no doubt see you again, Captain Leroux.' The man called Soulogne strode out of the cabinet and past Justin without observing him, and the gaolers glanced up at him as he walked to the front door. Justin took a deep breath, stepped forward, knocked, and entered the room. Leroux looked up at him with a mixture of mild irritation and curiosity. He was sitting at a desk, with papers and a quill and inkstand, his military coat slung over a wooden chair because of the heat. There was no one else in the room, which was small. A window looked out on the courtyard. The room smelt dusty, and the air was stale. There was a silence, in which Justin shifted his weight on to one leg.

'Well?' Leroux showed no particular sign of impatience.

'I would like to ask for your indulgence in speaking of a prisoner.'

'What will be the purpose in that? If he is a prisoner, then it is so for a good reason. What can you say that will alter that? More to the point, why should I listen to you?' Leroux picked up his pen and began to sign papers in a rote fashion, although he scanned each one for its content. 'You can shut the door as you leave, and I suggest you do that promptly, or you may end up joining him. Now, out. My men are not in the best of spirits, and would rather not be in this cesspit of a town.'

Justin got hold of the chair and pulled it towards him. He sat down, swinging the officer's coat onto his knees.

'My God, you are familiar, are you not? Are you tempting fate, man? What is it about this region that it breeds so many…'

'His name is Gilles. He is a boy, hardly a man. He was taken near Carnac, in the assault. He had joined like a young fool, thinking it was an adventure. He understood nothing of the game, of the campaign, of what was involved. I doubt if he had heard of the Republic, although he had seen soldiers before. He and his companion gave themselves up to your men.'

Leroux seemed interested, but not greatly. 'There are not many boys. Some of them are wildcats.'

'He is not wild, or not wild in that manner. Just foolish.'

'As are so many, boys or men. We have released the quiet boys who were with their mothers. What else did he do? I have no doubt you are hiding something from me. Quickly, man…'

'They say that he cut a soldier. Only a graze. They had made him take a knife…'

'Ah, the poor boy, they had forced a knife on him against his will, and the waif was somehow induced to use it against the Republic. No wonder he is still here. Get out of my room. I have given you more than enough time.'

'But there is more…'

'I don't doubt there is more, much more, if you got the chance to tell it, but you won't. Gaston! Mercier, where are you? Come and remove this bleeding heart and send him about his Breton business.'

'I think you will want to listen. I can tell you who his father is.'

'Well, how fortunate, but that can also be said of bastards in some cases. Mercier! So much for security in this cattle shed.'

'He is a bastard. And I can testify…'

Perhaps there was something in Justin's tone at this moment, or the perception had gradually been dawning on him, but Leroux put down his pen and looked at him closely. 'I don't know your voice, but I'm damned if I don't recognise that face. And I think you know mine, unless I am much mistaken. A sordid bar in Quiberon, and you had the temerity to make me sweat for a while. And you were with that woman. She is a dog-face if ever there was one, and she stood me down once in some dirty village.' Leroux stood up. 'Well, well. And would I be mistaken if you had a nasty smell about you? I was chasing one like that throughout the brambles and dung of this country from Josselin down, but never caught hold of his leg. I wonder if you would be he.'

Justin had been aware of this danger, but he now wanted to turn this sharpened interest to his advantage. He had to turn the trick, but his hands had to be deft. 'I do not know you, Captain. Faces are misleading. The boy has a father…'

'Damn the boy…'

'You will not damn him when I tell you who he is. His mother worked at an estate, and a man of the nobility, as it was then, took advantage of her. She left the estate, went back to her village, and had the child. She died not long after. The Baron provided for the boy, and another woman took him for her son.'

'And then?' said Leroux, still staring intently at him. 'This had better be good.'

'I am that Baron, or I was. Of Kergohan.'

'So you are the bastard's father, and you want to have him back, to save his skin? How very touching. Have you no legitimate heirs, Baron?' Leroux's tone was scathing, and the name of the estate had failed to register with him.

'No, his father has none. But he does have a daughter. Her name is Joséphine.'

Leroux's eyes went very wide indeed, and he placed the ends of his fingers on the top of the desk. 'Is it now? Kergohan, you said. So this boy, you say, is the son of whom, precisely?'

'Of my mother's cousin, Captain. Of Laurent Guèvremont.'

'And I have your word for that? Is that all I have?' Leroux was concentrating, quite stunned by what he had heard, and sensing this was to his advantage, but he had not worked it out yet. Justin had expected this. It was a question of how much weight his word would carry, and how much that of others. He would rather not introduce the others who were close at hand, and there was, of course, no document, no tell-tale ring or pendant given to a sweetheart as in the stories. He suspected that the captain believed him, but was perhaps seeking corroboration.

'My mother knows the truth. And so does the former steward of the estate, whom Laurent has had removed somewhere, as I am told.'

Leroux sat down, as if to digest this information. He put his elbows on the desk, and rested his head in his hands, his thumbs scratching his chin slowly. His strong suspicion was that this *émigré* was telling the truth about the boy, but concealing the reasons for his own presence in Brittany, and, he was sure, in Quiberon too, with that peasant woman. He had to calculate quickly, and it did not take him long to make up his mind. 'I will release the boy. Think yourself fortunate. I have citizens in here, not just from Auray but from other towns, who are telling me that there should be no clemency for any that have taken up arms. The Republic is aware of these forceful and reasonable views. As you may know —' and here he looked at Justin — 'the women have been released already.

We may count this boy as a child. I think I heard of the incident in which he was involved. The soldier had his wits elsewhere, or it would not have happened.'

He brought his hands down and reached for a release form, writing the date and his signature. He stood up, walked to the door, and opened it, and then spoke to one of the gaolers on the bench.

'Get me Mercier, and tell him to bring two soldiers with him. He is probably counting the breadcrumbs to make sure there is no waste. Bring him. I do not expect to wait.'

By the time he had finished, Justin was standing, carefully replacing Leroux's coat on the chair. He said nothing. Leroux looked at him, and his face was set. He went back to his desk, took up his pen, dipped it, and went on signing papers. The room fell silent apart from the scratching of the quill, and the sound of Leroux's boots shifting under the desk. The air was still and heavy. There was a knock, and in came a bald man, flushed, his head shining, wearing brown breeches, a brown coat, and a rather crumpled cravat above his collar. He ignored Justin.

'My apologies, Captain. I have sent for Martineau.'

'Take this man with you, Mercier, and search in the index for where we have the child this man will describe to you.' He looked again at Justin. 'We have the place and date of his capture, I assume, and we know the nature of the assault that lies against his name.'

'Yes, Captain, it should be straightforward. We have few children…'

'He may be a boy, perhaps even entered as a young man. No doubt he lied about his age. This man will then be accompanied by Martineau to wherever he has been incarcerated. He will have the boy's release paper, here.

Martineau will see the boy released. Go and get on with it, and send Martineau here to me, now.'

At the same moment Leroux handed Justin the release paper, Mercier tried to get out of the door, and a bulky figure in uniform forced his way past him, muttering apologies, and came to attention in front of the desk. Justin cast a glance at Leroux, and followed Mercier out of the room.

'At ease, Martineau. Shut the door. Now listen carefully to what I have to say.'

Justin left the prison with the two soldiers, who had been instructed to take him to where Gilles was being held. He had been told that it was down towards the river in Auray, which a Breton would have called the *loc'h*. The heat was at its height, and he felt light-headed.

And now it had fallen to him, as he had ultimately insisted, to be walking through these narrow streets in a town he thought he knew, but which had changed so much, as the Terror had changed the country into a place of fear. The two tall soldiers chose to go one in front and one behind, something which Justin observed but to which he did not respond. As they passed briefly down the main street, with people stepping aside for the soldiers, close to Les Halles he was distracted momentarily by a closed carriage that came past. It was strange in these disturbed times to catch a glimpse through its window of a young woman so well dressed, sitting easily against the cushions. They quickly turned off into a dark *ruelle*, cutting through some of the poorer quarters, until they came to a small square. Here, on one side, there was a townhouse, walled and with decorated iron gates, that must have belonged to one who was now an *émigré*. A guard was sitting on an upturned barrel, with another at his shoulder, their muskets leaning against the ironwork, and the one standing hailed Martineau with an obscene reference to his mother.

The gates creaked open, and Martineau made as if to push the soldier off his barrel, and with his other hand to cuff the one who had insulted his parentage. The gate eased shut behind them, and they made their way across the paved courtyard to the imposing front door, equipped with a lion's-head knocker. Someone had been looking out, because the door swung open before they reached it, and Justin was hit by that same fetid smell he had encountered in the prison. His heart was beating fast now, but his energy had returned, his senses alert, pointlessly, to every sound. Once again there were gaolers in the hall, local men, who looked curiously at Justin, and off to the side was an office. It was like a mirror-image, unnervingly, with an officer sitting inside, but on this occasion talking to another officer who was lounging on a chair.

Martineau made a semblance of coming to attention, and the officer behind the desk looked up at him, while the other picked at his nails without interest.

'A release paper, sir, for one Gilles, name unknown, but from Kergohan.'

The officer reached out his hand for the paper, took it, and for the moment held it without reading it. 'Kergohan? Where in hell is that? Good God, there could be many Gilles, corporal. How am I expected to find this one?' He glanced at the signature. 'Is Leroux off his head?'

'Some nest of pigs in the back of beyond, Captain. Ask this one. He knows.' And with that, Martineau lost interest and relaxed his posture, staring out of the window.

'Well? Kergohan, or wherever? One Gilles without a name? Who are you, anyway?' The questions were addressed to Justin, who had remained near the door.

'He is a boy, Captain. And I am from Kergohan myself.' Justin's voice was low, despite his excitement, because he knew that he needed to see his way past these people. It was a last step, and he had to take it cautiously.

'A boy? There are no boys in here. What do you think we are?'

'A young man, then. I can identify him. He is fifteen years of age, but he will be acting older.'

'I think I know who you mean.' It was the other officer who spoke, still preoccupied with his nails. 'A mouthy little bastard. He stabbed Thibeau, as I recall. Didn't do a very good job of it, more's the pity. Why on earth are we releasing him?'

The officer behind the desk stood up. 'After weeks in this posting, you ask me that? Cloarec! Come in here.'

Justin stood aside as one of the shrewd gaolers came in. There could be little doubt that he had been listening to every word, but his face expressed a question.

'Lieutenant Vernier here will instruct you.' And with that, the officer sat down again at his desk, and fingered the release paper idly.

'The boy, the lad, we have him at the back of the building. Answers to the forename of Gilles. From Kergohan, it seems. You know him.' It was a statement rather than a question.

'And what should I do with him, sir? He is sullen…'

'I don't care about his temperament, Cloarec. Fetch him here, of course. Quickly now. The captain wants this done with.'

Cloarec left the room promptly, and a door banged shut at the bottom of the entrance hall. Martineau shifted his weight, and reached inside a pocket of his coat for another paper, which he held in his hand. The two soldiers looked at each other. The officer at the desk started writing, making an entry in a ledger. Lieutenant Vernier passed his time in scrutiny of Justin, still sitting on the chair with his legs stretched out in front of him. Justin looked nowhere in particular, hoping that the sound of his heart could not be heard in the silent room.

There was a noise at the end of the hallway, and a brief word, seemingly from Cloarec. Some steps, and a scraping of clogs at the door. Justin looked down into the face of Gilles, whose eyes were wide with astonishment, and whose lips were trembling slightly. Neither said a word.

'Gilles of Kergohan? Come and stand in front of the desk. You must understand that the Republic is exercising clemency and granting your release, despite your hostile actions against its armed forces, and the injury sustained by one of its soldiers. You will, I have no doubt, be duly grateful. If we catch you again involved in anything similar, there will be no mercy. You may now go.'

The officer waved his hand dismissively, and Vernier kept staring at Justin, as if waiting for him to make a move, which he now did.

'Gilles,' he said quietly, 'you may come with me.'

'Corporal Martineau will see you past the gates. Now out, all of you.'

Gilles kept his eyes on the floor as he went past Justin and out of the door, and Martineau flicked his head to indicate that Justin should go in front of him. Cloarec stared at them as they left the room, until Lieutenant Vernier saw him and pointed to the doorway. Vernier stood up and walked to the window, which looked out on the courtyard. He saw the small party make their way to the gates, which the guards opened. He saw the boy step outside, and then Martineau place his hands on the iron bars and push them shut. He watched as Gilles turned back, and placed his hands below those of Martineau on the gates, gripping them tightly and shaking them. The guards rammed home the bar, and Martineau and his companion took the man from Kergohan by the arms and walked him away back towards the house. The man twisted his head and shouted something to the boy, who screamed back at him, trying to shake the gates.

Vernier stood back from the window and waited. The man from Kergohan came in, flanked by the two soldiers. His face was pale, and his eyes were staring, which in some way satisfied Vernier. Martineau left his companion holding Justin, and came up to the desk with the paper still in his hand. He passed it across to the officer, who looked up briefly at Vernier as if in surprise, and then at Justin, before opening it and reading it. He spread it before him on the desk.

'Justin de Guèrinec, *ci-devant* Baron de Kergohan, I am arresting you on this written authority as an *émigré* who has returned to France to take up arms against the Republic, for which the Convention has decreed the penalty of death. Since we are not in reach of a guillotine, you will be executed by military firing squad in due order, along with others now imprisoned and guilty of the same offence. You will pass in front of a tribunal for final condemnation before execution. Cloarec!'

The gaoler came into the room.

'Take this man away, and see him shut in. I hold you responsible, as always. Treat him with some respect. He was once of some importance here.'

Cloarec stood aside for Justin to go out of the door, and then followed him. The door at the end of the hallway opened, and then thudded back into place. Martineau made to salute, as did his companion, and they both left the room. Lieutenant Vernier watched them cross the courtyard. There was no sign of the boy at the front gates. He breathed out and scratched his nose.

'It is gratifying to see that Leroux has not lost his style, nor I my instinct for a rat.'

The officer at the desk grunted. He was too busy with paperwork to pay any attention.

Leroux had given himself time for some reflection. What had been brought to him, what he had been told, had astonished him, and if he admitted the truth, it had left him unsure of what course of action he should pursue. Fortunately, he held all the good cards, and the trick lay in not playing them too soon. Releasing the boy was easy, because he was no good to him dead, and these peasants did not go far from their hovels, so he would know where to find him. What troubled him slightly was corroboration. Yet he knew that the former steward was still alive, taken away by Le Guinec and Guèvremont, because they had told him that much, smugly confident of their cleverness. He even had a good idea of where they were keeping him, and so could find a way to extract some kind of written testimony from him. He could even threaten to send to England in some manner to Guèvremont's cousin, who must be the mother of this *émigré* baron, and Guèvremont would not like that. But, in any case, in the new Republic he might do just as well, perhaps even better, with testimonies from the villagers, some of whom would know the truth because they would have known or be related to the boy's mother.

Even so, was he sure of what exactly he wanted from Guèvremont? The man might be influential, that was true, but the existence of the boy would need to become an embarrassment, a hindrance to the man's ambitions, if it was properly to be of service to Leroux. Here he became angry with himself, because he could not quite perceive how it was all to his advantage; and yet he felt that for a soldier like him it was a godsend, if only he could see how to use it properly. In the circumstances, it had been easy to channel the flow of that frustration and anger by condemning the man who had the temerity to bring him the information. What did they say, these Christians: 'Daniel into the lions' den'? His duty was to put down all enemies of the Republic, under the strict governance of the law, and it gave him satisfaction to demonstrate that the old arrogance would not provide safeguards in these new times. So that part was easy…

He was interrupted by a knock at the door. Mildly irritated, but relieved to be released from his own thoughts, he pushed back his chair and clasped his hands behind his head.

'Ah, Captain Leroux, this is where I find you.'

The voice was by now familiar, and it sent a shaft of excitement down his spine before he became guarded. He stood up, and unconsciously brushed down his coat and breeches.

'*Mademoiselle* Guèvremont, to what do I owe this honour? What is your business in this miserable house of correction?'

Joséphine Guèvremont came to a halt in the doorway, expecting that this framed her to best effect, an assumption in which she was not mistaken. Her pale blue satin gown was restrained, in keeping with the emergent fashion, but it gave a splendid impression, setting off the paleness of her slender arms and hands, one of which rested lightly on the small brass doorknob. Her hair was gathered, relatively inconspicuously, by matching blue ribbons, but Leroux could not keep his eyes off her face, which transfixed him, as she well knew.

'Captain Leroux, I make a point of visiting only the finest houses, and before the estimable Republic placed its booted feet inside its doors, it belonged to an acquaintance of my father's. I have been here many times. My father always thought the man proud and disdainful, and had contempt for the extent of his debts. I suspect that now he owes no one anything, except perhaps something to his maker. Unless, that is, he is cowering abroad with the Princes of the Blood. But I presume that you will invite me in? Or do you want me to continue to shelter you from the draughts from the front door?'

Leroux moved to the door, and caught a hint of her perfume. This was a mistake, because it drove him mad. He murmured something about taking a chair, and closed the door behind her. Joséphine walked to the centre of the room and looked down at the wooden chair, which had probably been brought up from the boot-boy's closet.

'If that is the chair you are offering me, then I fear I shall decline, Leroux. Instead, I shall stand by the window, where people may see me, and envy you.'

She duly crossed to the window, but saw the soldiers standing outside the guard-room by the gate, and staring, a position they had been occupying since, to their amazement, she passed through the gates from a carriage. Joséphine decided that this was not the audience she had in mind, so withdrew to look over the papers on Leroux's desk.

'My, my, quite the little bookworm, Captain, and I had taken you for a man of action. Every one of these a detention or a death, I presume. Your Republic seems remarkably fixed on death, Leroux. We have heard chilling stories of that dreadful instrument in Paris. I even hear that they carry it around with them, much as the travelling players used to carry their stage. It is a degenerate age, if we are come to such forms of entertainment. But, I forget myself. You may offer me a glass, Leroux, and I am sure my chatter alone was preventing you from doing so. My preferred choice is Meursault, which I am sure you have somewhere, for you will have brought it with you. No? I see you have not.' There was a silence. 'What is the matter, Captain?'

Leroux had gathered his wits, settled his passions a little, and had decided to put the desk between him and this Venus. His hands ran idly over the papers. 'I have no Meursault. No drink of any kind suitable for a lady. This house is not what it was…'

Joséphine looked into his face, and relented a little. 'It is of no significance. My father did not wish me to come here on my own, into the prison, but I reassured him that I should be in safe hands with Captain Leroux. But he insisted that I take our man with me. He is standing on the steps outside. My father only agreed because he himself will be here at any minute. I believe he wants to talk to you about the prisoners, probably about more death, since that seems to be in fashion. He does not want the military to let them go.'

Leroux looked up sharply. 'Let who go?'

'What, have you been lenient, Captain? Let one slip away? I should not have thought it of you. No, I believe he means the Bretons, not the *émigrés*. Those who have been marching in the fields and forests.' Here she yawned.

'Ah,' said Leroux, uninformatively.

Joséphine smiled sweetly, which of course tortured him even more than her wit, and wandered once more towards the window absent-mindedly. 'Oh, Captain, what with my gaping and your "ah", I fear we shall not reach the heights of polite conversation.'

'I am sorry, *mademoiselle*.'

'As am I, Captain. You must understand that my way of life has been disrupted by these wars. There is hardly a town left in this region where polite society has the confidence to flourish. But there is my father now. I shall go to meet him. A welcome at the front door might be encouraging. You may take my arm.'

Leroux crammed his hat on his head, and they reached the door of the room. Leroux was stretching out a hand to open it, when Joséphine placed hers on his arm to restrain him briefly.

'My father is not averse to the military, Captain, but it is a matter of rank. Do you understand me? One must have ambition. Shooting *émigrés* in the marshes like so many ducks may not be enough for him. Or for me…' She smiled at him again, which at this proximity was devastating. 'You may let me go in front of you, but be sure to follow me to the door. Stand where he can see you, just below me on the steps. And, Captain, hold your hat in your hand like this.' She took it from him. 'Or, perhaps, under your arm. There, that will do very well.'

She swirled out of the room, and Leroux stood stock-still for a moment, his hat under his arm, staring after her. He breathed in and swallowed. He now understood his own absolute confusion, and what it was he wanted from Guèvremont.

The rows of prisoners filed slowly through the streets of Auray, led and followed by groups of soldiers. The line was long, and they walked with their hands tied in front of them or behind their backs. Auray had never seen anything like it in living memory. These were the noblesse, men who had exacted complete deference from all who came their way, who had sneered at tradesmen, humiliated peasants, demanded and received crippling rents from tenants while they themselves ran up debts that they refused to pay, never walked when they could ride, on horseback or in carriages, reckoned themselves the proper companions of dukes and princes, dressed in a manner that marked them out, that separated them without question from the rest of humanity.

That at least was the view of the burghers, who if they watched the sombre procession did so from discreet windows, while raising a glass to the health and future prosperity of the Republic, each one remembering a slight or an insult that he had had to bear without demur, until now, that was. So there was much satisfaction, and no pity at all. Out on the street, there were those who did not share that view. For some, these were the patrons who had sheltered them and their families, providing work and a place to live, remembering their names, placing a hand on the heads of their children, offering a return for loyalty over generations in security. Their estates were a home made of field and woodland, of which the manor was the owner. But a manor might provide, even in hard times, and see justice done, a better overlord than any hard-faced tradesman in the towns. Hand in hand with the Church, these prisoners were the fathers who looked after them, and saw them through from infancy to the grave.

Those who felt like this had come into the town, fearful and resentful, some with recent memories of taking up arms, many who still knew of those who were under arms. For the most part, they kept quiet, while alongside them the townspeople stared and wondered when it would end, because this was not the first occasion, and neither prisoners nor soldiers paid their way. Their lodgings were commandeered, and much of their food disappeared all too readily. They had to make do and make way and look out for themselves with too much care and worry.

The file of men had nearly reached the parish church of Saint Gildas, making its way north to the marshes where the killing was done, to the dug earth and the bored but nervous soldiers who were checking their cartridges. Those looking on had begun to thin out by this stage of the journey, and the prisoners were lost in their own thoughts, hardly a word passing between them, just the trudge of many feet. There was no need for orders from the guards, because these men despised the idea of orders, unless they gave them themselves, and their pride guided their steps.

Suddenly, in the routine tramp of feet, there was a loud cry of warning, which no one understood at first. Then more cries echoed around, and with a racket of rattling wheels on stone paving a pony came thundering down a side street, pulling a cart full of empty barrels. One of them had already fallen and was rolling behind it, banging against the side of the crammed houses. Neither cart nor pony had any human hand to restrain it, although a man could be seeing running some way behind and shouting.

Those at the back of the file of prisoners broke out of their reverie. The guards at the rear also woke up from their marching stupor, and looked to save themselves. The wild-eyed pony came careering out of the side street straight towards them, but then seeing so many people and smelling the fear, it abruptly pulled up, kicking and then swinging away at an angle. The prisoners began to scatter into doorways for safety, and one or two of the guards tried to grab the harness, but at the same moment the barrels broke loose as the cart turned sideways, some shattering as they fell to the ground, and others rolling wildly, knocking over soldiers and prisoners alike.

Justin had heard the sounds as if from another world, and then had sprung awake as the man next to him nudged him with his shoulder. He saw the cart, heard the shouts, and watched mindlessly as a barrel ground over the outstretched leg of a soldier and rolled at an alarming speed directly towards him. At that moment a hand with immense strength grabbed his arm and pulled him sideways out of its path. He felt his hands miraculously freed, and a voice thrust to his ear. 'Run!' it said. He was too stunned to take all this in, but the same voice said, 'Follow him!' and the hands took him like a child and made him face an alley, giving him a final push. And there, in a shaft of sunlight dipping between two houses, was Gilles, who reached out and grabbed his hand. The two of them started to run, Justin in compete wonder, while Grosjean took his beard and his bulk to hold the pony at its head, lift up the overturned cart, earn thanks from the soldiers, and prove himself to all to be a good citizen.

Justin and Gilles ran, and then walked, and then ran again, down a lane that led behind the church back into the centre of town. The hubbub faded away, and Justin came to his senses, blessing the boy who gladly embraced him, wiping the tears from his eyes, and remembering what he knew of the alleys and *ruelles* of the town. At times they walked arm in arm, like father and son out for a stroll in the sunshine, greeting those they passed in Breton with a pronounced accent — just tilted towards the town and away from the country which surrounded it. They crossed the main street at one point in just this fashion, and then ran some more, always heading down towards the *loc'h* and the bridge across it, below the old chateau walls. That much Gilles had told him, with some mention of a boat, and by the time they reached the bridge with the suburb of Saint Goustan on the further side, they had begun to feel the threat relax.

Yet they had not seen or heard the hue and cry that had resulted from the accident. The guard had counted its file of prisoners, duly cursing those who had let the cart get out of hand, and found at least three missing. They had no idea of who these were, because they had no index of names with them, but it was enough to set soldiers running to call out others, and start a sweep through the town. They hardly knew what they were looking for, but perhaps hoped to find forlorn and frightened characters lurking in the shadows with their hands tied, to make their task easier and their own inevitable disciplinary punishment lighter. Just as they had crossed the bridge, Justin and Gilles heard the sound of men running down the hill, calling out to comrades who were quartered across the river to comb the streets. One or two who had been standing at corners came into the square at the bottom of the hill, but Justin and Gilles had slipped away up and into the lanes of Saint Goustan.

They stood breathing heavily in a dark and narrow recess that lay between two houses, hardly the width of a man, waiting to hear of any pursuit. It was a matter of chance which way the few soldiers on this side of the *loc'h* would run, and how hard they would work. Their inclination might be to think that this was someone else's responsibility, and that one *émigré* more or less would not make their lives any more difficult. Gilles pulled Justin's sleeve briefly, and pointed up the hill. Sure enough, there were cries, and feet running along in the street above them. So they nodded to each other and stepped out of the cranny and into the lane. It led to the quay at the far end of the village, where smaller boats were moored.

As they approached the quay they saw the backs of two blues, who were gazing up at the town opposite, following the course of the hue and cry. The two soldiers heard them and swung round, at first with casual interest, but then with suspicion. 'And where are you off to?' one asked. The other took a step forward, swinging his musket around.

Gilles and Justin watched in astonishment as a giant with a huge black beard put his finger to his mouth, which was displaying a large grin, and crept like a cat just two short paces towards the soldiers. He had come suddenly and silently around the corner where they had been standing. It was likely that he had been watching them. The soldiers were still close together, and the giant's hands closed mercilessly around their necks, and brought their heads together sharply. There was a crack, and one fell to the ground and lay there like a stone, while the other writhed and moaned, bringing his knees up to his chest with the pain.

Grosjean took their muskets, and gave them to Justin and Gilles. Those same large hands hurried them along the remains of the quay to a small rowing skiff, in which there was another man, his hand on the painter. They laid the muskets in the bottom of the boat, and he shoved fishing nets and pots into their hands, motioning to them to sit down, and pushed off from the shore.

The water was calm, the tide on the turn, taking them slowly out and down the *loc'h* in the direction of the sea. The man rowed, not urgently, but as a fisherman might row, all the while scanning both shores, which gradually fell away. The heights of Auray disappeared behind its steep slopes, and the village of Saint Goustan became a cluster of roofs. On its quay, the figure of a bearded man watched patiently, slowly diminishing in size until he might have been taken for a person of normal stature. He then gave a brief wave, and turned away up the hill to the side of the village.

The noises from the town were muted, and the oars dipped and splashed lightly. Gilles and Justin looked at each other. They had reached more open water before they heard the distant rattle of musket fire, drifting down from the marshes above the town. There were four volleys, one after another, a chilling distance apart, and then there was nothing except the lap of the water as the rower allowed the tide to pull them down the channel.

CHAPTER XVIII: IN THE GARDEN AT CHITTESLEIGH

The apples were rounding nicely now, mottled with yellow on some of the trees, a deep, vibrant red on others. The pears, always Arabella's favourite of the autumn fruits, were fully shaped, or so it seemed, but rock-hard to the touch, some lying forlorn on the path the gardener kept open in the orchard even in the high summer, the birds barely touching them. It was not yet time for the harvest, but the weather had settled into that benign and bland season, as if the world was, for a few weeks, content to drift along like the few clouds that slipped almost imperceptibly across an open sky. Day after day could pass dreamily, hardly a sound to disturb one's reverie, an ease that would satisfy deeply if it were not for the longing that remained, no matter how gaily time was spent in company.

Arabella paused and kicked a pear. She was wearing satin shoes, and the pear was harder than she had imagined. Despite being on her own, she resolved to moderate her language and nurse a slightly stubbed toe. She looked round, and her glance fell on a tree stump that stood close to the path. It was a tree that had grown old and infertile, she assumed, and had been felled to go for logs for the kitchen hearth. It was close enough to serve her purpose, and she lifted her foot on to it, pulled up her dress above the ankle, and rubbed her toe. Although the satin of her shoe was slightly scuffed, it was not seriously stained.

She shook out her dress. It was a morning gown of light blue taffeta, edged with lace and with a delicately pleated bodice, which she felt matched the colour of her eyes, or so Grace insisted. The girl had been most attentive this morning, and had tied on an attractive net bonnet of a mildly deeper hue, expressing herself duly satisfied with the result. Arabella had indulged her today, as she did from time to time, on other days being brisk if not peremptory about the labour of dressing, which she thought to be a trifle exaggerated. The net bonnet still troubled her, and she was tempted to remove it, but she knew that if she left it in the orchard it would be forgotten, and she disliked carrying articles of dress with her. She was now in sight of the windows of the drawing room. To her amusement, Amelia was smiling and waving through them, and apparently trying to mouth some words, with the help of some incomprehensible gestures. How like her friend! She had parted from her only a short while ago to spend some time alone. She saw Sempronie come to the window and remonstrate with Amelia, taking her arm and leading her away with a wave to Arabella.

There was now time for a leisurely walk through the scented roses, an entrancing and diminutive avenue of blooms, with many of the colours she liked to see in fabrics. It might be that it was late for some plants, but others were flourishing, and the gardener had enticed a second flowering from several that had displayed early. The path delighted her, as it had always done, and she laughed as she displaced a small bee from one of the more odorous shrubs, leaning forward to catch the scent on her way back up to the arbour. Here there was a magnificent climber with vivid, deep magenta roses climbing up to the sky on gently waving stems, and spreading out in a bush on either side of the frame as if to welcome the traveller into a scented room. The gardener had kept the archway open, and allowed for the spread of the ladies' dresses; but as she slipped through the opening, Arabella's gown snagged on a trailing thorn. Quick as she was, she stopped before it tore, and turned her fingers to the task of liberation. With a sharp gasp, she realised that she had punctured one of them on a thorn, and so stuck the finger unceremoniously in her mouth to avoid any blood staining her dress.

It was at that moment that she heard a step on the path behind her, and her face flushed as she realised who it was.

'Perhaps you would allow me to disentangle you? Unless, that is, you would prefer me to fetch your maid.'

Arabella took her finger out of her mouth, still blushing furiously at the picture she must have given, but realised that she could not move without either tearing her gown or, in her confusion, probably puncturing another finger. Damn the man for coming up on her like this! Was he always to catch her unawares, making her feel like a naughty schoolgirl? 'You have, sir, caught me at an awkward moment, it is true. My maid will not forgive me if I get blood on this gown.'

'Allow me, then.' Justin bent forward to detach the taffeta from the unruly thorn, and then stood back. He reached into the pocket of his old frock coat and pulled out a handkerchief, which he offered to her for her finger.

'You are most kind, sir, although I will not thank you for coming up on me as if by stealth. I had thought my hearing good, but you eluded me.'

'I offer my sincere apologies, and if I was responsible for your hurt…'

Arabella drew the line at this idea of maidenly flight from the intruder into the toils of a prickly bush, a suggestion which struck her as bordering on impertinent. 'Nonsense. A woman may snag herself on a thorn.' She gathered her dignity and launched into a more formal acknowledgement of his unexpected presence. 'I see you are returned, rather earlier than I was given to expect. I must offer my apologies. I would far rather have greeted you alongside your sister and your mother, and had intended to do so. Perhaps we may now return to the house?'

At that, Arabella stepped forward, and Justin stood back for her. As she passed he glanced at her face, and caught a glimpse of the loose curls on her neck. She seemed angry with him, again, and this would not do. He strode after her and spoke with some urgency.

'Miss Wollaston, I believe there are things that should be said, and they may be better said if you will grant me an audience in the garden.'

Arabella halted in front of him, but replied without turning round. 'I do not know to what you refer, sir. I am sure your mother and your sister would be glad to afford you the opportunity for a brief conversation with me, if that is your inclination. As it is, they will be missing us by now, and I do not think it either polite nor strictly proper…'

Justin had known that he would have to be forthright, to conquer the obstacles that he had built up between them. So he did not hesitate to step forward and take her by her forearm, if only to turn her gently round to face him, and then release her arm quickly, stepping back as he did so. Arabella complied, but became irritated as she sensed the blush returning to her cheeks. Her decision was to say nothing, but to face him and leave him to say what he had to say. The sooner it was done the better.

'Would you care to sit down? The seats are clean, and will do no damage to your gown.'

If that was what he envisaged as the setting for whatever little speech he had in mind, then so be it. She was resigned to not getting back without having to listen to him, and remarked to herself how often men were like that. So she brushed a few stray leaves from the stone bench by which they had halted, and sat down primly, a resource on which she drew when she wished to bring an unwanted conversation quickly to an end. It was surprisingly more effective than interjection, which only encouraged them. She took care to sit fully in the middle of the bench.

Justin looked first at her knees, then at her feet, and then at the top of her head, which was still covered by the bonnet. He then risked looking at her face, but she sat motionless, and her eyes were on the ground. He did not feel nervous, but he was still in doubt about how to express himself. As he looked past Arabella's head, he saw the unmistakable figure of his sister at the window of the drawing room, but she turned away quickly when she saw him looking.

'Miss Wollaston, I am greatly in your debt. I have been astonished to learn just how greatly, and indeed my whole family adds its thanks to mine. What you did was highly courageous, bold, and unselfish. We could not have expected…'

Arabella stood up and brushed down the skirts of her gown, placing the handkerchief delicately on the bench. There was a tiny spot of blood on it, and she tutted as a light breeze wafted it away into the circular walk behind them. 'Well, perhaps we may now go in. Your expressions of gratitude are appreciated, but your sister is waiting. There seems little reason…'

Justin stepped forward, almost barring her progress, and waved his hand in impatience at himself. 'Arabella, please look at me.' She did not. 'I also owe you a profound apology. I have been a complete fool, and behaved like a boor, unforgivably, and I cannot say…'

At the first mention of her name, Arabella's manner softened, and she stood quite still, while her fingers unlaced the ribbons of her bonnet. 'If it is unforgivable, sir, then I know not what we shall do. But I see you flatter me with the use of my name, so there must be some contrition.' She paused and played idly with the ribbons of the bonnet, before then looking him resolutely in the eyes. 'If you refer to the incident I have in mind, then I think that we can come to an understanding. It did, I confess, haunt me dreadfully, and I marvel now at the levels of embarrassment to which I was clearly prepared to subject myself. To trespass in the house of a friend…'

'But as we both know now, your suspicions were well-founded, your actions sound and selfless…'

'Sir, if you use such words any more, I shall have to consider myself a saint of some sort, which I am not. I acted like an impetuous girl, and I should never have presumed to enter your room…'

Justin was not to be deflected by this young woman's modesty. He persisted. 'Had you not entered my room, had your suspicions of that agent not been aroused, then who knows what might have come to pass? And when I think of your daring at the White Hart in Okehampton, I can barely … hold myself back from laughing!'

Here Justin was so taken that his shoulders shook, and he had to sit down on the bench to recover from his fit. Arabella looked at him in astonishment. He rocked backwards and forwards, and then looked up.

'God alone knows what Mallingham made of it! Why, it makes me…'

While she gazed at him, a smile hovering around her own lips, he stood up on an impulse and came to her, placing his hands on her shoulders. He had noticeably stopped laughing.

'You brave girl. I can hardly…' And he put his hands around her head, and kissed her impetuously on the lips.

Her bonnet dropped to the ground from her hand, and she rested her fingers tentatively on his arms. She swam for a moment in an intoxicating sensation, one that far exceeded any pleasure she had ever had, and then pushed him gently away from her. 'I think, Mr Wentworth, that this demonstration far exceeds the gratitude that you have mentioned, and in any case is hardly appropriate for one you choose to address as "girl".' She picked up her bonnet, determined to maintain control of the situation at least, if not of herself. 'We shall, I believe, agree on cool reflection to say no more of this, and thankfully those who may have been watching will be kind enough not to mention what they saw if we do not do so ourselves. It might perhaps be best if you leave me now, and walk through to the house in advance, and on your own. I shall wait for a while.' *To compose myself*, she thought, *if that is a remote possibility.*

Justin decided to stand his ground. He realised that he had been shutting her out of his feelings for a ridiculous length of time, treating her disdainfully and coldly because he was frightened of his own passions, and what he mistakenly thought was her fragility. She was stunningly beautiful, and his heart leaped at the thought of how she had pursued Le Guinec, been disbelieved by all, and yet had been so steadfastly loyal to him in his absence, when she had had nothing from him in return. How he might say all of that to her, he did not know. He took the plunge. 'Bella, I am in love with you. I have been an arrogant fool, and I must have hurt you so many times. Look at me, standing here in my old frock coat, making yet another mess of…'

He did not get to extend his self-accusation, because Arabella had heard quite enough by now. She stepped right up to him, grabbed him by the collar of his coat, and wordlessly invited him to kiss her again in a manner that suited her inclination, and the racing of his pulse.

After a timeless interval, in which she put her head on his shoulder, and they breathed in air that had never tasted so vital before, he took her hand in his and led her to sit beside him on the bench. She was now more than content to leave her hand precisely where it was, and they sat silently for some minutes in the glorious peace of the late summer.

'I have been to see your father,' he said.

'While I myself have been in Bath, because it was my father's opinion that I needed some distraction while he sorted matters out here. It is not impossible that he was right. I found the walks refreshing, although I would not give my horse the waters to drink.'

He laughed again. 'I owe you an account of our conversations. They were amicable, surprising, and ultimately resolved.'

'Yes, he wrote to me at Bath of much that he has probably now told you. But I should hear what I can from you, in case there is more.'

Justin looked at her and smiled, and then felt himself completely exhilarated when she looked back at him, her own eyes shining. He resisted the temptation to take a curl in his finger and twist it, and concentrated on his narrative. 'Well, you may know that the steward, Le Guinec, was sent back to France, with the instruction that he was never to return, and the warning that if he did he would be imprisoned as an enemy, or worse.'

'Yes, I know that.'

'What you may not know is that he admitted nothing before he was put on board ship. But your suspicions were correct...'

'And Amelia's sharp eyes, her detection.'

'Yes, her detection. The letters purportedly from Mael Sarzou were undoubtedly forgeries. He was either forced to write them and sign them, or they were written for him, and then he signed them. But as Melia noticed, the dear old man gave the wrong signature, in the hope that would arouse suspicion about the letters — as it did.'

'But your letter, or the letter supposedly from you?'

'Another forgery. As was my signature on it.'

'But how did they obtain your signature? That always troubled me. Was it from the letters in your bureau?' Here Arabella's voice dropped a little, but she need not have worried.

Justin laughed again, and squeezed her hand, and then became grave again. 'You should not remind me of what an oaf I was to you. When I think back, I wonder how you could ever forgive…'

'If you ask me any more to forgive you, Justin, then you may be certain that I shall not forgive you for doing so.' Her tone softened. 'But do you know how they found your signature?'

'I believe it was from a reply I had sent to letters from my mother's cousin, Guèvremont. He will have kept my response, and his letters to me were indeed those in the bureau in my room.' Here he could not resist stealing a glance at her. 'He wrote to me a year or so ago. It is my belief that this whole scheme was prompted by that correspondence. It gave Le Guinec the idea for the substance of his forgeries, so that when he met Yeo he could suggest that he had something to show him that was incriminating.'

Arabella shifted on the bench, and her tone was hard. 'Ah, Captain Yeo. I hardly dare ask…'

'I am told by your father that he treated you abominably. That also included lying to you, and probably to your father. In the end, he proved gullible, and fell into the trap set by Le Guinec. Under questioning, he came out with it all to your father, who was incensed.'

'So Yeo happened on Le Guinec when he came first to Okehampton?'

'I believe that he had been observed by agents before that. But the man at the manor here took him to see Yeo, since he might be expected to have information, and that is when it started to go wrong.'

Arabella looked directly at Justin. 'Do you believe that, Justin? Is my father blameless?'

Justin sighed, and briefly put his hands on his knees, arching and stretching his back. He left it a while before replying. 'I do not wish to think otherwise of him, Bella. He had meant to shield me from suspicion. To that end, he got together with Yeo, who I am convinced also meant well, and they drafted a plan. They wished to convince others that I was … a man of sound opinions, like themselves. Your father was also responsible for a ring of agents who were keeping watch locally, linked to the militia and heaven knows what. It perhaps…'

'Had gone to his head. He had changed, recently. It was distressing. He should never have entertained such a scheme as this, using a family friend. It is abominable, but I still doubt that he can see that.'

'I am quite sure, Bella, that your father knew nothing of the intrigue set in motion by Le Guinec, even if he knew of the man. Yeo was duped into believing that Le Guinec had evidence of treachery, and as so often it was the existence of suspicion that made deceit possible.'

'And I dare say that Yeo thought he was clever enough to keep the full story from my father, until he had possession of the evidence and could produce it. What is the matter with these men? They foster distrust, and then fall into believing what their common sense should tell them cannot conceivably be true.'

'Well, fortunately Haworth was always inclined to dismiss the rumours beginning to circulate against me anyway, for which he deserves a great deal of credit. That he nearly sent me to my death in Brittany in order to demonstrate my loyalty to all doubters remains another matter. Your father told me that Haworth was in favour of disciplining Yeo sharply, but in the end they both agreed to pack him off on a commission to the fleet in the West Indies.'

'So that is that.'

'Not quite, my love. You must answer me this.' And he laughed again. 'Where did you get that pistol? I had no idea…'

'My father gave it to me. It is of the kind that we ladies keep in our muffs, to deal with unwanted suitors. A Queen Anne pistol, if you prefer, a little beauty, crafted by one Theophilus Clemmes, of Shug Lane, as I recall. Before you ask, I was taught to shoot by my father, although my accuracy on the day hardly did Le Guinec the disservice he deserved. What are you doing?'

Justin had swung himself off the bench and was now on one knee before her, his hand on his heart.

'Justin…'

'I have it on good authority from my sister that you once disclosed to her that you would never accept a man who did not go down on one knee before you to ask for your hand.'

It was Arabella's turn to laugh. She tossed her bonnet carelessly at him, and rose to her feet. 'Oh, I assumed that you had agreed it all with my father when you spoke to him, as men expect to do. Asking us is about the last thing that they manage. Up, sir, get up! Now kiss me again, and withal you may get something more than my hand. In due time.'

He did not need further bidding. They left the bench and began to walk slowly, arm in arm, towards the house. Their eyes were on each other, so they did not notice Amelia and Sempronie through the windows in front of them, dancing across the floor of the drawing room at Chittesleigh.

A NOTE TO THE READER

Dear Reader,

I hope you enjoyed reading *The Baron Returns*, which is the first novel in the Wentworth Family Regency Drama series.

As you will see from the inscription to *The Baron Returns*, and from various posts that appear in my biographies and on my blog, I was intent on following my mother's lead, the popular author Alice Chetwynd Ley in setting a story in what I had always regarded as her period, generally called the Regency, but which stretches out to embrace Georgian times in the later eighteenth century, and then into the nineteenth with the Napoleonic Wars. This is the era that belongs in the first instance — and in the imaginations of all who read romantic fiction — above all to Jane Austen, who managed to direct our attention and sympathies on to people leading their domestic and social lives in the home counties of England. My mother was perhaps a little more interested than Jane in the effects of war on the home population in a number of her novels, in spies and indeed in smugglers at times. But above all she liked to write about heroines of the feisty kind, independent in mind and will, who were not above falling for a dark, handsome stranger.

So I inherited history by inheriting that period, if I was to write something in her honour, as I wished to do. Being naturally predisposed through growing up in England to see history all around me, I had no difficulty in imaging characters caught in the middle of great events; but I wanted them to be working out their own lives and purposes with as much intimacy and discretion as Austen might have given them. Whether we like it or not, we live with what unfolds around us, and for the characters in my books coming to terms with what is demanded of them by society or events, or with the harsh demands of survival, takes place in what must appear to us as an historical period. The characters do not often see it in that way, and perhaps few of us really ever do either. Yet some of these great events appear like earthquakes: the tectonic plates underlying societies shift, and the result is uproar and turmoil, changes that may be drastic but some of which may prove to be beneficial, at least to some.

So it was that in 1793 England and France went to war, after the new French Republic had executed the King of France. At almost the same time, in the far north west of France, the rural population rebelled against the Republic, in anger at the attack on royalty, the aristocracy, and the established Catholic church, and probably at the overturning of a way of life with which they had been familiar for generations. The rebels in Brittany came to be called the Chouans, and they were devoted to monarchy and the old church and its priests, and were eventually supported by the British government.

That is the context for the events in the novel, which is set in 1795, when the exiled French aristocrats and royalists attempted to unite with the Breton rebels by making a landing on the Brittany coast at Quiberon and Carnac. Many no doubt hoped to repossess their property and estates, which had been confiscated from them. But Justin, who is by his mother's title the owner of the manor at Kergohan, has no real hope of that happening. Instead, his mother's cousin, the merchant Laurent who has fine houses in the Breton towns of Pontivy and Auray, has managed to assert an interest in the manor, trusting that he will be able to persuade the Republic to grant or sell it to him.

You need to imagine that the English navy is on station in the Channel, while on land the militia and at times the yeoman cavalry are active, with the fear of a French invasion and of treachery within Britain provoking treason laws and trials, harsh reactions, and suspicion, potentially even of one's neighbour. In the streets or at assemblies, the women encounter soldiers, or at least young men in uniform who may as yet have seen no engagement with the enemy, and so they meet gentlemen more widely outside their immediate social circles. But little still is expected of a gentlewoman outside the traditional domestic duties and responsibilities and subordination, although a spirit of independence is beginning to stir, while amongst those who have leisure and literacy the chance to be moved by women writers — in the imagination or even in matters of politics — is perhaps greater than ever before.

The countryside of Devon and Brittany lends itself to romance and intrigue, and living as close as I do to Dartmoor there are always magnificent views to take your breath away, or alternatively to inspire you to start filling the landscape with characters. It is all too easy in such a setting to dream of smugglers down at the breakers' edge in a rocky cove, or a caped rider driving his horse hard across the wild moorland, probably in the teeth of the wind and the rain. There is nothing wrong with that: but the familiarity of those well-used images can lead you quite quickly into a dead end. We have du Maurier's *Jamaica Inn* and Winston Graham's *Poldark*, and they are glorious; but there is little to be gained now by treading too devotedly in their footsteps. Gossip is good too, and people repeatedly working hard at sex in awkward costumes, but I'm not sure I would aim to match that Netflix chutzpah.

So what's new? For me, if there were two beautiful and beguiling places such as rural Devon and Brittany, then the answer was to join them together in telling the story through characters who firmly belonged to them. So Justin Wentworth and his sister Amelia and their mother Sempronie came into being, people with a foothold in both places, both countries, both sets of beliefs and attitudes. And the action would take some of them across the Channel, from peace into war, from trust into suspicion, and back into a past that contained disturbing secrets. Then the cast expanded, from the Breton girl who was now a woman who knew about that past, to the boy who was unsure who his father was, to the locals in Okehampton and Hatherleigh in Devon, the newly Republican citizens in the busy towns of Brittany, and the country people whose loyalties still lay elsewhere, and who fought grimly to keep them. The unfolding story will continue into the second novel in the series, *Heir to the Manor*, with the lives of the women characters from the first book encountering love and threats in Devon and Brittany, with much of the action in the naval city of Plymouth, and the arrival of new characters from Saint-Domingue in the Caribbean, tracked mercilessly by ruthless men from the plantations. There will be more on a range of topics — from bread ovens to actresses to manors and manners — in posts on my blog, called 'Welcome to the land of Kergohan', which can be found on my website: **grahamley.com**. I hope to meet you again there, and thank you once again for reading *The Baron Returns*. If you enjoyed the novel I would be grateful if you could spare a few minutes to post a review on **Amazon** and **Goodreads.** Alice Chetwynd Ley's Regency novels may be found at: **saperebooks.com**.

Graham Ley

Sapere Books is an exciting new publisher of brilliant fiction and popular history.

To find out more about our latest releases and our monthly bargain books visit our website:
saperebooks.com